REPORT TO MEGALOPOLIS

HOPE

REPORT
to
MEGALOPOLIS

or The Post-modern Prometheus

TOD DAVIES

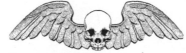

EXTERMINATING ANGEL PRESS

EXTERMINATING ANGEL PRESS
"Creative Solutions for Practical Idealists"
Visit *www.exterminatingangel.com* to join the conversation
info@exterminatingangel.com

Exterminating Angel book design by Mike Madrid
Aspern Grayling maps by Alex Cox
Typesetting by Christy Collins, Constellation Book Services

ISBN: 978-1-935259-31-2
eBook: 978-1-935259-32-9
Library of Congress Control Number: 2018903443

Distributed by
CONSORTIUM BOOK SALES & DISTRIBUTION
(800) 283-3572
www.cbsd.com

PRINTED IN THE UNITED STATES OF AMERICA

CONTENTS

EDITOR'S NOTE

This is the fourth book in The History of Arcadia. There were only supposed to be three. I thought only three would come to me in those various ways that Arcadia was able to send them. Arcadia, of course, being a world spinning in the same space as our own, but at a different speed.

First was *Snotty Saves the Day*, looking like a children's tale, accompanied by the footnotes of an Arcadian physicist that argue other meanings.

Then *Lily the Silent*. Her world leapt into being from the strange transformations of the characters in *Snotty*.

Then came another transformation: *The Lizard Princess*. In which a girl becomes a queen through finding herself half-animal.

These three tales come from the older generation of Arcadia. But it's the younger that sends us this fourth. In the form of a memoir written by a member of the old.

Its narrator opposes any change to his world, especially any hoped for by the young. He fights to retain power for everything he has lived by. And it might be that, in this, Arcadia is not so different from our own world.

To those who object to 'fantasy', on the shaky grounds that it doesn't reflect the 'real' world—whatever that might be—I say this: the world that we know is not the only one that can exist. As human beings, we float free in eternity and its unlimited possibilities. There are other living worlds than this small one of our own.

Arcadia's living world has many allies, some in unsuspected places. And I very much suspect that in our own world, our young generation is at work finding new patterns, as much as the young Evolutionaries of Arcadia are at work in theirs.

A list of characters involved in this story might be of help, so this follows. And at the end of the book, a family tree, along with a table of transformations the inhabitants of Arcadia undergo. Because that is the strange thing about Arcadia: as the story grows and changes, so do the characters.

DRAMATIS PERSONAE OF "REPORT TO MEGALOPOLIS":

Aspern Grayling: Scientist.
Born in Arcadia, educated in Megalopolis.
After losing his family in a Mega invasion of his homeland,
identified solely with the more powerful side,
putting all of his talents at the service of Megalopolis,
and its secret ruler, Livia.
Creator of Pavo Vale.

Livia: Autocrat.
The Great Witch of Megalopolis, ruling through the Council of Four.
Mentor to Aspern Grayling.

The Council of Four: Nominal rulers of Megalopolis.
Peter, Gordon, Anthony, and Alastair, archrival of Aspern Grayling.

Lily the Silent: First Queen of Arcadia.

Sophia the Wise: Second Queen of Arcadia.

Devindra Vale: Physicist, academician,
counselor to the queens of Arcadia.
Founder of Arcadia's Otterbridge University. Mother of Merope Vale.
Adopted mother of Shiva Vale. Grandmother of Shanti Vale.

Merope Vale: Witch. Daughter of Devindra Vale.
In love with Aspern Grayling. Surrogate mother of Pavo Vale.

Pavo Vale: First Emperor of Arcadia.
Creation of Aspern Grayling, born to surrogate mother Merope Vale.

Michaeli: Lord High Chancellor of Arcadia.

Faustina: Eldest daughter of Michaeli.
First wife to Pavo Vale, no issue.

Aurora: Youngest daughter of Michaeli. Mother of Shiva Vale.

Shiva Vale: Artist. Adopted daughter of Devindra Vale.
Wife of Walter Todhunter. Mother of Shanti Vale.

Walter Todhunter: Biologist. Gardener.
Foster son of Francis Flight and Amalia Todhunter of the Small House.
Husband of Shiva Vale. Father of Shanti Vale.

Shanti Vale: Evolutionary.
Daughter of Walter Todhunter and Shiva Vale.
Best friend to Isabel the Scholar.

Isabel the Scholar: Founder of the Evolutionary Movement.
Academic. Best friend to Shanti Vale.

To Mike
Thanks, Doc

To the Editor of Exterminating Angel Press:

Hello from Arcadia.

You know we've found through experiment that what travels most easily between worlds is our common language. Which is story. So we send you now this strange diary, the story of a great man gone wrong. We found it, my friend Shanti and I, in his papers after his death. He meant it to be his vindication. A confession of a kind. Do not take everything in it to be of face value. It is the self-justification of a brilliant but unbalanced man. Not evil, though it may seem that way at times. He was once my teacher. I knew him well. I mourn him and what he could have been. He was a man not so much vicious as violently confused, lost in following an out-of-date road map. A one-dimensional map, like those he himself drew of Arcadia.

Research shows your world faces challenges like ours. Any sharing of information can only do us both good. You might see in this confession of a man working single-mindedly for power what we do: the sign that the old ways are fatal to new life. To the fearful, this might be impossible to stop. But my generation, mine and Shanti's, is not afraid. We are determined, and we have a lot of hope. We know that to change, we need a new pattern. A new multi-dimensional map. We here in Arcadia are trying to find and follow one. If on reading this, you have any aid to offer, we will put it into use. And we will be grateful.

Please send useful stories by return mail.

In solidarity,

Isabel

Known in Arcadia as 'The Scholar'

PART ONE

THE WITCH QUEEN

To the Lady Livia

I saw Devindra's ghost last night.

We both know what that means. Research has shown these phantoms to be projections of the unconscious mind. And we know when my unconscious mind projects Professor Devindra Vale, a serious threat has arisen to my safety. And to my work.

Sitting in my laboratory on the False Moon I saw her, in that beautiful space that you, lady, built for me, prying the cash for it out of the jealous hands of the Council of Four. Alastair was furious, but there was nothing he could do. "Research," you said blandly, and all pretense that you, Lady Livia, are no more than a counselor to the state of Megalopolis dropped, for that one moment only, before the fig leaf of the Council's power was readjusted, and the meeting went on.

Of course danger threatens from that quarter. I write here, under what can be called nothing but house arrest. Alastair made sure of that. "Treason," he said. I don't know how much the others believed what he had to say. But you had made sure I would have my laboratory. You didn't listen to the whining from Alastair about my supposed disloyalty. He has so little imagination that he thinks someone born in Arcadia could never serve the purposes of Megalopolis.

"Not that he can help it," Alastair said in that silky voice he uses to deploy his most poisonous venom. "We...er...*dispatched* his mother, her pal, and his sisters too as I recall from the files, didn't we? His family? We in Megalopolis. During the First Invasion. What were you, Grayling? Thirteen?" he said, turning to me, in feigned compassion—idiot, as if I'm not fully aware that compassion has no place in matters of state, as if I haven't seen the files that list the certainty that my mother and sisters were enemies of the state. "You saw it all, I understand. Tsk. Regrettable necessity, can't make an omelet without breaking eggs, blah blah blah."

A sly smile at his own joke. No one else laughed; they looked to you, Lady, to see if it was safe to even crack a smile.

1

Speaking to me, an insult, as if I were a boy again. I, who have grown old in the service of Megalopolis. Even with all the possible enhancements available, it is no small achievement to reach the active age of nearly a hundred. An achievement worthy of respect. But showing respect was never Alastair's way.

So I held my peace. You and I exchanged a look. We know Alastair's ways, you and I. I stayed silent. That's the best way to thwart the man.

"Of course you say it doesn't affect your work for us, and I believe you, Grayling—oh, I believe you knew nothing of your womenfolk's 'patriotic' work."

Ah, the inverted commas on "patriotic." Nice touch, Alastair.

"Scholarship boy, as I recall from the files," he drawled. "Physics, biology, chemistry, the whole lot—we talent-spotted you young, did we not? Gave you all the benefit of a City education. Teachers pleased, warms the heart the recommendations in your file—oh, we checked you out thoroughly, vetted you within an inch of your life, no unsound thinking there. No silly ideals."

Dramatic pause here. His eyelids lowered, his voice went bureaucratically flat, his instinct to kill leading him on. And he said, "But—and I ask this with all sympathy for the boy, for the man—can you be trusted not to feel the teeny-weeniest smidgen of rage? Seeing the family topped? Home for spring break, only son expecting to be welcomed into the bosom, witnessing regrettably necessary judicial execution… unpleasant, what? Bound to leave a bad taste. No matter how many years ago. Bound to interfere with your *reasoning*. Is that not true?" He leaned back and looked at me. The others looked at you, Lady, but your expression gives nothing away.

Am I angry that he questions my loyalty? No. Pffftt. An almond for a parrot. I am angry that he questions my judgment. But I hide my anger, as I have learned to hide so much. From everyone but you, Lady.

"How loyal can he realistically be? I ask the Council," Alastair pleaded.

But I smiled, for I could already see he'd lost his case, and the funds for my research were secured.

Although not the confidence of the Council. Not that. As we see now. "Confined to quarters for the duration." I know what that means. An attempt to steal from me what power I have rightly earned by my work.

Alastair loses more than he knows from this, charm boy that he is, for now I know precisely where my enemy—and the enemy of my life's work—lies. I have known all these years enough to protect my projects from his interference. I have known enough to protect my greatest triumphs from his malice, and from the more hidden envy of the rest of the Council.

So that envy, that malice, has led them to banish me from their present deliberations. I'm to hunker down in my laboratory and prepare them a "report." That it is crisis time, I know well. All previous attempts to win over the tiny patch of our world known as Arcadia to the purpose of Megalopolis have failed; of course you and I know why. Perhaps only you and I, Lady Livia, which is why, in preparing this report for the Council, I report only the most secret portions to you alone. The censored version can be distributed as you see fit. But this, the franker, unexpurgated version, is for your and my eyes only. Two copies alone will exist: one in your hands, and one remaining in mine. A secret report on how best to achieve our mutual goal. Which is to overcome the Queendom of Arcadia, swallowing it for the future good of Megalopolis. Which is the same as the future good *of the entire world*.

The same goal as that of the Council. Though I think they mean to get there—if get there they may—through slightly different means. They wish to add to their own glory, rather than to that of a former scholarship lad from the backward land of Arcadia. No matter what impressive, even spectacular, scientific discoveries have been his.

More: they hate me because of that spectacular discovery—for showing them up. Alastair in particular. They sit there in the Council Room, lounging, apparently informal, the four of them having been raised together and schooled together, the products of intermarriage between the

3

most elite families in Megalopolis. You think your advocacy of my own work has helped me there? No. I'm the cuckoo in the nest. They'll push me out if they can. But my work will prevent that.

Here then will be my own secret history. You'll be my interlocutor and final judge. Not the Council of Four, not the ambition-blinded Alastair. You alone will decide if what I lay before you is worthy of the reward I ask. You alone will determine the worth of the goal. A goal worthy of a new generation of heroes. It would not be too dramatic to call them supermen. Men aspiring to be not just greater than their fellows, but, yes, to be gods.

For if gods are to exist, must we not create them ourselves? Must we not *become* them if our destiny is, as it must be, to rule over Nature, over Death herself?

The world has been torn apart. Megalopolis has been destroyed once, by a Great Disaster whose origins—natural or manmade—are still a matter of debate. But as I have always argued, whatever was the cause of that earthquake, that explosion, that tsunami that set Megalopolis back a hundred years at least, and caused the flight of her best and brightest to this, the False Moon—this was *creative* destruction. We have an opportunity now to create something new, something never before seen in the history of the worlds.

A world truly built on the strength of the individual, and on him alone.

If it was calumny that Alastair threw at me that day in Council, there was a kernel of truth in what he said. The day I arrived at my birthplace in Arcadia, as I watched the flames consume the home of my childhood, the pyre of my mother and my sisters, I felt, to my surprise, a burning within myself. A funeral pyre of everything weak, sentimental, and small.

In its place, rising up in me, throbbing and straight, came this revelation: that to risk life on behalf of a noble project is the greatest task a man can achieve. The reason—the sole reason—to be a human being.

My resolve stiffened in the days that followed. I had in that moment become a man. For I realized that a life here, a death there, are small prices to pay in the battle against the common enemy: the weakness of our kind.

I resolved to create a radically new type of man, surpassing the men around me as we surpass the extinct ape. All I desired from that day forward was to be free to experiment undisturbed in pursuit of that goal.

No one knows more than yourself, dear Lady, what I have sacrificed for my project. In every instance, at every turn of my long and, if I may be so immodest, illustrious career, I have preferred the glory of Megalopolis to every enticement offered by my family and my birthplace, the tiny land of Arcadia.

For nothing tranquilizes the mind like a steady purpose—a point on which it may fix.

Don't I deserve to accomplish that great purpose for which I have staked my life? For soon, I will be dead and gone.

Dead... Devindra is dead. She should be gone. That's what "dead" means. Why does she dog my footsteps now that I'm at the end of my endeavors? At my age, I should be able to rest, if not on my laurels, then at least on my certainties. And of all my certainties, the fact that dead means dead has always been at the top of the list. What an irony that my own unconscious should project an image of she who was the greatest barrier to my work when alive!

There she—it—was, last night. The projection sat before me, waiting patiently in the shadow just outside the pool of lamplight on my work table, as if these were the old days, when Devindra herself often waited on my work, waited for my attention to turn from it to her. When I had my small revenge on her for the many times she ignored me in favor of some hopeless student's problem, or some unattractive child's hurt.

Amusing note: I pretended, as I had then, to be too caught up in my own deep meditations to attend to her. Not Devindra now, but my invented image of her! At this it seemed the ghost smiled a dim smile, as if in memory of other times.

After a while, I put down my pen. A moment's pause, and I shut off the light, folding my hands on the table before me.

Starlight came through the windows. And the slanted light of the Moon Itself poured in, striking through the ghost to the wall behind.

I know such projections mean danger. But from where was the danger to come? I used a technique that has worked in the past: addressing the shade as if it had a reality of its own.

"Well?" I said. "Pleased as I am to see you, Devindra, I have little time to spare at my age, as you know. What is it you want to warn me of?"

Silent, unwilling to divulge its secrets, the ghost shook its head. It wore Devindra's favorite turban, which glowed blue-green in the light of the Moon Itself. Turquoise. Her favorite color. The color of the mountain lakes of Arcadia.

Perhaps not a warning, though surrounded by enemies as I am, a warning would be rational enough. Perhaps only a momentary misconnection between my aging brain cells. As you know, dear lady, at almost a hundred, I begin to slow down.

There are advantages to this. As I find myself close to a slowly opening door to nothingness, I find the fears I had for so many years drop away.

That shade and I sat in silence, until, finally, I turned back on the light with a gesture of annoyance, and got back to the work at hand. I couldn't help remembering how irritated it used to make me years ago, when Devindra wouldn't give me an answer to some question. As if it was too absurd to deserve one. She was never discourteous, Devindra. But she could be ruthless when needed. She was a woman, but she was also a scientist, and it was never plain to me which took precedence. She claimed neither did, but that was clearly impossible. For to be a scientist is to put all feeling aside—or, at the very least, put it in permanent second place. And Lord knows, I have yet to see a woman—barring yourself, Lady Livia—who is able to achieve that.

But my report! I must remember the supposed goal of my present banishment from Council. Here, then, is the first installment thereof.

REPORT TO THE COUNCIL OF FOUR OF MEGALOPOLIS ON THE LAND OF ARCADIA:

History of Arcadia

The early history of Arcadia is obscure.

No written records exist from before the year 1, in which year I myself was ten years old. It is a fact, though no Megalopolitan theory accounts for it. No Arcadian admits to any but the haziest memory of what went before. Is this disingenuous? It may be so. I myself was already at school in Megalopolis, and have no way of remedying this blank.

Many inevitably inadequate theories have attempted to explain this curious circumstance. I myself believe the explanation most Megalopolitan scientists accept: that some enormous cataclysm occurred in the days before year 1, traumatizing the entire population into a form of group amnesia. A small group of Arcadian scientists argues that there is no physical sign of such an event, and postulates a group emotional trauma. This theory, originally proposed by the late Professor Devindra Vale, suggests that there was a sudden radical shift in Arcadian culture, leaving the population incapable of remembering past experiences that provide no pattern or schema with which to understand their present. Her studies of legends, folklore, and fairy tales gave rise to this line of thought, inadequate and eccentric as it appears to most reputable academic circles. Nevertheless, it must be admitted the thing is strange. As far as I know, there is no record in Megalopolis either of Arcadia until the year 1. None of our historians has been able to account for this, other than by assuming the land was of so little worth as to be beneath notice.

I propose another line of thought altogether. Arcadia was always a small, insignificant part of Megalopolis, though separated from the empire by a series of mountain ranges, variously passable. But its very insignificance meant that it thought itself alone, and formed its own culture, its own way of life. It came to our attention—and by "our," I mean the empire—when it dared to pretend to a separation from our global reach. Although this took some time, valuable time wasted as Arcadia formed itself and considered itself a sovereign land.

By year 4, in Arcadian time, Arcadia as a declared independent state was finally noticed by Megalopolis. While it was undeniably a backwater, the plentiful resources it contained made it a prize worth winning. Thus the First Invasion occurred. Our attempts to "conquer" Arcadia failed at that time. The Great Disaster called all able-bodied soldiers back to the home country, needed as they were to help move the more important members of the population up to the False Moon. Afterwards, there was no will to spend in occupying a resistant land.

At that point in Arcadian history, the country consisted of a relatively sleepy population, inhabiting what early Arcadian records refer to as "a necklace of villages." These villages were under the governance of a system of local magistrates, who met together four times a year in times of peace, and when emergency required it. But after the Great Disaster came the Great Migration of many hundreds of women and children, fleeing from the Marshland of Megalopolis, over the Ceres Mountains into Arcadia.

This population influx resulted in a spurt of cultural and economic growth. Among the most notable of the refugees was Professor Devindra Vale, who had been trained in the elite Megalopolitan technical college, a prize student of our famous Professor Roderick Corman. Her great gifts were recognized by Arcadia's first queen, Lily the Silent, who took Vale as her chief counselor.

On arrival in Arcadia, Professor Vale was already pregnant with her only child, Merope, who has been of such service to Megalopolis. The father was never named.

Professor Vale continued her service to Arcadia in acting as chief counselor to Lily the Silent's daughter, Sophia, who ascended the queenship upon the death of her mother. This young queen, amusingly surnamed by her fellow Arcadians "the Wise," refused to make any crime at all a capital one—including the murder of her own mother by a wandering madman. It was under this overly tolerant reign that Arcadia consolidated its power as a Queendom, if not an outright matriarchy.

Further: Arcadian culture diverged from Megalopolitan in its embrace of superstitions of all kinds, which will be covered in more detail later in this report.

To the Lady Livia

We know who Merope's father was, though, do we not? Professor Corman, notorious throughout the Megalopolitan academic world for... er...*collaborating* with his more attractive female students. And in the case of the more brilliant of them, actively stealing their ideas and presenting them as his own.

Devindra was both brilliant and a child of the Megalopolitan Marsh, where the women were known, before the flood, for their tremendous sensual charm. She would not have escaped either Corman's attentions, or his intellectual thievery. In fact, you might say she was the victim of a twofold rape, for I know his theory of story as the building block of culture had its origin in her work. That work was interrupted by the Great Disaster, and her flight over the mountains into Arcadia.

As you know, dear Lady, Corman was assassinated by another of his female students, in a fit of "post-partum depression," as the coroner's office tactfully called it. It can only have been his just deserts.

Devindra chose flight over murder, and gave birth to Corman's child in Arcadia, in the midst of the upheaval caused by the restructuring of the country's administration and educational system that she and Queen Lily embarked upon.

Her daughter. Merope.

Perhaps it would amuse you if I should attempt a description of Merope, as she was in young womanhood. She grew into an almost comical inversion of her own mother. Short, squat, po-faced and pinchy-mouthed, dressed in such abominable taste that the casual observer might rightly conclude that every mismatched article of clothing, every clashing pattern, every garish color and dirty piece of trim meant hatred. And indeed the aggressive, intentional ugliness of everything Merope said, looked, and did meant revenge. Revenge on Devindra. For Merope, to deny all forms of beauty, elegance, *symmetry* was to defy her mother. Better, it was to make Devindra look foolish in the eyes of the mob, for

9

who could find it anything but laughable that she would continue to love and protect such a foul-mouthed, puling, awful daughter.

It was Devindra's one blind spot in an intellect otherwise characterized by clarity and light. She loved that stupid girl, in spite of all the evidence that the object of that love gave in return nothing but malice, spite, hatred, and betrayal.

So Merope.

Merope who hated her brilliant, beautiful, virtuous mother, who offered herself to me in the most degrading possible way, and who made possible my greatest achievement.

So should I not show a becoming gratitude, instead of indulging myself in mocking the poor woman? Without her, Pavo Vale could never have been born.

REPORT TO THE COUNCIL OF FOUR OF MEGALOPOLIS ON THE LAND OF ARCADIA:

Geography of Arcadia

Four different mountain ranges form Arcadia's natural borders. To the north lie the Samanthans and their foothills. To the west, the permanently snow-capped Donatees. To the south is the Ceres, and at its northern foot lies the Arcadian Ceres Marsh. To the east, the Calandals. Mt. Macillheny, a landmark from far off on the Megalopolitan side, is in this range.

In total area Arcadia is approximately 3,000 square miles. "Approximately," because there is no way of accurately measuring the mountain ranges that mark its boundaries. The Samanthans, in particular, have never been accurately surveyed.

Of that area, about 2,800 square miles comprise a valley that is roughly quadrilateral in shape, running lengthwise east to west. Within the valley nine towns are situated. The smallest, Amana, claims a population of about 7,000, while the largest, the centrally located market town of Walton, has around 15,000. All told, between the towns and the scattered farms and homesteads located in the mountains, the entire population numbers around 108,000—though this is growing.

The towns, in order of size, are:

Walton—popularly called "Market-Mad Walton."
Paloma—known for the artistic leanings of its inhabitants.
Mumford—the present capital of Arcadia, called "Learned Mumford."
Amaurote—home of the archives of Arcadia, called "Flower-covered Amaurote."
Eopolis—known for its practical know-how.
Wrykyn—known as "abstemious Wrykyn." This is an obvious joke, as the inhabitants there are much addicted to what they call "the good life."
Cockaigne—known for its great beauty.
Ventis—known as a center of agriculture.
Amana—a smaller community, known for its "expertise" in healing.

11

The population of Arcadia may politely be described as "mixed." Mass emigration from Megalopolis to Arcadia, on the event of the Great Disaster added, through widespread intermarriage, many varieties of the City's minority populations to Arcadia's. As a result, unlike in Megalopolis, it is impossible to identify the class of an inhabitant simply by their looks. Indeed "class" has a different meaning in Arcadia, referring more to the profession, talents, and activities of an individual than to their position in a social/economic structure.

Natural resources are many. Forests, protected by statute from the hunt for all but two months out of the year, team with game. Vineyards line the foothills of Arcadia, laid out by the occasionally eccentric theories of their individual owners, rather than along scientific lines. Rivers abound with trout, crawfish, catfish, pike, and eel, but these are left to reproduce naturally, with restrictions on their catch—in contrast to the rational replacement of the inefficiencies of nature with fish farms, which were such a feature of Megalopolitan husbandry in the days before the Great Disaster.

Arcadians live not just in their towns, but also in the many old farms that lie outside town limits, tucked away in the mountain ranges of the Donatees and the Calandals.

The people of the mountains tend toward an independence that may need control. Each mountain range features its own style of inhabitant. The permanent snowcaps of the Donatees seem, paradoxically, to nurture a gentle people, given to solitude, while the drier and hotter range of the Calandals produces a quarrelsome, stubborn, and sarcastic folk.

In closing, it's worth pointing out that Arcadia is, to a certain extent, held in place by the pressures of Megalopolis surrounding it. This threat enables all its many disparate parts to gather themselves into a whole. As we seek to attach Arcadia as a client state, and to take control of the Key, this is a fact worth pondering.

To the Lady Livia

"A black-haired child of the Calandals" is what you once called me, I hope with affection. I am still your child, am I not? Although now a white-haired one! But still as fiercely individual, competitive, and stubborn in pursuit of my goals as ever.

"It formed you," I remember you telling me, for I was something of a pet for you. Plucked by your talent-spotters from the mountain valley ranch where my mother and sisters toiled, I became a scholarship lad at the most elite technical college of Megalopolis, and then, after the Great Disaster, of the False Moon. You spoiled me, Livia. You took such care that I lacked nothing; school holidays were spent with you, under your eye. How envious were my schoolmates, who had nothing but their own families to coddle them. It was subtle, the way you pitted all of us against each other, but it was a success. We all worked hard to win your approval. I suppose saving your greatest signs of approval for the bumpkin lad from the Calandals was your way of whipping my schoolmates on to greater achievement. A good plan, in its way.

I think there was real affection between us. I'd always been an odd duck in my family. A woman-run farm family, for I have no memories of my father, and my mother never spoke of him. In any case I was unlike my mother and sisters, who were all blunt, outspoken, hard-working, tied to the land. My mother crooned more gently to her favorite cow than she ever did to her only son. She trusted her best friend, Polly, who unaccountably lived with us, more than she trusted me. In truth, they never understood me, any of them, and it was something of a relief when you appeared to adopt me, even discounting the fact that my mother, undoubtedly led astray by Polly, became a traitor to Megalopolis, secretly running a resistance to it in the mountains. With my sisters! How ashamed I would have been, all those years ago, if you hadn't taken me under your powerful wing. It was as if I was the hero of one of the fairy tales that Devindra studied so closely, who finally found himself of royal, rather than peasant, blood. I know, I know. I can see you smile

13

again. "Yes, Aspern," I can hear you say. "You always were a fanciful child." That's the Arcadian side of me, is it not? The side you felt was too lacking in Megalopolis. The side you hoped to partner with a more rigorous regimen of technical thought—to produce prodigies. To create a future never before imagined.

I think that strategy was a success. Although I wonder, as I look up and see Devindra's ghost, sitting there patiently: is this too big a price to pay for having imagination? Imagining a ghost? And such a ghost as she. But never mind that now.

As for my technical ability, no one in Megalopolis could doubt it. Alastair hates that fact, and loathes your insistence that I join in the Megalopolitan competition for precedence and glory. Myself against the Council of Four. Aspern Grayling, the only outsider allowed a vote in the secret conclave! That strategy of yours, of pitting us against each other in the race for technical innovation, has not just worked, it has succeeded brilliantly. There were inevitable mistakes, of course. For example, in the scramble to create a self-sustaining energy source, which may or may not have caused the Great Disaster—though scientific opinion is still divided on whether or not that gigantic tectonic upheaval and flood would have occurred without our experiments. We will never know for certain.

A shame we lacked, then and now, the Key.

But then, there were our triumphs. The creation of the False Moon, where what was saved from the Disaster is tended carefully, surpassing what had been achieved down below.

Creative destruction. How often have you and I sat in your rooms on the False Moon, meditating on the richness to be found in that simple phrase?

How often, in my years spent back in Arcadia, pretending to be the loyal subject of its queens, have I had to bite my tongue when faced with the spurious dreams that opposed that dynamic process. The New Idealism, Devindra called it. The New Partnership. That foolish doctrine that a world of partnership could possibly replace one of dominance and hierarchy. It was all the rage at Otterbridge University, the school she worked so hard to establish along with the first Arcadian queen.

But I was happy to work with her then. In the early days, when you sent me back home to finish my education in my native land, Devindra and I labored side by side. All for Science! "And Art," Devindra would add. She always insisted on linking the two, to my annoyance.

We made so many discoveries, she and I. I still feel the nostalgia of it. How many of our experiments ended in theories and facts taught not just at Otterbridge University, but in the research centers of the False Moon. Though you'd never catch Alastair admitting any of our theories as the root of much of his own work. Water culled from dew, fuel from common weeds, these useful innovations had their start in my chats with Devindra in her famous Tower by the Lily Pond, in Wrykyn.

And there were the higher flights as well. I'll admit Devindra was indefatigable. She insisted on using her own skin for cultures in our experiments on healing. Remarkable woman.

Ah, the ghost smiles again. A secret smile. Funny I imagine that. How amusing, the things the unconscious gets up to!

REPORT TO THE COUNCIL OF FOUR OF MEGALOPOLIS ON THE LAND OF ARCADIA:

Education and the University System of Arcadia

The Arcadian educational system was originally developed as a royal project of Queen Lily the First, and was continued after her death by Professor Devindra Vale. In year 40, this activity culminated in the establishment of Otterbridge University, a federation of colleges, each endowed in a different town.

The colleges of Otterbridge University are:

- Yuan Mei College, in Ventis. Originally Yuan Mei Agricultural College. I have suggested to the Council that this location should be converted into a Media Center once Megalopolis is in charge.
- Paloma School of Arts and Sciences. Formerly Paloma School of Art, Drama, and Dance, but latterly very famous for its physical sciences department.
- Walton College. The college where Neo-Rationalism or, as we call it, Neo-Fundamentalism was born. I myself was a fellow there, under the patronage of the Lord High Chancellor Michaeli.
- Juliet College, in Mumford. The oldest and best endowed of the colleges. Where Lily the Silent and Devindra Vale began their project of Arcadian education.
- St. Vitus College, in Wrykyn. Home of the so-called New Subjectivity, otherwise known as the New Idealism. Location of Professor Devindra Vale's famous study, "The Tower by the Lily Pond." Most renowned, some say undeservedly, of the colleges.
- Eisler Hall, in Amaurote. Keeper of the Arcadian archives. Famous school of library arts and sciences.
- Bel Regina College, in Cockaigne.
- Eopolis School of Ecology and Business.

- Hanuman School of Healing, at Amana. Formerly Hanuman School of Medicine, then Hanuman School of Medicine and Veterinary Medicine, in collaboration with Yuan Mei College, and finally Hanuman School of Healing.

Eisler Hall in particular is known for training archivists and librarians for its own extensive library and archives.

The Archives at Eisler Hall, in Amaurote, contain the following materials:

- The Public Records Office of Arcadia
- THE ANALECTA ARCADIA (collected literary excerpts or passages)
- THE ACTA ARCADIA – a collection of legends.
- THE VITAE ANTIQUAE SANCTORUM, containing the ancient *Legendus Snottianacus,* as well as the *Maud Cycle.*

Arcadian educational theory proposes *three* forms of Truth that can be perceived, analyzed, and used. The first two we in Megalopolis know well: Truths of Reasoning, where a rational mind, analyzing the situation before it, can be fairly sure of its conclusions, even if unable to prove them utterly. And Truths of Fact, those facts that no one not under the influence of drugs, intoxicants, or madness can dispute.

To these Arcadian education adds a third: Truths of Imagination. It is contended that a knowledge of the world of imagination is of all intellectual tools the most fruitful. The belief that underlies all Arcadian education is that there is not only an objective truth to be observed in the world around us, but also the truth of *the world inside.*

While this belief has no part in Megalopolitan thought, it must be admitted that it has lain behind Arcadia's ability to find and hold the Key. For that reason, it should not be passed over without due consideration.

To the Lady Livia

The rupture between me and Devindra was inevitable, I suppose, and not only because of our clash as to the proper uses of the Key, or due to the wiles of her ghastly daughter. You predicted it, when I would journey back under cover to the False Moon to report on what I had seen. You knew it was foreordained that she, the foremost Arcadian woman scientist, and I, the foremost male one, would fall out—mild phrase for so violent an occurrence—over the issue of cloning. "For," as you pointed out to me, "there are certain heights women will always refuse to scale." I pointed out to you, grinning, that not all women share this trait. "I am the exception that proves the rule," you said sternly, with a glint of amusement.

Of course you were right. There were many disagreements between us, Devindra and I. More and more as time went on. Any improvement of food sources, for example, any mingling of chemical with so called "natural" processes. Any animal experimentation outside of breeding practices. And any "tinkering," as she called it, with human genetic material. Any at all.

Tinkering! I still laugh when I think about it. Tinkering!

Of course when we discovered it was possible to clone an animal from a single parent, she expressed her reservations. And when I made the leap, years before Alastair, to a simple process where the same result could be achieved with a human, she balked. Not only balked, but used her considerable influence with Arcadia's first queen, Lily, to have the entire line of inquiry made illegal. Parthenogenesis, cloning, in any form for humans is forbidden in Arcadia. Without exception.

Old history.

Few things, in Arcadia, are forbidden absolutely in this way. Her action was much remarked upon. Battle lines were drawn. A group of young scientists, feeling the unbearable restraint, lined up behind me. Factions formed. There was a growing estrangement, both professional and personal, between Devindra and myself.

I regret that. I thought of my regrets last night, as I sat in silence with Devindra's simulacrum in the corner.

But I have done with regrets. Work is all that matters. Work and precedence. And so I must push on.

What matters now is my own—our own—project. That and the discovery, finally, of the Key. Just "the Key" they call it in Arcadia. But you and I—and the Council, alas—know it as "the Key of Power."

REPORT TO THE COUNCIL OF FOUR OF MEGALOPOLIS ON THE LAND OF ARCADIA:

Family Life in Arcadia

As in all cultures without exception, the family structure of Arcadia is its basic economic/political unit. This structure is overly fluid, heterogeneous, disorganized, and confusing.

In fact, the definition of the word "family" in the Arcadian sense would strike the Megalopolitan mind as strange, even as shockingly immoral.

For a family in Arcadia begins with a group of *any kind, of any number of adults*, and of *any mix of sexes* coming together for the purpose of functioning as a household unit.

Vows can be taken between or among any number of Arcadians, of any sex, who are willing to protect each other as members of the same family. What are called "First Vows" are meant to last for three years at the initial ceremony, then renewed—or reneged on, depending on the desires of the household involved. Subsequent vows are termed "Luna Vows" (see "Religion" below). These may also be terminated by mutual agreement, though generally are considered sacred and binding by the contracted parties.

The one exception to this is the case of *any couple partnership that has resulted in children.* In that case, the vows taken are permanent. No exceptions. The partners in this case may live apart, they may even form other bonds, but their vows remain intact as long as the child or children live.

Single parenting is unknown in Arcadia. If the biological mother or father dies, or for some reason is incapable of raising the child, the remaining parent joins another household, or is joined by another partner capable of helping with its nurture.

Children take the surname of the women they are born to—as, for example, in the case of my son, Pavo Vale.

To the Lady Livia

That last is amusing, is it not? Given what you know about the "mother" of my son. My own Arcadian "family" arrangement, as a single parent, was quite comfortable, at least until the final blow-up. Of course I had excellent quarters of my own at Walton College. As a sui generis individual, this suited me very well. But once I was a "father," Arcadian tradition insisted on a change in my domicile.

Though perhaps this was not a bad thing, even considering that regrettable incident at the end. So much was learned. So much was gained. In many ways, the grand home of Michaeli, Lord High Chancellor of Arcadia—the grandest, as you know, since most Arcadians regard grandeur, if not with scorn, then at least with amusement—was the best choice I could have made.

I needed grandeur for the nurture of my son. And where was it to be found in Arcadia but in the home of the Lord High Chancellor?

Michaeli was easy enough to manipulate for our own ends, as are all men who are secretly uneasy about their roots. This particular buffoon had owned a sweetshop in Cockaigne, from which the first Arcadian queen raised him to be her Lord High Chancellor. The choice of title was his, of course. Queen Lily was notoriously careless of that kind of thing, an error Arcadia makes too often for its own good.

Humiliated by his origins, he compensated with enormous, pointless displays of grandeur, along with endless ambitions for his children. Devindra and Queen Lily, and after Lily, her daughter Queen Sophia, were careful never to injure his fragile dignity, or to mention his antecedents in any way that might offend. Of course this solicitude made him hate them. And made him malleable to our cause. Until the... unpleasantness, that is.

He had his uses, though. For it was through Michaeli that you and I learned the uses of the Key. Yes. *The Key that resides, hidden, somewhere in Arcadia.*

21

Which brings us to the true nature of the Key, reluctant though we may be to admit it. I myself for years insisted its principle was an impossibility. I've had to retract my error. For this is the immutable fact: The Key connects everything that is.

And as Megalopolis hopes to control the whole, so Megalopolis must control the Key.

You know my own plans here. You know my ambitions for my son. You know the Council's secret wish to disarm him, and through him, me, and gain the Key for itself. And I think you know which side will prevail.

I wonder if the apparition in the corner does not warn of some danger there. I wonder if the danger resides within the Council's plan for Pavo Vale.

I wonder.

Art and Science in Arcadia

Arcadian uses of Art and Science are unsophisticated, even primitive, in comparison with those of Megalopolis. But at the bottom of both lurks the Key.

In Arcadia, it is difficult if not impossible to find the dividing line between these two quite different disciplines. The reason can be found in the underlying Arcadian belief system (for more on this, see below: "Religion").

A belief in what is called the "One" informs all aspects of Arcadia, and therefore all work in the arts and sciences. This belief gives all manner of productions a curiously egalitarian quality—in the crudest sense of the word. There is none of that individual genius so often shown in the works of Megalopolis: no extremes, no overwhelming drama, no bravura performance. No brilliant discoveries that dazzle the audience. The ideal of Arcadian art, and of its science as well, is what Arcadians call the "Golden Mean." The intended cultural purpose is to explore, to define, and to support what Arcadians call the "Good Life."

Arcadians believe that all artwork contains the history of the place in which it was formed, and by this I mean all artwork of any kind or quality. This is undoubtedly why Arcadian scientists spend so much time in the futile study of such childish nonsense as fairy tales, legends, myths, and fantasies. The late Professor Vale, for example, "pioneered" in this work.

Younger scholars seriously analyze art that runs from the low to the obscure. This belief that all artwork contains the history of the place extends to the Luna cards that are used for a form of Arcadian divination (again see below: "Religion").

Still, to be fair, while Arcadian literature and art are, by Megalopolitan standards, quite primitive, it must be admitted they have a certain charm when their adherents stop themselves from taking the stories and images in them as worthy of scientific study. At their best, they provide the kind of trifling pleasure associated with children's tales.

To the Lady Livia

Strange, isn't it, that the Arcadian belief in the primacy of imagination should lead to their possession of what Megalopolis most requires. This brings us back to the Key. Which dialogue must remain between us, you and I, at least for the time being. To discuss it in Council would be explosive—given how little we know of its properties—even should the Council call me back to its deliberations from my most recent exile.

What we do know is collected from a grab bag of Arcadian legend, fairy tales, and children's stories, along with measurements taken by myself in my research lab here on the False Moon.

This data has established a pattern of phenomenal surges of energy— earthshaking, epoch-making—and traced them to what was known at the time of the whereabouts of the Key.

I cannot emphasize this point enough: *we must treat the search for the Key with extreme caution.* Until we more fully understand its makeup and how to activate it, we must not make any precipitous moves that would lead to disaster. And when I say "disaster," I mean an apocalyptic nightmare that would make the Great Disaster look like a flood in a sandbox.

That hothead Alastair would have us charge into Arcadia, full bore and full blast, with all our might. As he puts it, "Threaten to blow them sky-high unless they hand it over."

I need not point out what uncontrollable forces that is likely to unleash.

It was Alastair, I believe, who authorized the First Invasion of Arcadia, resulting in loss of life on both sides, a fouling of valuable Arcadian resources, as well as *total failure* in its goal of making Arcadia a client state. If it achieved anything at all, it was a more firmly entrenched loathing of all things Megalopolitan on the part of Arcadia. What small success we have had in overcoming that disaffection has come from my strategy of "soft propaganda" aimed at the Arcadian young. My own son has had his successes utilizing such techniques in the gathering of his "Invincibles." If you recall, this was a project you yourself approved and financed, over Alastair's objections. And over his rage that the funding would otherwise have gone to his own experiments.

This is not to mention his experiments that very likely were the cause of the Great Disaster.

I can hear him now in Council. "I just don't understand your thinking, Grayling! We're bigger, we're stronger, we have more weaponry. Case closed. What the *hell* are we waiting for?"

And then his suspicious look. His attempt to make the Council—and yourself—doubt my motives.

"I know," he'd say in that nasty way he has. "We're waiting for that superman of yours. Your so-called *son*."

I invariably ignore his taunts, as the best way to deal with such idiocy. You and I both know that my strategy, the one of "soft propaganda," has worked far better than Alastair's force, even without considering the Invincibles. Case in point are the years I've spend straddling the divide between Arcadia and Megalopolis, the physical and the philosophical, working both in my rooms at Walton College, in Otterbridge University, and in my research center on the False Moon.

My whole project derives from this hybrid appointment, if I may call it so, from my years as professor, scientist, and leading intellectual in two such different atmospheres as Megalopolis and Arcadia. Of inestimable value was the cross-fertilization of ideas I benefited from by straddling those two realms. Even Devindra Vale used to say that such a hybrid approach resulted in increased creativity.

As I write this, Devindra's shade stands up, as if in distress, goes to the window and looks out, hugging herself—itself—as if chilled.

But what can chill a ghost?

Report to the Council of Four of Megalopolis on the land of Arcadia:

Arcadian Systems of Finance and Commerce

I've been asked repeatedly by my colleague Alastair to put a figure on the resources of Arcadia, as well as on its outputs, for use by the Council of Four in its cost-benefit analysis of a potential new invasion. But as I've said before, this is difficult, if not impossible, given the Arcadian system of finance, which is an eccentric mix of barter, trade, charity, and a kind of scrip.

To even use the word "trade" is misleading. What trade there is with the "outside" is the result of an elaborate system of barter mainly with the itinerant peddlers who make their way over the Ceres Mountains and, less frequently because of the nearness to Megalopolitan sentry positions, the Calandals. As the routes over the former are closed during the winter months, and those over the latter difficult of passage due to the patrols that watch over the daily transport to and from the False Moon, these exchanges cannot be called "trade" in the Megalopolitan sense.

Calls for this trade to be stopped by force are counterproductive. It is by those routes that I have made my way back and forth between Arcadia and Megalopolis. To lose the routes is to lose our paths of communication.

I know there has been a suggestion that I use the trade route over the Calandals for my own ends. I find the insinuation insulting, and unworthy of being addressed in this report.

Markets in Arcadia are basic. There is at least one market a week in each town, with a main market held mid-week in Walton, the largest in population and the most centrally located. But again, we are not talking "trade" in the sense our people understand it. An Arcadian proverb might make clear what I'm getting at here: "The wise woman prefers to have friends in the market than money in the chest."

Concerning the natural resources that are so abundant, and so necessary to a further development of the Megalopolitan project: It is written into the Arcadian Constitution, a joint project of Professor Devindra Vale and Queen Lily the Silent in the early days of her reign, that "Natural resources are common property." ALL natural resources, whether on "private" property or not—and it must be clear by now that "private" means something less than in the Megalopolitan sense—are under the jurisdiction of the Arcadian Sovereign Wealth Fund, and are regulated strictly in a way that would scarcely have been borne without a revolution by Megalopolis in the days before the Great Disaster. The emphasis is on husbandry rather than extraction, and there are many rules, enforced by popular opinion, regarding the conservation of wood, soil, water, and so on. All resources are "held in trust" for the generations that come after. All income is distributed evenly among the population, with no surplus remaining, with the sole exception of a sinking fund.

The change that the Arcadian system of finance and commerce needs, from which all other good will flow, is an alteration in basic beliefs about how society is motivated. The Arcadian idea is that society is powered by the prestige motive, rather than by the more rational profit motive understood to be the main engine in Megalopolis.

Arcadians have a constitutional dislike of the concept of abstract exchange. Its professors, starting with the late Professor Vale, have taught that abstract exchange in itself leads to an objectification of human beings. And to an Arcadian, that of all things is the most to be avoided. Presently. That may change.

A judicious and generous handing out of luxuries and inflated honors to certain key members of the Arcadian young would be a much more effective way forward. Indeed, my son and I have experimented with this as my own pet project, secretly attracting more than a few young Arcadian men to the goals of Megalopolis: our so-called "Invincibles."

These would be the example of an Arcadian of a new type, who may lead the way to our eventual domination. And of this type, there may be one who leads the rest.

To the Lady Livia

"An Arcadian of a new type." Oh, understatement, oh euphemism! What a pallid description of my greatest achievement, literally my greatest conception.

What a way to speak of my "son"! Not a computer, he. Not a robot. But a man. More than a man. A superman.

Let Alastair beat *that* with his pathetic attempts at autonomous "artificial intelligence," and his ridiculously half-baked "disembodied brain in a box." I argued time and time again in Council that these were, literally, dead ends. For how can we overcome the state of "being human," with all the frailty that implies, by avoiding the challenge of what "being human" means?

That's right: *the body*. The biological carapace that houses the software of the brain. That astonishingly sensitive feedback machine that calculates innumerable sensations, experiences, relations. How did Alastair—how *does* Alastair—expect to replace such a marvel with his binomial mechanisms?

The answer is that he cannot, no matter how much grant money he siphons off from the coffers of the Council of Four: grant money that could be put to far better use for Megalopolitan goals by investing in an actual human being.

An actual human being. This was where Alastair's vision failed him. Whereas you posited correctly that my heritage of Arcadian imagination crossed with Megalopolitan technological innovation would succeed where he had failed. I was able to build on the Mega thought that has gone before me. Mega scientists have long experimented with genetically "improving" animals to be more useful to man. Dogs, cats, pigs, even a lemur. I recognized one of these experiments in Queen Sophia's pet Leef. The corruption endemic in the laboratories of the Ruined Surface often led to animal experiments finding their way into the black market trade. Leef must have been one of these animals.

Perhaps it was just as well that Sophia found and adopted the creature.

For I learned much that was useful to me from observing Leef.

You know what I learned. I learned to create a human being.

You've seen my boy, Livia. My "son." A magnificent creature, isn't he? Doesn't he draw all eyes, all attention; has there ever been any to match his like?

There cannot be any to match him. For he is the first of his kind.

And I made him.

I made him what he is. I engineered the genes that built that bronze silk skin, that formed those solid muscles, that created that enormous head and those glowing violet eyes. I created those, through sweat, tears, and years of careful work.

All artificial. I manipulated chemicals to manufacture every bit of DNA contained in human chromosomes. I did this. For the first time in human history, I, not nature, created a human being.

And do not doubt this, the game was worth the candle. For in creating a human born free of the messiness, the chaos of Nature, I have created a free man. The rest of us, we organics, are tied by birth to our ancestors. To our families. You know what this means. Chained to traits, to expectations, to useless traditions and duties felt, literally, in the bones and sinews to be "sacred"—to be "human."

My boy is free of that. Liberated from the manacles of personal ties, unconnected to Nature, to the animal world, what can he not achieve? Think of the advantages of a man unencumbered by history. Unlike the rest of the mortal world, my boy is free of the unconscious storehouse of collective memory. He can literally act and be free.

Long as I have contemplated this ultimate good, I am still made breathless at the thought.

But you know all of this, you who encouraged me every step of the way, cheered me, most important of all, *funded* me. You deserve to have the fruits of my labor laid on your altar. So tell me, Livia. What can I tell you about the first man ever created by man, consciously, without a mother? A man, who, wielding the Key, might yet live to be a god?

29

REPORT TO THE COUNCIL OF FOUR OF MEGALOPOLIS ON THE LAND OF ARCADIA:

Religion in Arcadia

I have now arrived at the heart of this report: the Arcadian religion. Arcadians regard religion as a function of biology. Of Nature. They regard any "experience" of that imaginary being, "God," and any "experience" conveyed by the primitive stories of legends, myths, and fairy tales as being in relation to each other. Both "experiences" are considered as originating in the biological makeup of man, and their source is an absolute.

Its final revelation is in the family.

In a discussion with Professor Vale on this very subject, I pointed out that the concept of "God" for many Arcadians is the same as the immature experience of the "imaginary friend" so many of us know from childhood. I am almost tearful when I consider this, in sympathy for the deluded child who needs such comfort. Indeed, I remember something along these lines from my own childhood, which I can scarcely recall without pain. Mentioning this to Professor Vale, I was astounded at her response: "What makes you think your imaginary friend *wasn't* the voice of God?" I told her not to be ridiculous, the voice of the imaginary friend of my childhood sounded like what I imagined would be the voice of my teddy bear. For I, like all Arcadian children, had a teddy bear of which I was particularly fond, which burned with all the rest of my family's household goods in the First Invasion. "Well?" she said. "What did you think God was going to sound like?"

I mention this conversation to show the very primitive level of the Arcadian discourse on the subject, hardly even to be mentioned along with the Megalopolitan, if it were not for one very important—indeed, crucial—aspect of Arcadian religion. The Key. That same Key which we now seek, though for secular, rather than sacred reasons.

I will return to the Key after a brief discussion of Arcadian religious practices.

Religion in Arcadia II

Historically, many differing views of religion have joined together in Arcadia, blending more or less successfully. The source of this is undoubtedly the multitude of beliefs brought over the mountains after the Great Disaster.

These religious beliefs, of a seemingly endless variety, are more than curious. Forms of worship are many and varied, some cults so small that they contain only the members of one family. All Arcadians worship in *some* way, following one superstition or another, often passed down, supposedly, from an earlier tradition. There are even some in Arcadia who worship *trees*.

We should not be misled by this strange multitude of sects into thinking that no common religious feeling acts as a binder on the community. All Arcadians believe—or profess to believe—in what they call the "One." This "One" is the ground from which all else springs. Or, if not the ground, the substance. Or if not the substance, the Law.

I find this difficult to explain. Even after a lifetime of observing the varied forms of worship of this—even now I'm unsure what to call it. An animal? A mineral? A mycelium? A superhuman of some kind? I still find it impossible to explain in Megalopolitan terms.

But in order to come to a proper discussion of the Key, I must try. So I press on.

Arcadians firmly believe that all of life springs from this One, from which springs all wisdom as well. Arcadians believe that each individual receives an "idea" or even a "picture" representing however much of the One or its aspects—which are believed to be infinite—that they are capable of understanding.

Hence Professor Vale's frivolous remark about the "voice" of my teddy bear coming from God.

I will give you another example of the frivolity of Arcadian religious practice. The most respected Arcadians are those who have the greatest familiarity with an Arcadian fortune-telling deck known as "The Luna."

This "oracle" originally came over the Ceres Mountains with the diaspora from the Megalopolitan Marsh. In her lifetime, Professor Devindra Vale

31

undertook a serious academic and, she said, "scientific" study of these cards. "The Luna deck is primarily intended for meditation and reflection," she wrote in a monograph on the subject. "To use it, or any other form of divination, to predict the future is considered by the wise as not just foolish, but useless as well."

I have no memory of the Luna from my own childhood, which is what makes me believe it must have come from the Marsh. On the other hand, my sisters often kept secrets from me—not least of which was their activity in the Resistance. So if the Luna appeared in Arcadia any time much before I became aware of its use, I would not be in a position to know of it. It wasn't until I noticed Merope Vale, daughter of Professor Vale, hunched over these cards on more than one occasion that I inquired more closely into their meaning.

The word "Luna" is not an easy one to translate. It most likely comes originally from one of the barbarous dialects of the Marsh people of Megalopolis, from whence, as I've said, the Oracle itself most likely came. In Arcadia, even before the discovery of the cards, the word carried a variety of meanings. For example, as a color, it refers to silver gray. As an adjective, it is often used to describe a feeling, thought, or opinion deeply held, but difficult to define in normal terms. Arcadians would say, "It is a Luna vow," for example, to refer to a strong bond pairing.

I have had my own experience of this. But no more need be said about that here.

Instead, it is time to speak in practical terms of the Key. For this, the greatest superstition in Arcadia is at the same time an undeniable physical fact. Arcadians are blind to its real uses, to the endless supply of energy it can provide.

Arcadians do not speak of science when they speak of the Key. They speak instead of religion. They believe its purpose is to connect human souls to the souls of every living thing. To connect all families to all. The Key connects all to the One.

Arcadia believes it to be the duty of each individual in this world to "listen" to the Key through their own "soul," and to act in concert with what is heard in order to bring more growth to the intricate network it embodies.

Alone in Arcadia, my son Pavo Vale remains untouched by any super-stitions about the Key. He lacks any feeling of "the sacred" toward it. This gives him, and him alone, the obvious advantage that he may wield it for power, without the hesitance a typical Arcadian would feel at the "sacri-lege." The Key holds power scarcely explored because of this hesitation. But there can be no doubt of what this Power consists, for the Key gathers together the threads of energy making up the physical world.

It holds the unlimited energy of the One.

For whatever the "One" might turn out to be, the fact of the matter, upon which all our scientists are agreed, is that the forces associated with that vague concept are vast and enduring, past any energy source Megalopolis has yet used, or even contemplated.

The Key, then, is the hope of Megalopolis. To grasp the Key for Meg-alopolis is our goal. Unlimited energy. Unlimited growth. Unlimited boundaries. What the New Man demands can be taken from the Key.

As for where the Key hides, that is the question before us now. The claim that it connects all that "is," as Arcadian religion insists, may be discounted as superstition. But that it does in fact connect a vast network of energy cannot be denied.

To the Lady Livia

I well remember how startled I was to hear about an actual experience of the Key, one that I could scarcely discount. It was, to my surprise, the fatuous Lord High Chancellor Michaeli who shared a memory of his fear of the Key. *Terror* is not too strong a word.

It was over one of those endless glasses of Arcadian dessert wines he would push on his male dinner guests. But I know he was far from drunk. I must consider seriously all that he said.

As I recall, this was during a discussion at table of one of Devindra's more popular university lectures on the subject of the "unity" of all phenomena. I swilled the deep purple liquid in my glass—Michaeli was famous for the stuff, which came from a particular vineyard outside Amaurote—and said, "The idea that everyone and everything are inter-connected is, in my view, absurd on the face of it."

"Y-y-y-ye-yes," stuttered Michaeli in agreement. But I spotted—and disliked—a certain look of doubt. I pressed him to tell me of his reserva-tions, and after a bit of his usual hemming and hawing, he timidly spoke.

"B-b-b-but. I've s-seen it. The K-K-Key. T-t-touched it."

At this he shuddered. The memory was obviously an unpleasant one.

"*And?*" I demanded. For I was always able to force Michaeli to obey me, and I had no doubt of now being able to learn something of interest to myself—and perhaps to Megalopolis.

"H-h-h-horrible," he shuddered again. "I s-s-saw…I m-mean, I f-f-felt ev-ev-ev…all the th-th-things I'd done wr-wr-wrong. S-since a child." He looked at me in that doglike way he had, and I thought, not for the first time, that it was just like Queen Lily to choose a pompous ass like that for her Chancellor.

"I r-r-really d-d-don't w-want to s-s-say more," he said, looking furtively down into his own glass. Tossing its contents down, he refilled it with a shaking hand.

But of course I insisted. And he complied. He always did comply. Until the unpleasantness, of course.

Apparently it was in the days of the second queen, Sophia, the daughter of Lily the Silent, though why the idiot didn't tell me about it then escapes me. Having some appointment or other with her, he found her sitting on the floor of her study playing with her goddaughter, my "great-granddaughter," although she may someday be something more. This little girl, he told me, was playing with a large rose-gold-colored key.

"And I s-s-said it was t-t-t-too v-v-valuable an object to be a pl-pl-play-thing!"

Old fool, I thought. I knew he had hopes of forming an Arcadian Trea-sury, and he obviously thought everything of value should be kept there under his eye. In fact he had come on this particular day to remonstrate with the queen about her theory that the proper use of valuables was to hand them out to the Arcadian populace as soon as they were acquired. "Given soon as got," as she said, with that irritating light laugh of hers.

This was a sore point with poor old Michaeli, and when he saw the toddler playing with what was obviously a valuable heirloom of some kind ("b-b-b-b-belonging to the n-n-n-nation"), he lost what control he had and snatched it out of her hands.

"Th-th-th-that w-w-w-was wh-wh-when I s-s-s..., f-f-f-felt..."

"Saw what? Felt what?" That stammer of his tried my patience sorely. But bit by bit, I managed to pull the story from him.

He told me—I'm summarizing here rather than quoting—that the moment his sweaty palm grasped the Key, the walls fell away from the room. A wind blew through him. He could see himself at every age—and he didn't much like what he saw. Also, though he couldn't explain to me how this could be, he saw every person, every thing, every incident connected to himself.

"In the past," I said. "I assume."

At this, the fool actually looked terrified.

"N-n-n-no," he whispered. "N-n-not j-just the p-past. The *future*."

I should tell you that Michaeli, unfortunately, was a bit of a lush, and in fact his tragic end was the result of his combining a massive bender with an unfortunate desire for a swim in the Juliet River. So I think we might safely discount any testimony here that stretches credulity too thin.

He dropped the Key immediately, he told me. And the little girl, apparently unaffected by whatever powers it concealed, picked it right back up and continued her play.

This is important, Livia. I mean, that the "little girl" played so carelessly with the Key.

Sophia ushered Michaeli out of the room: "Go home and have a good nap, you'll feel much better after." I can just hear her!

He was so shaken by the incident, he said, that he'd told no one of it until that day. And once he had told me, many things that had been dark to me came into the light. The source of Queen Sophia's power, and her inexplicable hold on the hearts and minds of Arcadia, for example. The secret of the confounding paradox of Arcadia's lack of technology and Arcadian abundance.

For I have studied what there is known of the Key, and the result of my studies is this: The Key is, in reality, a physical embodiment of condensed force—the connector between the Unmanifest and the Manifested World.

It is, in short, the portal to Eternity. And as such, to eternal, unending Power.

I have been unable to determine where the Key originally sprang from in my researches. Nor have I been able to discover if it is a unique artifact, or if fellows of a similar nature and power exist elsewhere.

Nevertheless, dear Lady, I'm sure you immediately see with your keen intellect that the important point is that we have identified a key as *the* Key, and that we have a general idea of its location, for it was undoubtedly in the keeping of Queen Sophia, after having been found in the sea by her mother, Lily the Silent. We have no reason to assume it has ever left Arcadia. In fact, measurements of its radiation show it to be there, somewhere, hidden...who knows? Perhaps guarded, too, by those who understand the secrets of its workings, and the sources of its power, better than we do at present.

Perhaps kept, without the use of its power, by a person or persons unknown.

In other words, as I have said before, we must move carefully. For we must pluck the source of power from its hiding place without mistakenly turning its potentially destructive rage back on ourselves.

This is what that clumsy blackguard, Alastair, has failed utterly to understand. I tell you, Livia, I despair of the Council of Four if it does not allow me to handle this in my own way. There is very little time to do this, but if it can be done, it shall be done by me. And by Pavo. For I have a very good idea about where the Key resides at present, and of who is its protector. That little girl Michaeli saw playing with the Key is now a grown woman. Shanti Vale.

If Sophia left the Key to anyone, it would be to her.

More, Livia: Shanti bears the genes of my experiment. She may very well be free of bondage to the Key. She may be of the lineage I've created that can wield it and be free.

REPORT TO THE COUNCIL OF FOUR OF MEGALOPOLIS ON THE LAND OF ARCADIA:

The Future of Arcadia

In this report I believe I have made crystal clear both the valuable natural resources that Arcadia can provide to Megalopolis, and the difficulties in convincing Arcadia that its best future lies in peacefully handing them over. For at the present time, with most of Megalopolis still in a disorganized state after the Great Disaster that so unfortunately interfered with its previous strong forward thrust, Arcadia feels we have little to offer it. This will not always be so.

We should not be surprised to find that present-day Arcadia enjoys a period of unusual creativity and progress, even if that creativity seems primitive by our standards, and the progress derisory. The stimulus that comes from direct personal intercourse works powerfully in a small community, and this was always an advantage Arcadia had over the greater population of Megalopolis. Existing in smaller units, it has the advantage of combining the stimulus of intimacy with that of varied points of view.

I say this as Arcadia's fiercest critic. Speaking in all fairness, though, it is undeniable that the majority of people living within her boundaries find their lives less circumscribed than we might think. They want little in the way of change. No matter how deluded they may be, Arcadians are by and large a "happy" people. Or at least they believe themselves to be so, which amounts to the same thing.

This they ascribe to the Key. This same Key that was brought from Megalopolis to Arcadia by her first queen, Lily the Silent and disappeared at her death, only to be—and a mysterious silence is kept on this subject in the records—rediscovered somehow and returned to Arcadia by the second queen, Sophia.

We might think this mere propaganda, although our own scientists originally alerted us to a glow of energy emanating from Arcadia so strong that it could only come from some superior origin. As we know, Arcadia has such primitive forms of energy production and renewal that this beam could come from no previously known source. Scientists using artificial intelligence capable of parsing information to an incredibly finicky degree were able to determine that the energy was similar to that originally found under the sea by the Marsh. And after that, in information received and stored from the Arcadia of the first reign.

There was no doubt. It was the Key that emanated that strange and powerful energy. It is the Key that is emitting it now.

What that energy is composed of, what it is capable of providing, remains to be discovered. Suffice to say that we know now that it exists, although exactly where has been slightly more difficult to determine. Arcadia appears to believe it has reason to hide it from Megalopolitan eyes.

It is said in Arcadia that the Key holds the community together. But this particular glue is something we can dissolve, for it is the enmity of Megalopolis that enables the towns of Arcadia to avoid falling out among themselves. This will not last forever. Any threats of imperial violence must be replaced by "soft" propaganda: for example, a son of Arcadia's offering of a New Way. For this, you know my thoughts already about my own son, Pavo Vale, and his credentials as just the New Man to rule over Arcadia in Megalopolis's name. But let that rest for now.

To speak again of the Key. It is obvious that it is an object of real power. Of how much power our scientists will need to ascertain when we possess it and can analyze its qualities. But suffice it to say, such a small, backward, technologically stagnant culture as Arcadia could not present such a misleadingly vibrant face if it weren't for some superior force powering its national life. Such a force is the Key, a point which I and the Council of Four, barring some small disagreements, agree on. And scientific evidence bears this out.

When at last we do hold the Key, we will have in our hands a weapon par excellence with which to restore Megalopolis to its former greatness. But who, I ask, will be the one to wield it?

To the Lady Livia

And then, as if in answer from the universe—though of course that is my figure of speech, these things do not happen in this way—Pavo appears.

"They've called me in, Dad," he says in that attractive, swaggering way of his. He picks up a paperknife on my table and fiddles with it, puts it down, and pours himself a glass of Arcadian wine.

They—meaning the Council.

"For what?" I say, though of course I know.

He shrugs. "They say so they can figure out how much they wanna support us going in. BUT..."

He looks at me significantly. Of course I know what that means.

"And I?" I ask. But I know the answer.

"They want me alone. Not you." At this he whistles, and we look at each other with mutual grim understanding.

I scent a trap. Pavo does too. Pick us off, one at a time. Envy. Malice. We can feel it in a wave coming across the False Moon.

Is this why my unconscious calls up the specter of Devindra Vale? Does my fear of my enemies create an image of she who was enemy to my work, all those years ago?

Pavo grins. "You know me, Dad." He throws down the rest of the glass, sets it down, and goes out.

I await developments. But in a clash between the Council and my creation, I can scarcely doubt the outcome.

Enough of this "Report," then, and any pretense that I have service to give to the backward thinking of the Council. We move on alone, Pavo and I.

From now on, this history is for you alone, Livia. You alone will judge me. You alone will weigh my plans in the balance and see if I deserve failure, or the success I've coveted for so long.

Why should it be as I write these lines that I feel a clutching at my heart, a sharp pain in the center of my breast, a strange weariness. Is it fear of my enemies? Or something else? Do I protest my belief in my impending triumph too much? Am I overly proud, should modesty be my watch-word, am I punished for feeling overpleased with myself? Has arrogance made me careless, as Devindra often said?

Devindra's image still sits in the deepening shadows as the False Moon turns and the light of the Moon Itself fades away and dies. It seems to me—am I unwell? Overtired? Worn out with overwork? Here at the greatest moment of tension, when the dice are cast, and we wait to see the result. Why does this specter still haunt me? I'm sure that if the fairy tale is true, that after death something remains of the soul, then after passing through that unknown portal Devindra would see all that her mortal limitations had not allowed. Surely she would see the importance of my work for humanity, the sheer imagination, the wonder of it! Surely, then, she would have to admit I was right.

Here I have another confession to make, Livia. Last night I ignored my strict training, indeed, my entire system of belief, the foundation on which the whole of my life and work securely rests.

I laid out a Luna spread.

Yes. The Luna. That impious pack of fortune-telling pasteboard, of mysterious, doubtless ignoble origin, that informs the so-called "science" of my native land. More than its science, its history as well.

Why, you ask? I can even now see the pained look of disappointment cross your face, and yet, Livia, I can't help myself. In penning this report, I seem to come closer to borderlands I have avoided with signal success the whole of my long life.

Why, I hear you say. Why even fool in jest with the silly, discredited things? And yet this is no jest. I have never felt further from a jest in all my years. So much weighs in the balance. Perhaps I clutch at straws.

You understand me. For in times past, you have taken more than a casual interest in the Luna.

Why was that? I still want to know the answer. I still ponder the mystery of you, Livia, who controls Life and Death in Megalopolis, which is to say the civilized world—of you being fascinated with a pack of pasteboard regarded with veneration by the savages of Arcadia.

"Tell me the meaning of this one, Aspern," I remember your asking, one forefinger tapping at the card of The Bride.

Why did I have a sudden thought that this was not the image that captured you, but that your subtlety led you to pretend an interest there? Why did I think your real gaze was turned to that most mysterious of the Luna's minor arcana, The Changeling?

"Is this," you purred, "how Arcadians foretell the future?" Your amused scorn was palpable. I answered, perhaps intemperately, "Queen Sophia, so-called 'the Wise,' says that no one should seek to know the Future. For the Future is not immutable. To predict it is to change it, in ways that cannot be controlled."

And the past? Can the cards tell you the truth about the past?

I heard your angry intake of breath. With a flick of your forefinger, you sent The Steed skittering off the malachite tabletop to the floor.

I put the cards away that day, but your anger made me thoughtful. A children's game that angered the great Livia. Surely there was some mystery there.

So it has been a secret study of mine, Livia: the Luna. It has been in the Luna that I have remembered things, and feelings, long forgot.

I tell you, Livia, I wonder at myself. Devindra's ghost sits with me still, sinking farther into the shadows of the corner of my research room, and I find myself wanting to follow her, phantom that I know her to be. To pull her back into the light. To keep her with me, even as a phantom. The force of this feeling has come on me slowly, as I've written this report. Why should that be? I'm frightened, Livia. I haven't slept since writing these words. I feel she's with me, though she will not speak, she will not touch my hand.

In allowing Devindra's ghost to take control of my mind, in leaving her be in the dark side of my room without shining the lantern on her form to dissolve it—have I come too close to the borderlands?

It's dangerous to wander near the borderlands, I know. It's far too easy to wander away from the boundary line, risking loss even of one's own self. It seems to be like death, if not Death herself. Although I could be mistaken. What I feel could be simple fear of my approaching and inevitable end, the understandable fear of an animal body—that same animal body which I created Pavo Vale to defeat.

Why do I not turn on the lights now? Ah, this is the most frightening thought of all. I do not because I fear to lose her, Livia. I fear to chase away this ghost, which is all I have left of Devindra Vale.

This is something I have to confess about myself and Professor Vale. In our early years, we would find ourselves having the same dreams. And the same nightmares. For we had, one mad spring, taken the Luna vow. It was only through the most severe discipline that I managed to break that tie.

Or thought it broken. For she sits there, or her simulacrum, wrapped in a filmy shroud that covers her face. Am I going mad, Livia? No. I am as sane as I ever was. She is there, whether phantom or strange reality—that is a veil I cannot pierce, even with an intellect as keen and seasoned as my own.

I should sleep now. But I am afraid of dreams, Livia. And—I confess—I fear to wake and find the ghost is gone.

No. Instead I will relate the whole history of my creation, the truth of my great achievement, the story of my scientific life. For it occurs to me now that I never knew, when Devindra was alive, how I longed to explain myself to her. Is that strange? That I longed to be understood by her. I am old now, and they say the old remember early memories better than the day before yesterday. The ghost sits there, and I remember her beauty. I remember I loved her.

Why is it I have this sense of impending doom, of nearing disaster? It grows on me as I write these pages, Livia. And yet, it cannot be so. My plans are well laid, my strategy well laid, my actions put in motion. Yet as I sit here, in the darkening of the Moon Itself, a strange fear almost overmasters me, as if its larger force could crush my personality in a vise. I, struggling against it to regain my balance, swing this way and that.

I will regain my balance. Be sure of that.

Devindra's ghost watches me, patiently. She wishes me no harm. I believe that.

She seems—strange! strange!—to guide me now. To light a tunnel I can dimly see ahead, if my feet would only touch the ground, sending me to hurry down it, away from this imagined—surely imagined—approach of destruction.

In my mind. It's all in my mind.

In my mind, she holds a lantern. A dim reflection from it falls on her face. Its expression is one I remember. A look of worry. Almost of care.

When Devindra was with me, when she was alive, I took that look to be one of assumed superiority, for one feels concern only for an inferior, does one not? It annoyed, then finally enraged me. And yet, I must admit to a weakness. What would I not give to have her here beside me, alive, that kind look on her face, that light in her eyes?

Does that make me weak, Livia? Yes. For I am all too human. Pavo Vale is more than human. I made him for that.

Sitting here in my room on the False Moon, I watch, grateful, as the light of the Moon Itself shrinks, fades, and disappears. For I require night now, in which to make my confession.

Did I say "confession"? The word formed itself before I knew it, but when I look at it now, black on white, I find it should stand.

Disaster impends. This can't be so, and yet the fear of it touches me. I know not what kind, from where, or how, but I have an irrational terror that it nears me. It is this fear I must battle now, in my waiting for Pavo's return. For fear is the last infection I can allow myself now.

To find its antidote, I must go back. To the beginning. To trace the road that led to our being here.

I must—as Arcadians say—look back to look forward. To the day I had waited for, for so long. The day that Pavo Vale was born.

PART TWO

PRIDE

1.

I will never forget the horror of that day—the mingling of horror and triumph. Impossible to thrust away the events, how they affected my mind, all my future hopes and fears. Oh! Livia. Only to you would I confess it. And to the shade that sits before me as I write.

Merope and I had agreed it would be I alone who would midwife the birth of my sons.

"Sure thing," she'd said, with a feline smile. "I don't want any of those stupid women fussing over me. For sure, not Ma."

She smiled again, a little wider, showing those overly small, overly matched, overly white teeth that had always had such a repulsive effect on me. I remembered looking over, as I lectured at Arcadia's Walton College, to where she sat, squat and enigmatic, staring at me unblinking, though she, unlike her mother, could never have understood the subtleties of my concepts. I knew her constant presence to be a slap at Devindra rather than a tribute to me. For the strongest emotion Merope ever showed was a hatred of Devindra Vale.

"It'll be our secret, Doc." She cackled at that, slapping her thigh, snickering at some private joke.

She was sure such a great secret would bind me to her. As if I'd ever have been fool enough to put myself in thrall to Merope Vale! She was a bad seed if ever there was one. All the better for me, for my plans. There was no other female in the whole of Arcadia who wouldn't have reacted to my proposal with horror. Merope, though, would do anything, commit any crime, torture any innocent, as long as she was sure it would wound her mother.

So it was that she slunk into my laboratory at Walton College, in Arcadia, where I performed the operation. I implanted the precious fertilized eggs, grown in a dish of science-grade crystal smuggled over the mountains from Megalopolis.

The same crystal makes up the windows of my room now, through which I look to the dark face of the Moon Itself, when it has turned away from the sun.

Merope enjoyed the operation. This further repelled me, though I kept my feelings to myself. She grinned that grin of hers—I still remember it with a shudder—and her protruding eyes seemed to start out of her head as if on stalks, like those of some insect.

Oh, she enjoyed it.

"Won't Ma go crazy?" she chortled when I had finished. She climbed off the table and slapped her stomach. I winced, needlessly—it was too early to damage what I'd done.

"Glory be!" she said. "So what happens next? The least you could do, Doc, is take me out and give me a really good feed."

She yawned. There were those teeth again. "In fact, you're gonna have to feed me real well the next few months, ha ha." Slap, slap on the stomach again. "To make sure the sons and heirs are tip top, eh?"

I gritted my teeth, Livia. You can imagine it, I'm sure, you who have so much fastidiousness, you who have such distaste for vulgarity. It was a chore, but I did it gladly. I watched her with care—Merope Vale!—I protected her from winds and rains, I escorted her to dinners carefully chosen for taste and nutrition. I even tucked her, god help me, into bed. All to assure myself that the vessel carrying my children was rested and well.

Of course, as her pregnancy became more apparent, the whispering began. It was popularly supposed—and why not? I had foreseen it—that I was the father of her unborn child. Or rather, *children*, for I now knew that Merope carried not one child, but three. Triplets. Of course I was known to be the father. What was not known, and what would have had us hauled up before the Arcadian magistrates' bench, was that Merope, stupid girl, was no more their mother than a barbarian slave-girl wet-nursing an infant king.

I was hard pressed to tell what Devindra thought of all this. That she and Merope were estranged was clear. That Merope flaunted her pregnancy and her attachment to my person—hanging on my arm in the most revoltingly intimate way whenever we appeared together in public—was all too obvious. But Devindra had become ever more opaque to me since our earlier days of comradeship. What feelings she had she kept to herself.

As for me, my main feelings were of shame for being associated with trash like Merope, and triumphant pride as her pregnancy proceeded, healthy and unhindered, toward its successful conclusion. Confusing times, Livia. I might almost have been the mother, my moods ricocheted so, a caricature of the hormonal disturbance of pregnancy, from despair to elation and back again.

By the time her birth pangs started, I was beside myself, finding it ever more difficult to control a passionate longing for the children to join me in *this* world. I did control it, however. I doubt any observer guessed, in those turbulent days, what a havoc of paternal solicitude was playing with my hopes and fears.

I appeared as urbanely acerbic as ever, though, and the inevitable whispers happened well away from my hearing. Such was the healthy fear I inspired in the university world.

The wait was near intolerable. It was the closest I had ever been to a breaking point. The tension, the suspense of forcing patience was almost too much. I yearned to have done with a Process demanded by Nature and grasp instead the manmade Result!

I think I have never hated Nature and her dreadful inefficiencies as much as I did in those tedious, yet terrifying months.

Then, just as my nerves were at their tautest, so that one more pull of suspense would surely break them, the thing was done. And done quickly. Though not without tragedy.

I had challenged Nature. I had yet to best her.

With the birth of my sons, I would be on my way to that goal. And to reach that goal, I, a man, could hardly have lusted more.

2.

It was a dreary night in early winter that I finally grasped the result of my long work. With an anxiety that almost amounted to an agony, I acted as midwife to the birth of my sons.

My sons. Mine alone.

It was one, I believe, in the morning. The rain hit the windows in a dull monotone when Merope's birth pains, and her cow-like bellowings, finally ceased. I gathered into my arms first Marcian, then Lionel, then Pavo—the last. For I had named my sons long before, while they were still in the womb.

But horror awaited me. Horror in the midst of triumph, as happens all too often in this still unconquered world. For while Pavo, third and largest of the infants, cried with a lusty vigor, and Merope, bleary-eyed, belched and looked about herself, Marcian and Lionel were ominously quiet.

Their limbs moved, so feeble! Then, as I watched in despair, they ceased movement altogether. And the slight rise of their tiny chests stopped. Never to start again.

"No, no!" I cried in spite of myself. I grasped Lionel in the dim light of my rooms—for I had not wanted the attention of any casual passer-by—and saw what I took to be a shadow on his chest. Further ghastly investigation proved it to be a cavity, a hole, where his infant heart should have been.

Gasping for control, I turned to Marcian, who gave one last pitiful mewling cry, and breathed no more. Clutching him to my heart, my fingers, inadvertently probing, discovered the awful fact of his misshapen head, an incomplete covering of his delicate skull. As he breathed his last, I made the vile discovery that Marcian was born without a brain.

"Oh for pity's sake, cut the cord, will you, and shut that kid up," Merope squawked from the table. For in my confused and grief-stricken state, I had left Pavo attached to the vessel that bore him. Thanking I knew not what or whom that he still cried, and that he kicked lustily out like a babe far older than one newly born, I cut his cord and snatched him up, to the heart where I had held his dead brother only moments ago.

Merope gave a hideous groan of relief, and her legs, grotesquely akimbo, fell back on the pillows of the table.

Eyeing her with loathing, I cradled my one living son and rushed from the room, to sit on the floor by the wood fire in the hearth, of the type that primitively heats Arcadian homes. I chafed Pavo's little body to warmth, willing him to life, leaving Merope and his poor dead brothers behind me, in thought as well as in deed.

I spent the next torturous weeks nurturing the child myself, feeding him the milk I harvested from a scowling Merope, hugging his small body to my chest, protecting him from drafts and winter weather. It was spring before I felt the ground settle under my feet, before my confidence was assured: the boy would live!

It was left to Devindra to bury the ones who hadn't. It was Devindra who performed the rites of the dead for my failed experiments. I had no time to give to anything but the successful one. For it is in the success of Pavo Vale that the future lies.

3.

I'll confess it irritated me, the way Devindra treated the graves of Marcian and Lionel. She tended them as if the dead had some meaning. This more than irritated me. There were times…well, anguish is not too strong a word to describe my feelings. Anguish all the more bitter and unendurable because its source eluded my grasp.

Why should I care? I asked myself. True, she had enraged me by taking it on herself to give the fetuses a burial with all the superstitious ritual with which Arcadia surrounds death. But then, she had believed the failed experiments to be Merope's children. Her grandchildren. What flowers she placed on the graves—tight little blossoms that would never open once plucked—what shiny pebbles, what quaint wooden toys of the type that Arcadians find odd pleasure in making during winter months when outside work claims less time.

Devindra did all of this. For, of course, Merope never went near the place.

Was my anger a form of disappointment in Professor Devindra Vale, the finest scientific mind I have ever known, with the exception, always, of my own? The sentimentality, the foolish waste of time that could have been spent in nobler technical pursuits, the sheer childishness. All of this served to convict Devindra in the court of my own judgment.

And yet—there was something. Something else.

It was this mysterious "something" that eluded me, that led me to keep silent when Devindra buried my failures in the earth. She asked if I didn't want to join her in tending the graves, and if I was a trifle brusque in my refusal, I believe I held my scorn in check well enough. I saw a kind of doubt in her dark eyes as I responded that I had no wish to feed any suspicions about the boys' conception and birth. Not, at any rate, till the time was right.

She took this to mean I was not ready to acknowledge my relationship with Merope. Laughable! And she forgave me! She accepted what she believed was the fact. I wondered, did she not feel the humiliation entailed in the whispers that she had been supplanted in my esteem by her own daughter? Did it bother her in the night? Did she remember, even, that we had taken the Luna vow?

Her image looks at me as I write this. And the eyes—those eyes bring me back to that time. This is a shade, I tell myself, not Devindra herself, long dead and gone. But still…those eyes…

She had the audacity to bury the corpses in the Queen's Garden, which can be seen from the main reception rooms of the Queen's House, where I, as counselor to Michaeli, the Lord High Chancellor, was so often bidden—or found it necessary to invite myself. So over and over I was forced to view small changes made atop the graves.

I would stand in the Queen's Reception Rooms, listening with feigned respect to the pronouncements of that callow young woman, Queen

Sophia, as she attempted to flatter me into submission to her womanish take on Arcadian law. Already irritable, I would look out the window over her shoulder to see Devindra—Professor Devindra Vale! Founder of Otterbridge University! Inventor of the Claraudioscope!—on her hands and knees, dirtying the orange and turquoise dress that matched the turban on her head, wielding a small spade and planting lavender shoots. For lavender, in Arcadia, is considered the herb of the dead.

"What, Sophia? I'm sorry, I was woolgathering there."

She wasn't fooled, though. They called her "the Wise"; it should rather have been "the Cunning." Turning, she smiled faintly as she spotted Devindra. Then, as if it reminded her of something else, she turned back to me with a serious look.

"It's about Pavo," she said. I could tell by the way she picked each word that she knew she was on dangerous ground.

"What about him?" I said, still suave, as is my usual manner with upstarts and fools. "He's perfectly well. It suits us both, living with Michaeli. And I have plans…"

"Yes," she said, cutting me off. Outside, Devindra stood up and stretched, rubbing her hands against the small of her back. The orange drapery of her dress, I remember, shone in the sun.

I looked at Sophia with suspicion. Did she know I had begun to speak with you, Livia, about the lad's education, about the need to send him over the mountains to you to learn all the skills of war and dominance that Arcadia could never provide? No. I'd been too clever. She couldn't know about that. Of that I was confident.

"You know he's been tested."

Ridiculous, of course. All Arcadian children go through a series of tests—"games" they call them, which are carefully observed.

"Yes, of course," I said, impatient. "I assume he astonished the invigilators. He usually does."

No surprise there. There was no competition, feat of skill or intelligence, where my boy's precocity did not shine.

"Yes," she said. And then was silent for a moment.

"On guard, Aspern!" I thought to myself in exasperation. "What's the girl up to now?"

"Aspern," she began again, looking once more out at Devindra, who was now, to my anger and embarrassment, arranging a wooden horse and a plush stuffed dog on the graves. Sophia followed my look, her eyes filling with those spurious tears she seemed to find so easy to conjure up.

She wiped her eyes on the back of her hand, and continued.

"In strength, in agility, in grasp of abstraction, Pavo's quite beyond the other children. Both of his age and much older."

"Yes, yes," I said, impatient. "No less than I expected."

"But, Aspern, I'm afraid..." Then, feigning some kind of deep feeling, she handed me the report of Pavo's auditors. It was all there, I was pleased to read. The highest possible mark for everything on the report's first page. A low mark, lower than one would expect, for "creative thought," but I didn't let that worry me.

I knew Sophia watched me as I turned the page. Just then, Devindra entered, brushing the dirt off her hands. I saw them exchange a look.

I had been discussed!

Annoyed, I returned to the business at hand. There, on the second page, was the inexplicable. Astonished, I held up the paper and read aloud: "Altruism. Zero. Empathy. Zero. Spiritual Understanding. Zero. Care for Nature. Zero." I put the paper down. "What is this?" I said. "These aren't the usual categories."

Sophia and Devindra exchanged another look. Sophia took a step back, as if it had been agreed beforehand that Devindra deliver the coup de grace.

"True," Devindra murmured. "But it has been noticed..."

"Hah!" I said savagely. "I notice the lack of subject in that sentence. Who has been damning my boy behind his back?"

"*I* noticed, Aspern," she said more loudly, and more firmly now. "I saw that Pavo is missing…something. It was I who ordered the extra tests."

"Hah!" I snorted again. But I cursed myself silently. I should have expected this. By Arcadian law, as Pavo's "grandmother," Devindra had full rights here. I needed to tread carefully. Schooling my expression, I said, "May I ask what you think a lad of outstanding physical and mental attainment, a superb physical specimen of Pavo's caliber, could possibly lack?"

Another look passed between them. Damn the women, I thought.

"A soul," Sophia said.

"*What?*" I shouted. Devindra stepped forward again.

"Aspern," she said earnestly. "Sophisticated testing that I have developed…"

"You're testing for a *soul*? Have you gone mad?"

"He doesn't have one," Sophia said flatly. With no hint of embarrassment, mind you, at having put forward such a demented idea.

And Arcadia called her "the Wise"! Absurd! Absurd and dangerous, too.

I took a deep breath and controlled myself. "How could Pavo have a thing," I said calmly, "*that does not exist.*"

Another look. Even more infuriating. Was that a shadow of an "I told you so" that passed over Sophia's face?

"Nevertheless, Aspern…"

This time I forestalled her. "Professor Vale," I said. "Devindra. I must protest. You, a scientist, party to this *mockery*…"

Devindra spoke. There were tears in her dark brown eyes, those eyes so dark they looked black. This sent me into a tailspin of exasperation. Were these women completely insane?

55

"Aspern," she said. "There are ways…we know the secret…it has been discovered…I have discovered…" She paused as that dratted Sophia handed her a cloth on which to blow her nose. She looked at me with those liquid black-brown eyes of hers and said these astonishing words: "We know how to give Pavo a soul. And with your permission, we will."

I stared at the women. They stared back. I clutched at my hair in my frustration. Was *this* the land of my birth? If so, the sooner we turned it over to Megalopolis, the better.

The better for Science.

The better for Technology.

The better for Pavo Vale.

The better for *me*.

It was an automatic response on my part to cast on them one final look of scorn. And without speaking, to go.

I spent the afternoon of that day in the foothills of the Ceres Mountains, clocking Pavo as he ran the fastest mile of his career to date. He came to me, glowing with the exertion, saying with that endearing certainty of his, "Proud of me, aren't you, Dad?"

Yes, I was proud. So proud that I made a silent vow. I resolved then and there that his inheritance should match his amazing talents. I resolved he should inherit Arcadia itself.

For its own good. As well as the good of Megalopolis.

As well as my own.

Of course, all this happened later, much later, after I had officially taken Pavo into my care.

But first, let me go back a bit more. To his childhood. And his growth to man's estate.

4.

The boy despised Merope. That was clear from the start.

I had no choice, then, but to acknowledge him and take him into my own care—even if I had wanted such a choice that was so far from my private thoughts. For her part, Merope was alternately smothering and sulky with the lad. "Fine," she finally said. "You take the little creep. Better you than my ma."

For that was the choice. Devindra, distracted though she was by the myriad details involved in the founding of Otterbridge University and the management of its system of colleges, even in the midst of *that* she noticed Merope's supreme unfitness for motherhood.

"I blame myself for it," she said when she arrived at my rooms to discuss the matter. Her lack of pride irritated me. She never paid due attention to her own dignity, in a way that would have been positively injurious to her career in the more rigorous academic circles of Megalopolis. *She* came to *me*. A basic error in any hierarchical structure. And not one word of reproach for what she must have felt as an injury: a bastard grandchild, although Arcadians, provincial as they are, think little of such distinctions. I did venture to murmur, with a pretense of sympathy, that Merope's...er...*fall* must have been reason for some upset, but all she did was look surprised. Then, of all things, amused. Did I perceive a hint of anger? Was there some thought there of the partner of Merope's disgrace? But no admission of hurt came from Devindra.

"Don't be silly, Aspern," she said in that annoyingly tolerant way both she and Sophia had. "I was born the same!" Worse, of course, though I'd forgotten—her own mother having been one of the "washerwomen" of the Megalopolitan Marsh, who served the needs of the scientists at its nearby laboratory. Who knew what Devindra's paternity was? Though judging from the power of her brain, quite a brilliant mind must have stooped to the use of Tilly Vale. "My dear mother," as Devindra would call her, seemingly unashamed of her parentage. It was Tilly Vale who Devindra called on now.

57

"She would have known the best thing to do with Pavo," she said, ridiculously enough. "Normally I would never suggest parting a child from his mother, but in this case…"

"Oh for goodness sake, Devindra," I said in exasperation. "Face facts. Merope is a disaster. For all she is your daughter."

A mournful nod.

"I would like to raise him myself, Aspern," she said, hesitating. "It might make up for the mess I've made of his mother. Too many cares…I didn't spend the time…"

I wasn't having any of that. Let Devindra take over my greatest project? No hope there. I knew how to play on her own feelings; after all, hadn't they once most concerned me? So I brought out the full panoply of manipulation. "A boy needs a father…I can give him the attention he needs…suitable arrangement with Merope…etc."

As so often happened, annoying as it always was, this barrage of reasoning was met, not with the spirited resistance you would think proper, but with a look of deepening sadness. Talk about manipulation! This had been one of my main complaints about our earlier relationship. She would never argue. Even when it was clear that I was inviting her to an exchange of views, if the tone took a more aggressive turn than she liked, she simply gave in to whatever demand I made. I used to test her, making my demands more and more extreme, just to goad her into response. But there was never a response. She simply drifted away, treating me with a distant courtesy I found more disturbing than the anger I had hoped to arouse.

"Yes," she said now in that polite tone of hers. "Of course you're right. He'll want to be with you. A boy would want to live with a brilliant father."

That must have been a passive aggressive dig on her part, since her own daughter had not been content to live with a brilliant mother.

But that worried me little now. I had won my point, and, to my surprise, with very little effort. It always surprised me how, when I was expecting a battle, Devindra disarmed me with unexpected agreement.

I now had near complete control of the project, thanks to that unexpected bit of spite on Merope's part—for as you know, in Arcadia, a child is expected to live with its mother until it reaches the age of reason, which in Arcadia is relatively late. Thanks to what Merope inelegantly called "Ma's hovering" over the boy—which I suspected was ill-disguised envy at the attention Devindra paid him—the silly girl "split" on me. As she phrased it.

"What on earth do you mean?" I said, trying to keep the irritation from my tone.

"Told her the whole whack," she smirked. "She got on my nerves, going on about the kid. She doesn't like the way he's turning out. Well, she didn't much like the way her own kid turned out, what makes her think she's gonna like one that doesn't have a thing to do with her? I mean, really."

I stayed calm. I stated what to her must have seemed an obvious fact. "You told her the boy was a clone."

"You betcha!" she grinned.

"A clone of my own," I said. I was thinking fast. Was this for good or ill? For good, I calculated. In the main.

"Yep," Merope yawned.

"How…how did she take it?"

Merope's little eyes, too close together as I'd always noted, widened a bit at this. "How d'you *think*?"

"Badly, I would guess."

She gave a hoot of unattractive laughter. "Badly? That's a Class A understatement. How do you think she'd like that kind of wacky interference with"—here she pursed her tiny mouth into a caricature of her mother's more dignified tones—"*natural processes, the unexplained of life.*" She laughed again. "Don't be daft, Aspy. She went nuts, of course. As nuts as Ma ever gets, anyway."

I understood it all.

Parthenogenesis…cloning…was and is forbidden by Arcadian law with a strictness rarely applied to any crime short of murder. But Merope was safe from prosecution, and she knew it. Devindra's maternal guilt over her daughter's appalling personality, combined with the exaggerated respect Arcadia always gave the mother, on top of the general compassion felt for the parent of such a daughter, meant that Merope was safe. And if she was safe, so was I. As was Pavo, my most valuable treasure, for in Arcadia, he would pass as the grandchild of Professor Devindra Vale. The great Professor Devindra Vale.

An irony I will share with you, Lady Livia. And only with you.

For it is as you have often hinted you suspected. Pavo Vale, my ultimate achievement and success, is as much beyond the mere cellular and mechanical tinkerings of Alastair's prize scientists as the sun is beyond the moon. Pavo is no mere clone, like the many "half-children" as we call them, being raised in the nurseries of the False Moon.

No. Pavo is unique. Pavo stands alone. For Pavo Vale is an entirely manmade, synthetic creation. He is parentless. *And yet he is human.* He was made through the chemical manipulation of the human genome. *My* manipulation.

For I discovered—oh, how much toil and agony was involved—*how to create a human being*. Your help was needed, and you gave it, amused, without question. I have often wondered how much you knew as I worked to synthesize the DNA contained in human chromosomes. I have often wondered if you, unknown to me, looked over my shoulder as I worked, in that way you have, Lady, of knowing all that happens. And of encouraging all that can happen.

I have often wondered if it is you I have to thank for my ability to create Pavo Vale. For he is, literally, a creation. He was not born of man, but by man. He has no history. And without that past, he is not a man.

He is a god.

5.

I took care to keep Pavo away from Devindra after that. In any case, it was time to prepare him for his entry into full manhood—which for him came early, as did most things, at the age of twelve. But for four years I had the training of him without the interference of women…always excepting you, Livia. But then you have the mind of a man.

Every day he grew in strength, and in those lofty attainments of manhood appreciated in Megalopolis, if not in Arcadia. Leadership. Firmness. Self-Assertion. Innovation. Ruthlessness. You'll remember his year at the boarding school on the False Moon, how he was the darling of his teachers, how he could have had his pick of the aristocratic half-children living there. Your own little pet—was she called Gilda? I can't precisely recall—was mad for him, and to this day I'm not sure what they got up to when my back was turned. But as you know, I was having none of that. These half-children, formed by Alastair's inferior knowledge of cloning technique, so frequently have something seriously wrong with them, even if what that might be isn't immediately apparent. I couldn't risk an alliance with one of them. My project needed an established lineage of healthy offspring.

A line of godlike men. But why beat around this particular bush? *A line of gods.*

To achieve this, I knew Pavo *must* mate with a fully functioning organic child, born naturally of two parents. This was an imperative. Without that, I risked losing everything I—we, Livia, for it has ever been a shared goal—have worked for without cease.

So my choice alighted on Faustina. Michaeli's beautiful eldest daughter. Her lineage: impeccable. Her father: my closest ally in Arcadia. Her dowry would be considerable, for her mother came from a Paloman family that cared, for a change, about such things. As a consort she would bring elegance and dignity, though as a daughter-in-law, I will admit she lacked spark. A bit cold, Faustina. That may explain why, after two years of marriage, there was no sign of the hoped-for child.

6.

I might mention here one odd thing about my lad. He hates the Moon. Not the False Moon. No, the False Moon he admires—as who doesn't?— as one of the miracles of modern technology. His loathing is reserved for the primitive, original moon, what Arcadians call "The Moon Itself." He complained to me once of nightmares, recurrent, and, to him, horrible. Though they mean something other to me, for a superman without dreams would cause me to worriedly review my calculations.

There is one small issue with his dreams, however. Both his own account, and sophisticated testing confirm that they, pleasant dreams and nightmares both, are remarkably one-dimensional. By which I mean flat, as if in a cartoon. Perspective is abolished. All occurs as if on one plane.

So it is with this nightmare he complains of. A trivial enough image, but for reasons I have still to determine, a terrifying one to him who is terrified by nothing and no one in waking life. Hormones? Diet? I have still no idea. An odd anomaly.

But I must tell you the dream. I feel compelled to list it here, as I feel compelled to write this memoir down, as Devindra's ghost sits beside me.

The nightmare, then. Pavo dreams he stands on one side of a clear, thick, flat crystal wall. "Like the bottom of a bottle," he complains, though when I ask how, without the effect of depth, he can experience thickness, he pettishly refuses to answer.

On the other side of the glass—so he reports with an uncharacteristic shudder—"pressed up against it," is an enormous, round, luminous, flat face. "Staring at me," he says. "Always staring."

Nothing else. Why this should make his heart race and his blood pressure rise, both, as I've seen in the lab, during the dream itself and the recounting of it, remains a mystery. He himself finds it impossible to explain.

There is one small clue, though I'm unsure of its importance. As I mentioned, his hatred of the Moon. But why would that be? Where does such a strong feeling come from? I have no idea.

And I have no idea why I mention it here.

Of course, he has his likes and dislikes, for after all, he is only human—even if superhuman. As odd as his loathing for the Moon Itself is his almost visceral hatred of an unassuming Arcadian plant biologist named Walter Todhunter. Nothing remarkable about the man: raised on a farm in the Donatees, clever with his hands, fond—over-fond—of practical jokes. His one accomplishment in life has been to capture the heart of and marry Pavo's daughter Shiva. Shiva, who will, I'm afraid, have nothing to do with either of us. Father or grandfather.

Her loss.

She's a sullen young woman, given to rating the arts more highly than anyone should.

Oddly enough again, the one woman—girl, actually—to whom Pavo has shown a sustained form of attachment is Walter and Shiva's daughter, Shanti Vale. In fact, and this is strictly between us two, dear Livia, for the nonce he is determined to marry her.

Yes! You're shocked! "*Marry* her!" you're saying. When he can have any woman he likes without going to the bother of raising her to his level? And indeed, the political marriage to Faustina ended with nothing but a useless amount of ceremony and the cost of her funeral. But my boy is determined here.

Of course I argued with him. I must even confess I had an unguarded moment, an involuntary feeling of revulsion that quite shocked me. The limits of my biology! But Pavo has no such limits. He is beyond the petty morality of lesser beings. And what my boy wants, he must have. After a moment's thought, I gave in to him with good grace. I agreed to help him to the best of my ability to have what he desires.

You'll have immediately spotted why we must keep this planned alliance under wraps. The Arcadians have an irrational hatred of this kind of match, no matter how appropriate. They would regard the marriage of a grandfather to his granddaughter with abhorrence. Of course, in Megalopolis, we would too, if not for the fact of the much higher status and power of the male, which allows him to choose whatever mate he desires.

"When you're a star," as you've often laughingly said, Livia, "we let you do what you want."

Devindra's ghost shivers and fades. The truth, Devindra? Not even your imagined image can bear it? Even now, your ghost cannot bear the truth?

7.

To return to Faustina.

I had begun to fear that my experiment had reached its limit, for she showed no sign of pregnancy—nor did any of the many women of Megalopolis who threw themselves at my boy when we ventured over the mountains.

I began to worry that there would be no new generation, and that I would have to think again—oh misery!—if my purpose was indeed to produce a lineage of godlike men. (No, not godlike men but, I repeat: *gods*.) It's true the lad was a mere fourteen years old, but he had matured quickly, marrying Faustina when he was twelve. And the women! When we would make our way in secret over the Ceres Mountains to meet with you and the Council of Four, it was all I could do to keep them off him.

Oddly enough, though, Arcadian women are not attracted to Pavo in the same way. Or even, though I often suspect myself of misinterpreting the data, attracted at all. I can only account for this, if it is indeed not a corruption of the test results, by a general lack of sophistication on the part of the typical Arcadian female. For the kinds of men most valued there,

here in Megalopolis would hardly be considered men at all. Industrious, yes. Well-meaning, yes, if you like a sickly sort of tolerance for the weak. Uncompetitive. An almost perverse refusal to fight for dominance.

Unlike Pavo Vale.

No, Arcadia as it was and is has no understanding of his vitality, of his tremendous value, of his veritable personification of the future.

Even Pavo's wife, Faustina, appeared to dislike him, and this after having been clearly dazzled by his prospects, which Michaeli and I were careful to put before her.

That may explain the barrenness of the marriage. Though not, of course, the troubling lack of fertility among the many girls of Megalopolis who trooped in and out of his bed.

Could the latter be explained by the environmental devastation of the Great Disaster? I wonder. More study is needed here.

So, as I say, I worried. I altered Pavo's diet. More protein, more phosphorus. Genetically modified oysters! Caviar! The raw meat of rare beasts! I tested his sperm count again and again, for of his potency there was no doubt. You yourself showed me the reports of your secret police affirming this. But still I could find nothing wrong. More than puzzled, flummoxed, near frantic, I attempted methods that you had discouraged, and that embarrass me now: massage, music therapy, aromatherapy, forced sleep. But Pavo only laughed at me. "Father," he said. "I've never failed you yet. And you have never failed me." His confidence touched me. I resolved to deserve it.

There is much, I admit, that I have sacrificed to be so deserving.

All unwittingly, I sacrificed Aurora, youngest daughter of Michaeli, sister of Faustina. The darling of her family. And, if I am to be completely honest—for I find it impossible to be otherwise tonight, sitting side by side with Devindra's ghost—my own darling, as well.

8.

Aurora was a pretty child. As charming as her name, she was a particular favorite with me, who had no favorites but my own son. "Tell me a story, Professor!" would be her inevitable demand whenever we two met in Michaeli's home.

I found, to my surprise, that it was my delight to do so. In what spare time I had, I ransacked my memory, along with the libraries of both Arcadia and Megalopolis, to find astounding tales with which to fascinate the adorable child. I'll even admit it: not only tales of scientific wonder did I relate, but fairy tales, legends, myths, as well. And these latter were her particular favorites.

Her green eyes, so strangely colored at the outlines with wine, the color of spring sprouting leaves (Shanti Vale has inherited these eyes), would widen with delight, sending a look like a spring day itself to me, as I related some scientific oddity, some amazing fact, or some half-forgotten children's tale. I confess I loved to see her intent and inward stare, for it was as if she had taken an image I'd given her—say, of the existence of untold millions of stars just beyond our world's grasp—and judged it from all angles in some perfect internal landscape of her own. A landscape, I was sure, that could never have been less graceful than her own fair form.

"The stars are so very far? Tell me again how far." When I did so, she'd chide me, "But if it's so, how can I hear them?" For it was her childish conceit, charming if misinformed, that all the universe was alive, and that much of it spoke to her.

A fantasy I should have corrected. But somehow, I could not. Soon enough she would grow old, I told myself, and lose that foolish freshness that I found such a breath of clear, cool air.

For a child she was. Six years younger than the haughty and reserved Faustina, but oftentimes seeming younger still, so determined was she to retain the right to silly jokes and sudden dances. "How are an Otterbridge professor and a cedar tree the same? Neither of them can ride a bicycle!"

For it was a joke with us that I was clumsy in the extreme at any kind of sport, and for some reason, with Aurora, the joke was funny, even if at my own expense.

Faustina, of course, was singularly unamused by this badinage, and would say something like, "Stop acting like a child, Aurora," or, "You encourage her, Professor." I admit it—I did encourage her.

Her silliness was refreshing at the end of another hard day's labor. Almost as if it was a *reward*. For by this time, Devindra and I were estranged, meeting now only as formally connected colleagues in the university system.

I do wonder now, tonight—and I'm surprised at the thought, which somehow seems not as strange as it should—if I wasn't a little in love with the child.

Was that what caused it? Was it my avuncular attraction to the pretty child that caused her to catch Pavo's eye? Or was she slyer than I had credited? Was it she who seduced Pavo? Was she the predator not the prey? Such things are known to happen, and in even better families than that of Michaeli, the Lord High Chancellor.

They called it a rape, those who were Pavo's enemies and mine. But surely it was a case of passionate desire? Others became my enemy, as a result, when I refused to condemn my son for, in his passion, being unaware of his own strength. And then there was my doubt of Aurora's role in their mating. Still, her father inevitably took a different view.

"She is twelve y-y-years old!" Michaeli cried piteously, clutching my coat for balance, demanding what he called "justice." His hysteria, about a trivial matter that could have been easily passed by, forced my boy to flee to you, Livia, over the mountains. I confess I found it difficult to forgive Michaeli for that.

"He is fourteen himself," I answered coldly. I was a miracle of self-control, staring the possible end to my plans in the face.

"He is a m-m-m-m-monster," Michaeli said. I ordered him from my

67

rooms, and he went, hangdog, never to look me in the eye again. We met, afterwards, only in groups. Never alone from that day forward.

I admit, though, Livia, I am all too human. When I thought of what I'd seen—for I had found them. I'd come for one of my usual visits, and gone, as was my habit, up to Aurora's nursery, for she still slept in the rooms she'd had as a small child. Blue and gold rooms, the ceilings decorated with the stars she and I had painted together, as I taught her to name each one.

There she was, bleeding and whimpering, holding, of all things, a stuffed toy to her chest in a vain attempt to cover what her ripped shift did not.

Pavo stood over her, glowing, glorious, naked, blazing, triumphant. I think I have never seen him before or since look as godlike as he did that day.

A moment later, fatally, Michaeli and Faustina followed me, and the emotional father overcame the otherwise rational man. "I'll k-k-k-kill him!"

What a scene, Livia. Faustina screeching, Michaeli lunging, Pavo laughing. And Aurora with a strangely bewildered look.

Of course I leapt to protect my project, pulling Michaeli off Pavo's throat, lest the stronger lad kill the old man and put us even further in the basket. With a word, I told Pavo to go, and eyes alight with laughter, he did.

My gratitude again to you, Livia, for sheltering my boy, while I worked for him back in Arcadia.

It was easy enough to keep them all quiet after that. Easy enough—almost too easy, I laugh a bit now thinking of it—to bring the story around to my own version of it: Aurora's unwitting seductiveness, her unconscious desire for her sister's godlike husband, the equally godlike desires of Pavo Vale, the unfortunate juncture of circumstance and opportunity, the inevitable—I stressed "inevitable"—result.

Do I feel ashamed of myself now? Perhaps a bit. I think I believed my own story then. But now…I wonder.

Of course I had my work before me: to calm the situation, and bring it under control. My control. For this, to aid me, I had Michaeli's terror of scandal, of losing any kind of face in public. That and Faustina's fastidiousness, which forbade her from complaining in public of her husband, lest any lesser being insult her with censure or, worse, pity. And Michaeli's wife, whose triviality and, truth to tell, fear of her magnificent son-in-law made her easy enough to tame.

If I felt any twinge of guilt as I went feverishly to work, it was toward Aurora. Used, as she was, to taking my word as gospel, it was all too easy to beat back any attachment she might have to childish feelings of hurt or injustice. She had been honored by a great man with a passionate love. That was how I bade her look at the matter.

Obediently, she tried. She followed. She stumbled, certainly, on the path, but I was careful to be there to catch her, to hold her up and set her feet firmly back on the path. My path, of course. I always made sure of that.

So sweet, Aurora. Always ready to take another's view as superior to her own. "I know I'm just a girl," she would say humbly. "But I think...," and then, faltering, she would be silent, as if realizing, with true wisdom, that her thoughts were neither here nor there.

She was a jewel, Aurora. In truth, she was now as beautiful and silent as the rising dawn that shared her name.

So silent was she, that it was some time before we—before I—became aware that she was soon to have a child.

9.

I tell you, Livia, my heart was in my mouth when I knew of Aurora's condition. I acted as the girl's doctor in all this, so it was I who saw the unmistakable signs before anyone else even suspected.

The girl herself was more and more quiet with every passing day. Though if she knew what momentous happening was within her, she gave no sign, said no word, to anyone.

So slender was Aurora, she scarce had begun showing by the second trimester. I held my breath and my tongue, hoping my luck would hold. Many things favored my design: her taste, since a child, for loose and comfortable clothing, as opposed to her sister's near-obsession with skin-tight wear. The self-centeredness of her immediate family: no one in Michaeli's circle ever had more than a cursory interest in the doings of their fellows. Most blessed of all, Aurora's increasing depression, which kept her to her own room, sitting silent and staring at the fire. Another piece of unexpected luck: it was an unusually long and cruel winter, keeping even healthy and happier young women than she by their own hearthsides. The absence of Aurora from the occasional festivity was easy enough to explain away and then forget.

Devindra, of course, had no notion, as of yet, of what had occurred. Soon, though, I reflected, it would be impossible to keep at least part of the truth not just from Devindra Vale, but from Arcadia itself.

I didn't worry too much about that. The straw I clutched at was the hope that the fact of her pregnancy wouldn't emerge until it was too late. For while ending a pregnancy, for one motive or another, is not unknown in Arcadia, it is rare, and considered only as a last resort. No Arcadian woman gives up a potential child without the kind of reason that elicits pity from her fellows rather than their scorn. But there is no Arcadian record of any termination taking place for any reason after the babe was developed enough to survive on its own, outside of the maternal womb.

Any child of Pavo's—a child of Pavo's! every time I said that phrase, my heart sang!—would, I reckoned, be strong enough to survive at the earliest possible date. If necessary, I thought, I could induce a premature birth and take the child into my own care.

Aurora, drifting daily into a world of her own, proved no hindrance to my plans. She said and did nothing to interfere with the development of Pavo's child.

A peculiar thing happened around this time. It was a cold and cruel spring, following that harsh winter, but customs remained no matter what the weather. It was Arcadia's habit to exchange small gifts of food on the vernal equinox. Decorated cakes, candies, breads—that sort of thing. I had forgotten it was Devindra's special delight to bring such presents to the young women of her acquaintance. Doubtless her own unsatisfactory relationship with her daughter was an additional motive. Aurora, as I've said, was a favorite with all who knew her, and Devindra was no exception. Before I knew it—before I could make up some excuse that would stop her—the dragon invaded my princess's chamber. And with the inevitable result.

"You must have known this," she said to me, after having been closeted with the child for half an hour. I admit, I gnawed a fingernail or two, counting and recounting. I was safe; I was sure of that. The child would be just old enough. The sentimental side of Arcadia would never consider stopping it from being born.

"Known?" I said, uneasy in spite of myself.

"That child is going to have a child of her own. A girl, unless I'm mistaken."

"A girl?" I said, this time aghast in all honesty. No need to feign my surprise and disappointment now. I hadn't bothered to test, so sure had I been that Pavo could sire nothing but boys. "Are you sure?"

"So she tells me."

"She? How would she know?"

Devindra gave me a strange look. "She's done the Luna, she says. It told her that. Among other things."

In my haste, I missed that last. I laughed out loud in my sudden relief.

"The *Luna*? That's a wild one. We're getting diagnoses from cards now, are we?"

Devindra looked at me now without expression. Then looked away. Then, gathering up her things, left me without a word.

What were you thinking, Devindra? Were you remembering long ago, when we thought we, too, might have a child?

To my disgust, when I did do the simple test I should have performed long before, I saw Devindra was right. The child was female.

It was a blow, of course. Not that I lost interest all at once—a child of Pavo's proved that other, more satisfactory, offspring could follow—but I did then leave the scene and return to you, in Megalopolis, to discuss our options. My plan was to return closer to Aurora's time.

But my plan was overturned. Too late to fret about that now. Too late.

10.

You'll remember there was a sudden thaw that spring, a warm wind that melted so much snow on the Ceres and Donatees Mountains that the water came rushing down in a flood. The Ceres Marsh was turned into a churning lake, extending for the first time in modern memory across the flatland, that one they called the Witches' Plain, almost to Paloma.

It was shortly after this thaw that the secret passes were opened, for the first time since the early winter when I sent Pavo over one of them to you.

I gnawed my fingernail again. I wanted to assure myself that he was safe, and up to no mischief—remember what had happened the time before that, when I had left him alone for a short time, the almost-scandal of himself and some half-children!—and I thought I could risk it. Aurora was not due for another three months, more than enough time to go over the mountains and come back again.

This was reckoning without two things: the sudden spring snowfall that closed the passes once again for seven or eight days at least. And Aurora herself.

Devindra told me later that she foresaw what Aurora would do. "Don't be daft," I said. "How could anyone?" She'd seen it in the Luna, she said. "What?" I said—I was overcome at the thought that I had missed my chance, and, raw from that knowledge, not as careful in my speech as I might have been. "You can foretell in those idiotic cards what a silly little girl might plan to do?"

Devindra just looked at me, as if my rancor was not worthy of particular notice, then down at the sleeping baby she held. She cooed to it the way women do in that disgustingly treacly way they have with children, and then said without heat: "The Luna doesn't foretell, Aspern. The Luna simply points. It's simple enough to make a judgment on what will happen next if you know how to read the signs."

The "signs" had apparently been this: that Aurora, roused by what I never knew ("by the thaw," Devindra said, but this is so ridiculously unscientific as to be unworthy of notice), became aware enough to ponder her situation, and to make decisions, foolish and unworthy though they were, for herself. Shortly after I'd left, she'd made her way to the Witches' Plain. She'd heard tales that there were women there who could "help" her. For she was bent on ridding herself of the life she carried inside.

"She was beside herself," Devindra said calmly, rocking the baby back and forth in her arms. "I could see that. I visited her every day." She shook her head. "You men have no idea what a torture it is to a woman to carry an unwanted child. It's as if a monster is growing there. An illusion, of course, but it has driven women to madness before now." She hugged the baby and kissed the top of its head, as if to make up to it for its mother's folly. "How much more," she said softly, "would it affect a girl such as Aurora?"

Impatient now, I demanded the story. "My right," I called it, rather sanctimoniously, but it succeeded in getting some sense out of the woman.

Aurora had crept out of Michaeli's house one cold night, heading for the Witches' Plain. She had heard that there was a woman living there who could "help" her rid herself of the unwanted child, even at the point where the child could exist by itself outside of her womb. Where she had learned this, I was unable to discover... Devindra said wryly, "Her sister always has had such a good figure," though what that had to do with it, I could not make out.

Child murder. There are no capital crimes in Arcadia, but there are crimes that receive no forgiveness there. This would be one of them.

Devindra, visiting Aurora as usual in the morning, discovered her flight, and somehow divined where she had gone and for what purpose. I think we might discount her blather about the Luna. For of course I then remembered: Merope Vale lived on the Witches' Plain. Still protected by her mother, but did her mother know what mischief Merope Vale was capable of? I had heard rumors myself.

"You knew she went to Merope," I said. At this, she blandly nodded, acknowledging the truth of my suspicion without conceding anything more.

"Merope denied having seen her. But there were, outside, in the patches of snow still left…drops of blood. Bright red. Like rubies. It hadn't been long since they'd been left." She shook her head sadly. "They made a path." She sighed, hugging the baby to herself.

"I hoped I was not too late, and as it happened, I arrived just in time to see Aurora walk into the Marsh, holding the child. I plunged after her, and plucked the child out of her arms just as she disappeared under the water, which churned so violently with the wind that I could not make out where she had gone. The Marsh was swollen with the snowmelt, deep in places like a lake. And then there was the baby. I could not risk my own drowning and the baby with me. I was forced to go back. I stayed by the edge of the Marsh for what seemed like hours, walking back and forth, frozen myself, keeping the child warm against my skin. But Aurora never appeared again."

Interesting point: when the body was finally recovered, it was found that Aurora had not drowned. I did the autopsy myself, over the hysterical protests of Michaeli. Of course I did the autopsy, had I not been Aurora's doctor? What I found was that in the freezing water of the new snowmelt, she had succumbed, almost immediately, to exposure. The herbs used to bring about the premature birth had caused a decisive loss of blood. She was always frail, Aurora. That and the cold were too much for her heart.

But before I got there, Devindra—curse her—claimed the baby. Wrapping it in her gown, she took it back to her Tower by the Lily Pond, days before I was able to get back over the pass and make a counter-claim. There, with all Arcadian custom and law to back her up, she claimed her grandmotherly right—though of course she was, or thought she was, great-grandmother of the helpless thing. It was impossible for me to demand any kind of custody other than visiting rights, liberal as those are under Arcadian law. There was no recourse.

I would have fought that custom, perhaps, had the child not been a girl. And if, when Devindra first placed her in my arms, the puling creature hadn't wailed and screeched, refusing to be comforted until back with her great-grandmother. It was doubtless just a moment of bad digestion, or a touch of the croup, but it boded badly for the future. And indeed, the chit—now named "Shiva"—never took to me, not even as she grew, but hid from me whenever I appeared, and shuddered if I tried to stroke her, or take her by the hand. I soon tired of such attempts, and let her be a project of Devindra's, rather than my own.

Pavo never asked about Aurora, or the child. He has always been one to look forward. Never back.

11.

I'm sure you remember our discussions at that time, Livia. Why had there been no child before this? Why now? Why *this* girl? Then it came to me—or perhaps this was your suggestion: this female, this Aurora, drew Pavo to her by his overmastering desire. Not just for any woman, any girl, but *for her*.

It was not just the will that was involved, we realized. It was the instincts, too.

Well do I remember our talks about the future of mankind. If men were to actually achieve the godhood that should be the inevitable end of their trajectory, all that makes up men needs to be involved. Recreated. Transcended. And as you so wisely pointed out, the experiments of Alastair and his cohort—his ridiculous "Brain in the Box" experiment, for example; his mechanical men—left out one important building block of mankind.

Feelings.

That was your insight, Livia. Feelings are what make man *man*. To make man more than that, they must be, not just tamed, but transformed and transcended.

Why is tragedy given us? Is it not to provide a test, an exercise, so that the spirit might grow to meet its greatest Fate? Isn't that the point of sorrow and strife: to force us to win through?

You and I have discussed this often enough, Livia. Sometimes playfully, often in full earnest. We have touched on secret matters, those hidden springs of human history that lesser men never discern. And the most secret of all is this: it is only by sacrifice of life that men can be saved.

Should I then bow my head in regret at the deaths my creation has caused? No. For the end redeems them. The end transcends our puny, emotional, sentimental weak humanity—our feelings. But this can only be achieved by way of our deepest desires.

It was Pavo's feelings that drew him to Aurora. His desire for her, which is a thing no machine, no matter how sophisticated, will ever be able to feel. And if he had desired this one girl, we reasoned, there would be another. And when Pavo Vale marks out another woman as his own, as you pointed out—you woman with a brain like a man's!—we must make certain he has her.

The crisis has come, Livia. He has found that woman now. More than that: she has the Key.

12.

To explain, I must back up a bit.

It was the year of the fake civil war, do you remember, Livia? My idea. We had worked out a rather ingenious, if I do say so myself, form of propaganda for the flightier Arcadian youth—magazines, pictures, all showing a more glamorous life in Megalopolis, hoping to lure them over the mountains. And lure them we did, though it was almost impossible to hold them there.

We had tried many methods, many ways to bring Arcadia back into the imperial fold. Pure force, which was Alastair's preferred option, failed us twice. After that, we used more subtle strategies. A show of our own grandeur: the False Moon shines above Arcadia as well as over our own Ruined Surface. Luxury goods meant to tempt, sent with the black market merchants over the secret ways of the Ceres Mountains. Our merchants, of course; the ones we had bought and paid for.

This worked only for a tiny sliver of the Arcadian population. No, there wasn't that much longing there for luxury goods.

Then there was the year we sent Pavo to Arcadia with the offering of a host of new technologies—forms of power generation that would need Mega technicians and spare parts to keep going. But the timing was bad. You'll remember after that came the years of charmed weather and incredible harvests for Arcadia. The new technologies were met with indifference—at best, with a polite "no, thank you."

That was the year Shanti Vale was born, to Shiva and Walter Todhunter.

Glamour, that was what we tried next. Exporting the possibility of Megalopolitan sophistication. We chose carefully among the Arcadian population, giving some of them special hairstyles, outfits, gewgaws. I argued it would act like a virus, and spread through the rest of the land.

I remember your laughing at me, at us. You said our plans were more as if we were trying to get Arcadia to pay attention to us, rather than forcing her to obey.

But you did agree, even with a slightly satirical look, that the very traits that defined Arcadia—her naiveté, her tolerance for other points of view than her own, her ready willingness to forgive a past injury—all worked in our favor.

It occurs to me as I write these words that Devindra Vale showed all these traits, and in their purest form. When she should have been strong in defense of her own point of view, she was weakly accepting of others. When it was clear an enemy intended her an injury, she forgave them and puzzled over where the enmity had sprung from, and whether or not she was able to transform it. She had, for a scientist, a quite remarkable way of looking at the world each day as if for the first time, expecting nothing but good to come, even from the bad. "It does come—eventually," she said to me once, with that strange complacency I always noted in her.

She claimed to have worked out the algorithm that showed this: that whatever evil came worked eventually for the good. She tried to show it to me once, to explain it, but at that point—it was around the time of which I now speak—our relation had degraded so much that I could barely bring myself to look over any of her work. Her work! It came between us. Her work was the enemy of mine.

All the more did Pavo, born and engineered to be the opposite of all the weak tendencies of Arcadia, hate and fear her.

Pavo hates all that is womanish and weak. That is to be expected: he was made that way. But why he fears such tendencies—and I am forced, through a scientist's inbred honesty, to admit he does indeed fear them—that I have yet to understand. But fear them he does.

But with Pavo we have this advantage; he never looks back to look forward.

With Pavo, it is always Forward March.

13.

When you suggested the obvious way forward for suborning Arcadia, Pavo immediately understood. "Ruptures," you suggested. "Destabilization."

We sat with you, for you had given us audience, in your rooms on the False Moon.

"Tactics!" Pavo growled. I could see you were pleased.

He jumped up and began pacing excitedly. "Explosions," he said. "Coming from no one knows where. Causing surprise and dismay."

"Causing maiming and death," I said, not to argue with the plan, simply to make clear what the results would be.

Pavo looked at me, surprised. "Of course," he said. "That goes without saying."

I remember you looked at me with an amused lift of your eyebrow. "What a piece of work is man," I thought you said. I could have sworn I heard it.

But you had said nothing. I puzzled over that for a time.

"I can organize it," he said, pounding one enormous fist into an enormous palm. "Me and a few of the boys."

"An insurgency," you agreed, amused and encouraging.

He meant the group of promising lads—the "gang," as you called it—he had gathered about himself, both on the False Moon and the Ruined Surface. What we call now the "Invincibles." For where Arcadia ignored, Megalopolis admired. He had no shortage of admirers, of adherents, in Megalopolis.

That is still true, as you know. I know Alastair has warned you that as Pavo becomes too popular with Megalopolitan youth, he will be hard to control in the future—that he is secretly building his own faction. "And from faction, it's a short step to militia, and from militia to army." Alastair should have a care to his own followers. The insults he so gratuitously spreads, the strategy of humiliating his people to cow them and make them obey, sometimes has unfortunate repercussions for his leadership.

Pavo is more cunning. His grasp of overarching strategy is, as you've said to me, impressive. His ability to gain the loyalty of his followers makes him all the more successful as a leader. In any contest between Pavo Vale and Alastair for the governorship of a Megalopolitan colony, I would think you would have no difficulty choosing.

True, Alastair points out that Pavo and I have a somewhat higher idea of the lad's future in Arcadia than does Alastair. True, I have suggested to you before that Arcadia would be of more use to Megalopolis if it believed it had chosen its own ruler, rather than had one foisted on itself. You have agreed with me to a certain degree, with your head cocked at that angle that usually portends slight argument with and adjustment of the plan laid before you. But with you, Livia, I have never had any hesitation in saying what I desire. For what I desire is for the good of Megalopolis. That is: I hope for Pavo Vale to be made emperor of Arcadia.

A neat solution to our problems. You agree? And as the sum of my ambition, it has the advantage of being the most efficient way of utilizing the resources of Arcadia that we so desperately need. What better way than to let the country believe it works for us of its own free will?

In my excitement, remembering our old plans, I forgot Devindra's ghost.

She sits there still, in the dark, but now so far back in the shadows that I can hardly see her.

Can I drive her away? Will she abandon me as I relate what comes next, what plans we made, what plans we implemented?

Is that what I want, I wonder. To have her leave me now? Or perhaps… yes, I think this is so. I am glad the shade sits here with me as I write. Devindra, or Devindra's simulacrum, will finally see the brilliance of my own completed project.

Having seen the brilliance, can she do otherwise than to forgive?

"Forgive what?" I can hear you say mockingly, Livia. I understand you. You scorn my weakness in thinking there is anything to forgive.

14.

So we planted the seeds of insurgency. Another aspect of strategy at which my boy excels. He has an uncanny ability to separate the weak-minded from the strong, and to woo the former to our cause. Boys, usually. The kind of boy ripe to take a man-making risk of any kind, the kind of risk there is little opportunity for in Arcadia. There, the risks are all against Nature; few are of the existential variety that young, frisky men like best. The ones where you risk all to gain all.

Pavo is a born leader in the fight to risk all. Men follow him where he leads. "Glory or Death!" he promises, and these are stirring words. For a certain type, anyway.

Old news again. He and his gang swept into the mountain town of Ventis, taking it over. Upheaval and havoc in Arcadia. I remember some of the schools shut down for a time. Certainly Yuan Mei College suffered. The insurgents laid waste to the countryside around Amaurote and Ventis; many vineyards were destroyed in the process, leading to a lack of exportable wine that year.

Amaurote fought back bravely, and in defiance of Arcadia's queen, who counseled peaceful opposition. You remember that, Livia. You called it "borderline madness," and it amused you at first, then angered you. Sophia's program included inviting aggressors into the homes of fellow Arcadians, listening to them rant, feeding them, and then sending them courteously on their way.

If attacked physically, Arcadians were urged to defend, and then to encircle. Escorting the aggressor to the edge of the city—"with all due politeness," the royal edict urged—and releasing them into the country-side. With, if you'll remember—this amazed us—a "bag of food for them to eat as they traveled." No alcohol. That was stressed.

As Amaurote watched its vineyards destroyed, it followed Sophia's strictures, almost without knowing what it did. It was a less an act of obedience to the monarch than an organic response to pressure, given the circumstances surrounding it.

Yet, strangely, this did have the effect Sophia had wanted. None of us, of course, believe this is why that attempt at overthrow failed. There must have been other forces at work we are unaware of. In any event, the band following Pavo seemed to simply melt away.

Still, we were on the right track. Twisting and winding, of course, but that's true of any road leading to a goal.

Once again, the Arcadian temperament offered us a way in. As I've said, your true Arcadian finds it almost impossible to bear a grudge. Why this is, I have no idea; there has been speculation among our people that it's something to do with the water. Alastair himself has urged more tests on Arcadian springs, "lest we unknowingly emasculate our own people by importing their water for our men to drink." As I pointed out, we can easily turn that to our advantage by leaving Arcadian water as drink for the masses. If the wine is affected, of course that is another matter.

In any case, as we had been canny about never revealing my own association with any disturbance (at least it never progressed past an easily deniable rumor), it was simplicity itself to reestablish both myself and my boy in the good graces of the Arcadian elite—if one can speak of such a thing.

Pavo was then thirty years old, at the height of his magnificence, his cunning, and his power. A golden boy he had been, and a golden man he became.

15.

I remember that day well. As I've said, the incredible weakness of the Arcadian view that humans are capable of change "for the good of the community" offered us our way in. This unfortunate position allows any common malefactor—though Pavo certainly was not one of these—license to commit any crime and still be allowed back in to the community. As long as certain conditions are met.

We had met those conditions. Pavo had made public penance for his role in that recent unsuccessful insurgency, showing the proper grief and contrition. Funnily enough, I didn't even have to make him do so. He positively embraced the chance to "show off," as he called it.

"Let's get this party started, Dad," he had said in that way he has that sometimes reminds me, regrettably, of Merope. "I'm itching to worm my way back in no matter how. Don't you worry about a thing, I know just what to do." Laughing, he said, "I got a whole bunch of lads love anything I do."

It was true. Pavo has a core group of supporters who count on him to bring Arcadia to a greatness she not only has never had, but has actively scorned under the weak governance of women.

Arcadians admire bravery of all kinds. Pavo has bravery, all right. He announced that he would walk barefoot over the Ceres Mountains through the snow, repeating his contrition, until he arrived at the square where penances were performed. (Although this rarely happened. Such a bovine group the Arcadians! What did they have to repent?)

Arcadians lined the foothills above the town of Cockaigne and watched in silence as he descended. He looked like a young god in the afternoon light. Lightning had struck in the mountains that summer, leaving behind fires in canyons that would not go out until the fall rains, and the sun shone bright red through the smoke. His bare chest and legs shone red as he strode down the hill, calling out his sorrow for the "impetuousness" of his "betrayal" of his native land. As if his deeds had not been meant to bring Arcadia to greatness!

At the Luna Square, he stood, and fearlessly proclaimed his guilt and his repentance. I watched carefully to see if he was believed, and of course he was—Arcadians do not lie easily themselves, and so find it difficult to perceive lies told by others. Pavo had no difficulty in persuading them of his sincerity. He is a born actor, as you have often remarked.

I watched him count the house, as it were, out of the corner of his eye. The faces that watched him were blank, stoic like animals that care not whether they live or die. Shanti's dull father, Walter, stood there grinning foolishly, leaning on a staff he had carved. He leaned over to exchange a word or two with a former student of mine, Alan Fallaize. I watched them closely to make sure there was no treachery planned toward Pavo, but Walter just laughed abruptly, and Alan, catching my eye, coughed, pretending not to do the same. Their faces returned to that blank look I find so annoying in my fellows, and when the

83

ceremony was completed—and by Arcadian law, Pavo was allowed to return to membership in the Arcadian community—they did not move forward to greet him, but disappeared into the crowd.

It had been a grand performance. If only Pavo had been able to restrain himself, if only he had moderated himself in his quest to gain Shanti Vale, if only he had not struck Devindra down. That made it impossible for us to return as anything but conquerors. But all this is the past.

Old news.

That day, Sophia was notably absent. Pavo remarked on it that night, as he lay back on my window couch, shading his eyes against the light of the Moon Itself. "Hiding from me," he said perceptively. "I don't think she likes your boy. But no use hiding. What I want, I get. That's the way you made me, isn't it? That's the way I roll."

Sophia had made no excuse for her lack of attendance, and when I taxed her with it, in a follow-up ceremonial visit where I meant to make sure of Pavo's freedom to come and go, she was in her library, dusting that endless line of children's books and fairy tales that she and Devindra had always thought so much of.

"Ah," she said absently. "I'm sorry I missed it. No discourtesy was intended, I assure you."

I was annoyed. This was scarcely enough. She was treating the entire matter as if it was of little importance: an insult, almost, to both Pavo and to me, his father.

"He may have been acting out of boyish exuberance, Sophia. But he did commit a crime in attempting a revolt. Surely that rates some kind of response?"

She looked at me vaguely. "Are you both happy to be back? Will you take up your old place among my counsels, Aspern?"

Astonished, I said, "Is that what you want?"

"Of course, Aspern, of course. I like to hear all sides, you know. All points of view."

84

She looked at me, I thought, a trifle sharply. "You have an alternative point of view, after all," she said. And then she dismissed me! Oh, not in so many words. Sophia, in her later years, had a way of using vagueness to get her own way. You would hardly notice you had done what she wanted, until after it had been done—I would waste hours trying to decipher what her courtesy and kindness had meant, and how it had maneuvered me into acting at her behest. Whether I had wanted to or no.

She turned vague now, and Walter and Alan entered the room. This surprised me, I hadn't thought their status had been high enough to lead to contact with the Queen. They seemed equally surprised to see me, but I didn't think much of it at the time. I hurried out instead. My purpose had been met: Sophia would not interfere with Pavo's activities, now that he had been, by Arcadian custom, shriven.

Walter and Alan watched me go in silence. I didn't think about it again until that last day, the day I met with Sophia to entreat her to consider the future of Arcadia—and that of Pavo.

16.

She was in her library again. This time Shanti was there as well, busy in some library-ish sort of task: cataloguing, or dusting, or both, whatever it is young women do in libraries. I didn't pay much attention then, which I rather regret now, except to note that she shuddered at the sight of me. No forgiveness from Shanti! In a way, that makes her a more worthy consort for Pavo. In those days, she had yet to be seen by him. Yet to be desired. Just another of those nondescript young girls Sophia seemed always to have about her.

"Yes, Aspern?" Sophia said distractedly. "What is it?"

I indicated I wanted to speak to her in private. A subtle toss of my head. But subtlety was always lost on Sophia. When she wanted to lose it, anyway.

She ignored me, and sat down on a chair, indicating I should do the same. The young girl pottered behind her. Sophia leaned forward, a bit tiredly.

"Sophia," I began. But the girl interrupted us. Just came smack up like that, barged in when I was mid-sentence. She knelt by Sophia and took up her hand.

"You don't look well," she said. Impertinence! Can you imagine a young girl saying something like that to you, Livia? Impossible!

Sophia patted her on the cheek, then bent down and kissed the top of her head. She whispered in her ear.

The girl looked at her sadly, stood, kissed her cheek, and looked a question.

"Yes," Sophia answered the look. "Yes, my dear, it must be."

Shanti hesitated—I was so irritated by the length of their parting that I could have shrieked with rage—then leaned down and kissed Sophia on the cheek. Yes! Kissed the queen of Arcadia, without being asked, without permission. This is the kind of useless and, indeed, counterproductive informality that will have no place in the reign of Pavo Vale.

She kissed Sophia, and was gone without a word. Sophia stared straight ahead, blankly. She held her hand vaguely to her cheek.

Then she returned to herself, and said briskly, "Well, Aspern? What is it?"

I launched into my mission. I spoke well, if I do flatter myself. I had rehearsed what I had to say. It was irrefutable. Watertight reasoning. Rationality in the highest degree.

"Sophia, it is time to think of your succession. You haven't been well—why look at you, you are pale as a piece of paper, when you're usually so brown. Your hair has turned white. Your fingers begin to tremble."

She smiled then, and held her hand up to see for herself. Her fingers did indeed tremble. But this appeared to cause her no worry, and she let her hand fall back again into her lap, looking at me with vague amusement.

"You have no heirs—no children."

Her look of amusement, did it deepen? I must have been mistaken, for in a flash it disappeared. She looked at me gravely, with as serious an expression as I could have hoped to find.

"You're going to suggest Pavo as my heir," she said flatly.

I'll admit this took me aback for a moment. Not only had I not been aware that she knew of my plan, but if I had known, I would never have expected her to take it so calmly.

"Well, yes," I stammered. "Yes, I am."

She shook her head. "Not possible, Aspern. At least—I think not."

"What do you mean?" I said. "Of course it's possible. All that's necessary is for you to write your will..."

She shook her head again, and that amused look returned. "Ah, Aspern. Still the same Aspern. Still thinking life is a matter of papers and proclamations." I sat there, aghast. What did this mean?

"Aspern, what will come after me will come after me. What I say about it now doesn't matter. It is what I've done that matters. If what I've done has been right, it will go where it will go. If what I've done has been wrong, it will right itself. Somewhere along the line."

Gibberish. I realized then the truth: that Sophia was, as rumor had it, dying. She was rambling, in the way the dying do. I quickly apologized for bothering her, and stood up to take my leave.

A door opened behind her. She turned and looked at it. She waved a hand as if to say, "I'm coming."

But there was no one there.

She rose from her chair and walked toward the door. As she approached it, she turned and looked at me one last time.

"Pavo can never rule in Arcadia, Aspern," she said softly. "For Pavo doesn't hold the Key."

Then, with a flicker of her eyelids, and a wave of her hands, she turned toward the door with an expression of…of what? As I remember it, I can only call it joy. Joy at what, or who, she saw on the other side.

I hurried across the room to see what was on the other side of the door as she walked through. But there was nothing there, Livia.

The door shut behind her, and I was left alone.

I had no recourse but to leave.

That night, I heard bells toll across Arcadia, echoing in the valley, calling to each other, town to town, between the four mountain ranges. And I knew Sophia was dead.

But where was the Key?

Thinking back, Livia, I wonder: is Pavo right? Did Sophia give the Key to Shanti that day? Why would she have done such a thing? And yet, thinking back, I can't help but wonder.

And it is Shanti Vale that Pavo Vale desires.

I know what you're thinking, Livia. Couldn't I have headed that off? What could be a bigger disaster for our plans than for Pavo Vale to desire a true child of Arcadia? Let alone, the girl thought to be the great-grand-daughter of Devindra Vale?

Let alone, the girl who is his own granddaughter.

I did try to head this off. I offered Pavo a woman of his own kind. I offered a woman made the same way that he was. All traits to be tweaked to produce the ideal mate. A goddess! A queen consort!

But he refused. He wanted no one else. He wanted…he wants…Shanti Vale. Shanti, the daughter of Shiva. Shiva, the daughter of Pavo and Aurora. Shanti, the granddaughter of Pavo Vale.

17.

Shanti was fifteen years old that year. The most beautiful child in Arcadia. More beautiful, even, than her grandmother Aurora had ever been, but with the same deep green eyes rimmed with wine. Tall, slender, whip-strong; her face, hands, and feet were molded for both beauty and use. Skin a brown-gold that glowed rose when its owner's attention was engaged. Hair a shine of crinkled bronze.

The child of Shiva, daughter of Pavo Vale. Shiva who has none of the brilliance of her daughter, let alone of her own father. Shiva who married the nonentity Walter Todhunter, with his commonplace name and interests. How they produced such a prodigy of intelligence and grace is one of the mysteries of nature.

Of nature, and of man. For if Pavo is Shanti's grandfather, I myself am her ancestor. For *I* produced the very genes from which Shiva, her mother, sprang. Shiva who was such a disappointment to me. Shiva who rejected her father and all he stood for, taking refuge with Devindra, hiding herself at home with her peculiar drawings and paintings. How she even met Walter Todhunter, I have no idea.

But marry she did. And produced a child. The one creature worthy to be consort to my creation. The one woman desired by him. The granddaughter of Pavo Vale.

Shanti Vale is…I really fail in my attempts to describe her. Beautiful, yes, but more than that. The possessor of an elusive charm. Jaunty, open-faced, fearless. The most popular young person among her contemporaries in Arcadia, but without appearing to notice this eminence herself. Undeniably attractive, her insouciance.

I flatter myself in describing her inheritance. Since I myself designed the genes that composed it.

She is young, but wiser than her years. Look, for example, at her choice of closest friend: Isabel Watson—"Isabel the Scholar," as Arcadia calls her. This girl is unprepossessing enough at first glance: short, plump, frizzy-haired. Short-sighted.

A superficial observer might think Isabel a strange choice of friend for the lissome, brown-gold beauty that is Shanti Vale. You might think

89

Shanti would rather have picked someone of her own "quality." But look more closely. For while Shanti, wherever she appears, leads without effort, she herself is a follower of one. And that one is Isabel. Who is more than worthy of being followed, I do assure you, Livia.

I warn you, too: beware of Isabel. She can be a danger to Megalopolis. A danger to my own plans. As if Pavo's lust for his granddaughter isn't dangerous enough.

I was there when it happened, when Pavo first saw Shanti.

As I say, she was fifteen at the time. Pavo himself was fifty-seven, heading upward to the height of his powers, as he was genetically engineered to reach a long and vigorous masculine prime. Fifty-seven was nothing! He could have had his pick of any woman in Megalopolis. There was really no reason why he should have been impressed by, or even known of the existence of, a mere Arcadian teenager, a child who showed no particular genius or promise of brilliance. But the heart wants what the heart wants.

There had been a long period before that year when Shanti's parents, Shiva and Walter, had barely appeared at court, or even in the common areas of Arcadia. Which was odd. Arcadians are a sociable people, by and large, given to surging in and out of the marketplace, the commons, and the Queen's House at the slightest hint of a festival, or even just a welcome. Sophia the queen was always, as you were fond of saying, "inclusive to a fault." She especially loved to have children around her. Strange that Shanti wasn't to be seen more often. There were times, almost, when I felt she was being kept from my sight—but that was surely an idle misunderstanding of mine, for Sophia was so easy to fool about one's true thoughts. She would have had no reason to hide just one particular child.

Still, there was the fact that she was rarely seen. Merope still appeared, now and then, sneering as usual, in the halls of the Queen's House. But Devindra's great-granddaughter and her family? Missing. They lived in a sort of semi-retirement, next to the father's experimental farm, outside of Amana, in the foothills of the Donatees.

What a place for the next empress of Arcadia to be raised!

I made an excuse to visit them once. Science, I said—I professed a desire to see Walter Todhunter's garden. Although that was a sly fib, the science part was true enough. I wanted to see how my experiment was faring down the generations. What was Shiva like? And her daughter? It was imperative that I know.

I gleaned precious little from that trip. The boredom! I barely had a glimpse of Shiva, who nursed the newborn Shanti in a room behind a closed door. That shambling Walter showed me around. I saw Shiva's art studio, and I admit the woman had some talent, though little ambition— her pictures appear, here and there, in Arcadia, on the walls of private homes, and sometimes in the public buildings of the town. But without fanfare, without even a particularly legible signature. Her work generally involves illustrations from Arcadian mythology, done in intricate colored pen. And she has designed a deck of the Luna that is in general use.

But of the artist, that day, I caught only the merest glimpse as her husband closed the door. She suckled her babe in a shaft of light. That was what I saw, no more.

As for Walter, surely I've described enough his unutterably commonplace personality. His glasses, his unkempt hair, his old clothes. I dismissed any information I had from observing him and his bucolic setting, for nothing I saw could answer the question as to why Shiva chose him, why the grandchild of Pavo Vale, who could have had any husband from among the elite of Megalopolis, chose a life of retirement in the countryside.

It makes one think.

This was during the time of the Great Harvest, when many Arcadian children were born. As you predicted then, while the economy was good, our ability to disturb the Arcadian status quo was limited. But finally, unrest, carefully tended, began to grow. The desire for manly risk reappeared in the population, and glamour, generally an unknown quantity in Arcadian culture, began to allure by its very unfamiliarity.

I look back with pride on how we took advantage of that moment. We stoked the flames of desire for growth beyond the limits of what Arcadia itself could provide. We were canny. I stayed put in my position at Walton College, teaching the virtues of risk, of transcendence. "How puny the goals of a culture that demands stagnant harmony!" was my thesis, and many of the new students, all male, were eager to hear lectures on the goals that truly ennoble a man.

It was in this period that Pavo drew around him the nucleus of what would become the Invincibles: a coterie of young men, all admiring, imitating, near worshiping his strength, his quickness, his courage.

We prepared, didn't we? There were those Arcadians who turned away from us, suborned by Devindra and her counsels of a womanish tolerance.

Then we had that piece of luck. Sophia died. An old wound, they said. And then there was enough disruption to open a door—because we knew it had been Sophia who kept the Key.

But where, after her death, had it gone?

"Shanti has it," Pavo told me, panting with desire the night after their chance meeting on the towpath of the Juliet River. "Shanti has the Key. I know it."

I believed him. She had it then, Livia. My belief is she has it now.

Ah, but that day. I meant to tell you about that day.

18.

We had been walking along the towpath together, Pavo and I, so that he could relay to me your many secret messages sent over the mountains after his attendance at your councils.

Of course, we used the time well for that purpose. But really, I have to admit the choice of towpath was more for nostalgia's sake than secrecy's. For it was the towpath that was a favorite haunt for us both, when Pavo was a small child.

He loved then to watch the barges on the river. He still loves it. I have to admit my fondness for the spectacle too. A colorful group, the Arcadian people of the barge. They love color, they love decoration; their free time not spent in ferrying the goods of Arcadia through the river transport system are spent in the frivolous creation of wood carvings and decorations—of ornaments almost outrageously imaginative. Centaur mastheads. Cherubs running up and down the mast. Foxes chasing rabbits along oaken railings. Stars and planets so real they seem to move on a wooden sky.

The names of the crafts, too, are fanciful. I'm almost embarrassed to say how appealing I find them: The Nonesuch. The Tall Tale. The Floating Enigma. The Catch As Catch Can.

We'd had our favorites, Pavo and I, when he was a lad. I would take him down to the towpath, where we would walk, foolishly skip stones, pretend to dream of piloting our own barge one day. Silly thoughts, of course, as if barge travel isn't one of the first inefficiencies that will disappear when we've thoroughly rationalized the system of Arcadian transport.

When we have the Key.

Of course, that was our main concern, Pavo's and mine, as we walked and talked that fine sunny day, the barges waving their colorful pennants in the breeze as they passed us by, both going downstream with the current, and upstream with the poles pushed into the rocks of the riverbed. For Pavo was no longer a child, but a man of fifty-seven—yet still built like the robust, vibrant, and golden youth he has been since the age of twelve. The genes I created are yet to be tested to their full extent, but Livia! I planned for near-immortality for the lad—or near enough as I could engineer back then, before his birth.

Over the years, you know well, I've been able to extend even what I managed then.

If his intended bride is twenty-two, and he is sixty-four, that is no great distance apart for such as Pavo Vale. Given that Shanti is not liable to live much longer than a century, even with the possibility of genetic enhancement, her husband will live long past the time when her own body will decay and finally fail. Past his own century mark, Pavo will not just live, but remain a young man till near then, as well.

So I see no problem with the age gap. Nothing to make the match ineligible on that account.

Grudgingly, I do say there's nothing I can see in the girl herself to render her a bad match for my boy. Oh, her parentage on her dull father's side, as I mentioned: a lineage of rural Donatees hicks, beekeepers, small landholders, farmers. Provincial bores. No ambition beyond a well-spread table, a sunny spot in the summer, and a seat beside a warm fire in winter.

But to look on the bright side, this could be said to add a certain stability to the girl's character, though leavened by more illustrious blood. Something not to be despised in a child born for an imperial fate.

She certainly looks the part, in any case. I mean, the part of the highborn virgin chosen for the highest honors. Although Arcadia puts no value on virginity, and Shanti, no matter how much we in Megalopolis might disapprove, doubtless shares this casual attitude. Nevertheless, she certainly looked the part that day, as she ran past us on the towpath.

It was, I discovered later, her habit to run there of a morning. Her fifteen-year-old body, long, lithe, bronze-gold, barely covered in those tempting garments that Arcadian maidens affect in warmer weather, her curling bronze hair pulled back, her small breasts high, her knees strong.

She looked every inch a mortal deserving pursuit by a god.

Pursue her he did. Before I had time to understand what was afoot, Pavo had taken off from my side, running after her as lightly as she, but with increasing speed—the speed of desire.

She was quick. She was serene. She had no knowledge of what fate had in store. As she ran, she slowed to admire the reds and greens and blues of the passing barges. It wasn't long until Pavo overtook her, then ran beside her.

In the distance I saw her head snap toward him, his head bend toward hers as they ran in tandem, fleet and lovely as two animals running down the same prey.

For one brief moment, that was my vision. Only to be shattered in the next.

I saw his arm snake around her shoulders, slow her, turn her toward him, his other hand holding her shoulder down. Didn't I know his strength? I could feel him, even as I broke into a trot to catch up with them, pressing her into a standstill on the grassy ground.

Then—and it was quickly done—his head bending to hers, pushing it back, his tongue searching out her mouth.

And a scream. Not Shanti screaming, but my boy! For she bit down as hard as she could on his tongue, at the same time bringing up her knee sharply between his legs.

His hand released, hers clenched in a fist, and flashed forward into his throat.

A groan. He bent over and retched as I ran toward them both. She saw me, and wheeled away, running hard for a downstream barge that had viewed the whole scene, slowing, then near stopping as the pole-man thrust his pole into the riverbed.

Shanti leapt from the towpath to the barge's deck. I could see her scramble, grab the pole-man's hand, and gasp out a word of thanks.

The pole-man looked back once before releasing the barge again to the river current, and I saw it was no man, but a girl. She pushed off now with surprising strength from the bank, and with the current on their side, the two girls soon disappeared into the distance.

I hurried to Pavo, where he stood still bent over, catching his breath. His back heaved, but I saw as I neared that the heave came, not from pain, but from laughter.

"What a leg pull, Dad!" he exclaimed as I neared, slapping one of his huge hands against a muscular thigh. "You promised me a queen consort, didn't you? There she is! That's the one I want!"

I explained hurriedly that this was impossible, not what I had intended, for I had recognized her from the brief moments we had shared an audience at court. I said that this was Shanti Vale. The daughter of his own daughter.

Not to be thought of.

"No," I said sternly as he stood there, gasping and laughing in the sun, the side of his face bleeding from where her nails scratched him. He limped to the water, still laughing, and rinsed off the blood.

"My *granddaughter*," he howled, laughing harder than before. "How perfect! How delectable! How thoroughly, completely desirable!"

Desirable. That made me stop, Livia. Desirable. I had been looking for the woman Pavo would desire, and it seemed I had found her.

My argument continued, but now it was half-hearted at best. As I told you, I offered him a woman of his own kind, built of genes of my own devising, of his own specification: passionate but biddable, strong but compliant. I offered him that.

But he persisted. He refused. He swore he wanted no one else but Shanti Vale.

19.

I suppose it could have been predicted. As Pavo loves Shanti—if "love" is the proper word for obsession, desire close to madness—so he hates her dearest friend. Hates her with a murderous hate that almost frightens me. More than frightens me, Livia: looms before me as an obstacle to all our plans. Make no mistake: Shanti's dearest friend will prove a formidable foe. For Isabel the Scholar, as she is known, has the sharpest, most restless, most creative mind I have ever known outside of my own and that of Devindra Vale. And it remains hidden, enigmatic, behind the thick lenses of the glasses she insists on wearing.

I should know, Livia. Isabel was my most brilliant student. So I say to you, Livia: be wary of Isabel the Scholar. I have seen the reports of Alastair that dismiss her as nothing more than a schoolgirl grind, lost in a haze of impractical ideas.

Once again, Alastair is wrong, wrong, wrong. Fatally so. For Isabel possesses a quality that Alastair, and his ham-handed minions, cannot imagine, and therefore cannot see.

And that is fore-vision. Yes, that's right. Isabel the Scholar has the faculty of knowing what is most likely to come next.

You'll say that that's impossible. And that is true, so far as it goes. No one can know the future with certainty. Indeed, in Arcadia, it is considered dangerous to try. The Luna, as I've said, is never used for "fortune telling." In fact, it's considered blasphemy to ever inquire into the future. The future, it is thought, is formed by free will. To ask what will happen is therefore meaningless.

In Megalopolis, by contrast, I remember a time where we all believed it was inevitable that we should have such knowledge. Feed our computers enough information about the past, so we reasoned, and they should be able to predict future outcomes. The race was then on, if you'll recall; in fact it was the origin of the bitter competition between myself and Alastair, our first battle to win a scientific prize.

And what did we find, we two? Both Alastair and I came to the same startling and unwelcome conclusion. No matter how much information we fed the system, it always—always—turned out later, when the prediction went awry, that there had been one small piece of information that we thought too trivial to include.

It didn't matter who "we" was. Whoever was responsible for the input would, inevitably, miss the one small item necessary for a successful prediction. The way the flaw would finally be discovered was when the small bit of information surfaced, was duly recorded, and then dismissed.

We discovered that the more complex the prediction needed, the wider

97

our prediction went astray. When we went back painstakingly over our work, we always found some tiny piece missing.

At first, we called this human error. It could not have been due to the quaint Arcadian concept of free will, since our science had already proved that to be nonexistent, a chimera.

Heroically, we kept at it—you continued to fund our investigations, both mine and Alastair's. We were dogged. We tried to stop the leak. Until the day it finally dawned that it was impossible to fix.

For it is inherent in the worldview of Megalopolis that something must be of too little importance to matter. It is inherent in our worldview that if something is to be great, there must be a corresponding thing fated to be small.

Our search for perfect prediction was a heroic search. But always there was that tiny flaw, unaccounted for until it had spoiled the rest.

You know this as well as I do. It's a fundamental scientific law, formulated simultaneously by myself and Alastair, five short years ago.

Here is what you don't know. The honor for discovery of that law goes to neither myself nor to Alastair. It was Isabel the Scholar who discovered what we now know as the Law of Impossible Returns.

As you know, that law states: "Perfect prediction is an impossibility as long as it is the goal. For there is no movement toward a goal without imperfection."

And where was this law first formulated? In a series of stories that Isabel wrote to amuse her friend Shanti!

"Stupid things these girls get up to!" Pavo said, showing it to me, who was first secretly stunned, then appalled. "Thought I ought to see what the silly things were up to," he said, yawning and tossing the papers aside. "But it's unreadable, frankly. I can't stand these fantasies. I like real stories about real science and real men."

He laughed. "Shanti's going to prefer a real man to this tripe before I'm done." He went out, still laughing to himself, flexing his muscled arms over his head in the sunlight of the doorway. For we were in Arcadia at the time. It was one of those periods where we were forgiven our errors and invited back. Ah, the advantages of Arcadian tolerance.

I have to say, though, that this time I rather regretted our return. For Pavo had left behind him, on the table before me, Isabel's little fantasy. In that story was the very piece needed to complete the puzzle that had confounded Megalopolitan scientists for three generations.

There was the Law, clearly stated, in the silly little tale Isabel had written to amuse Shanti. I had picked up the sheaf of papers meaning to toss them in the fire, but caught in a train of thought of my own, about that very mystery, found myself rifling through the pages absently until the words blared out at me.

The Law!

Gripped, amazed, astonished, I sank into my chair by the fire, fingers at my temples, reading the pages before me, carefully, one by one. I was stunned. Isabel had found the solution to future prediction. Oh, not transferable—not then, at least, not now, but once the work was done, the solution was embodied in her, in the abstract processes of Isabel herself.

As this astonishing fact revealed itself to me, another darker, jarring thought interfered, as if it had been trying to get my attention for valuable wasted minutes, as indeed it had.

Pavo. His casualness. His yawn. That flexing of his golden muscles. All of these were signs of intense, even unmanageable feeling building up in the lad, requiring release. Release, more often than not, in violence. After which, he was peaceful again, for a time. He scarcely ever remembered what havoc he had caused in the interim.

But violence against what? Against whom? My mind raced to all the possibilities. Anger, fear, envy…jealousy.

Why had he troubled to steal a letter written by her friend to Shanti? Why bother?

A cold cloud passed through my chest cavity. I knew Pavo. Jealousy of anyone, anything loved by Shanti. Jealousy of Isabel, who was valued by Shanti while he was shunned.

Isabel, who was loved.

The awful truth burst on me then, Livia! Would I have cared the day before, no, would I have cared fifteen minutes before what Pavo meant, what torment or mutilation he had in mind for just one more silly Arcadian schoolgirl?

But now, the agony! For it was the mind of that girl that I saw must be preserved at all costs.

Swearing, I leapt from my seat and ran, yes, bolted out the door after my boy.

But first, I took the parcel of papers and carefully placed them in my tunic pocket, securely over my heart.

I had little leisure to study them then. Events moved too quickly, and it wasn't until much later that I understood their entire significance. If indeed I have understood it yet.

20.

I am unsure how Devindra discovered the magnificent and transgressive passion of Pavo Vale for his granddaughter Shanti Vale. There could have been many paths leading to that end, for Devindra had a quickness in discerning the motives and desires of those around her. I couldn't say where, when, or how she first picked up the scent.

That she did is undeniable. And she undoubtedly signed the warrant for her own death. As well as for the permanent maiming of Isabel.

For Pavo brooks no interference with the fulfillment of his desire. What he wants, he must have, at any cost. Even at the cost of murder.

As I say this, Livia, I hear you murmur to yourself. For after all these years, don't I know you? You wonder, "How? It's obvious that he loved the woman Devindra Vale. What was the effect on him? What could have been the varied feelings, the suffering he must still feel in spite of himself, on finding that his great project encompassed her own end?"

I know you wonder this, and these are good questions, Livia. Cogent, incisive, as I have always found your interrogations of my motives and my plans to be. You look into the darkest parts of my heart and see me for what I am. You provide my art—for I must call it that—with its theater. Its lighting, its music, its applause. It is your attention, your understanding, your *acknowledgment* of my deepest feelings and desires that nourish me. Your apprehension of my whole is as necessary to me as water, as sunlight, as air.

As applause is necessary to the artist.

I feel you trace my memories back to that defining moment in my early manhood, that moment I would find impossible to bear remembering without you there silently watching, *approving* my courage in overcoming my own weakness in aid of ending the weakness of all mankind.

Of finding, for all mankind, the power that comes from winning the fight with Death.

That power, you've taught me, comes from the domination of our weaker selves. For we have weaker selves, we who have risen from the animal. Our attachments, both early and late in life, trip us on the road to that goal.

We greater men. We create, we destroy. We create again, anew. We destroy in order to learn the ways of creation. We destroy in order to create the ultimate creation.

I have done it, Livia. You know that. I have created the ultimate creation. The man without history.

Should I then bow my head with weak regret for the cost of that creation? No. The end justifies the means.

Do I say this to you alone? No. The ghost of Devindra looks straight at me now. It is *she*, Livia. No shade, no simulacra: it is Devindra herself. Does she accuse me? Does she say, "Look at my death, Aspern, for my death was your creation"?

It's strange. I feel there is no blame in her. The blame…I search myself, inside. The blame is there. A small hard nugget rubbing up against the inner reaches of my heart.

I wonder if it is not, as I thought, my mind that holds my value as a man. But rather my pain.

Or is it—I think it is—that I reflect on Pavo's future, on the future of my own project. I—you'll laugh at this, Livia—I think—in searching my heart now—for what should stop me at this point? I find other…thoughts. Other feelings. Other motives than those I've always thought I had.

I remember other pains. Other sufferings. Petty ones, certainly, their very triviality a reason for my forgetfulness till now. I wonder, though. If they were so very unimportant, why do they rise up now, as if in accusation? Why do they clutch at my heart?

Why, as I write this, does Devindra rise from her corner, letting her veil fall? Why does she take three steps toward me, her hand stretched out before her?

And why is it I shrink away from her? I? Who would be the least inclined to fear a shade?

And yet, I fear Devindra's ghost.

Why is it that now, at this point in my report, I feel a sickening in my stomach, and a crushing pain in my chest? As if some muddy fist is clutching my heart and giving it a gleeful squeeze? Who is attacking me?

Is it you, Devindra?

Do I really still need your approval? You who are dead and long gone? Is this the weakness of an old man?

When I look into my heart, I am surprised to find I envy Pavo. Yes! I am jealous of my own boy.

For he emerged full-grown, needing the approval of no one. He has no conflicts in his desires. He does not hate where he comes from in order to achieve what he dreams. No. I spared him that.

He need not sacrifice what it is he loves in order to become himself.

He is a god. I made him so. Let that be my reward for giving up what desires I had as a man.

He desires Shanti. Well, then. He shall have her. "My hand on it," I had said to him that dreadful day, and he had grinned back at me, his teeth shining sharp and white.

"Your hand on it," he laughed. He grasped my hand. "I would take her with or without you, Dad. But maybe that's the way to make you proud, eh? And you are proud of your boy, aren't you, Dad?"

I am proud of him. I say that, and the muddy hand grips my heart, sliding as it struggles to get purchase on it. The pain. Why should I feel pain in my pride?

Am I dying?

But Devindra's ghost shakes her head, and pulls the veil over her face once more.

No. I'm not dying. I am remembering. It is hard for me to tell, tonight, which of those options is worse.

How strange it is, Livia, that man cannot go straight for a goal, be he never so rational. My purpose here was to report on the land of my birth. But I find myself lost in a maze of my own making. I find myself speaking of the past.

Even that past twists and turns. I had meant, in this detour of mine, to relate simply the tale of Pavo's desire and choice of mate. From there I planned to pass on briskly to the death of Faustina, strangled at night in her own bed, Pavo freed both of her and of all suspicion—for everyone in Arcadia knew he was far away that night, with you, in Megalopolis. Your own testimony brought over the Ceres Mountains was alibi enough under the leniency of Arcadian law.

We were at one of our periods of détente, Megalopolis and Arcadia. Pavo's visits to you caused unease in some circles, but in others nothing more than a protest that all should be allowed free travel where they would. Liberalism works so often on our behalf.

I had meant to simply mention these events, passing over them lightly, and then to move quickly to my plan, the plan that must be completed quickly, to gain us—and Pavo—both Shanti and the Key.

But I find I cannot; where I wish to speed, my mind falters. My words dry up before they reach my pen. Other words rush forth, from other springs, other depths.

Devindra's ghost stirs now, Livia. Is it in sympathy? But how could she sympathize? How could she forgive me, the author of her death?

Yet I feel she does. It terrifies me. She stands before me now, her long dress blowing in a nonexistent breeze—for where would such a breeze come from, on this, the False Moon?

She moves closer. So close to me now that I can see the very pores of her dark skin. Her violet-brown skin.

She is as she was when I first saw her—yes, and first desired her! At the height of her beauty, her eyes shining, her mouth the curve of a bow.

Her dress lit by my candles, the color of crumpled autumn leaves.

One hand laid over the swelling of her pregnant belly.

She is as she was then. Devindra! We shared the Luna Vow, the two of us, walking under the Moon Itself and the sole star that could shine in the full moon's sky. The Lovers' Star, we called it. We walked there, by the edge of the Juliet River.

Devindra! Unable to help myself, I call out to her. I jump to embrace her. But she dissolves at my touch, shrinking back into the shadows, shrouded. She wants something from me. I feel it. But what?

"Risk," a voice murmurs. "Vile risk," she says. Evil words. For is risk not the essence, the foundation of man's liberty?

I risked your death, Devindra. And did it not bring me freedom?

Why, oh why, do you not answer me?

The Key. The Key means freedom for mankind. The Key, man's liberty, man's risk, Pavo's fate, Shanti—it all swirls together in my mind, and for a moment threatens to unman me altogether.

21.

Of course Pavo killed Faustina. I knew it at the time. Not only did I know, oh Devindra! I felt for him, not her. I felt his own anguish as he strangled her. For I had felt that anguish myself, and for you. I say that now, I admit it to your shade.

Why do you turn away from me? When we were young, we shared everything, every thought, every goal. How did it change? It must have been you that changed, Devindra. It was never me. Livia herself has said, "You never change, Aspern. I am pleased that you never change."

It must have been you, then. Why did you change?

Pavo, too, is always the same. He never changes. Faustina, though—she changed. She became spiteful, resentful, angry. She transformed herself from an adoring wife into a raging witch. How could Pavo live with that, with a woman who no longer saw him as the center of her world, a woman who rejected his manhood?

He had a right to kill her.

There were no other suspects at first. I worked hard to provide other men, other motives for her death. With Merope's help, I put it about that the murderer must have been a black-market peddler, one of the many who scurry back and forth from Megalopolis over the secret paths of the Ceres Mountains. Merope, malicious as ever, claimed loudly to have seen one of them skulking outside of Michaeli's house on the night of the... murder. Faustina was well known to buy luxury items unobtainable in Arcadia from such travelers—jewels, trinkets, lap dogs, and suchlike—so the doubt was well sown.

I knew differently of course. The boy had been with me that night. He

105

came to say he had arranged a secret rendezvous with his wife, to offer her whatever she wanted in exchange for a breaking of their Luna Vow.

He knew that no young woman truly of Arcadia would lie with him as long as that vow was unbroken. In Megalopolis it is different, and he had long dallied with many women there. For what woman could resist Pavo, himself a rare treasure? And with your patronage! He was irresistible in Megalopolis.

Not so in Arcadia. Once the Luna Vow is taken, unless it is severed, with the severance agreed on by both parties, it is permanent. Inviolate. Eternal.

Faustina must have refused. I know that.

Faustina did not love Pavo. I think she hated him. But hate is a strong reason for refusing to sever the Luna Vow. I know this myself, to my bitter regret.

I easily envision the scene, what must have occurred. Pavo slipping into Michaeli's house unseen, for having lived there as a child, he well knew its secret corridors, and the habits of the house.

I can see him facing Faustina, her eyes coming back to life with hatred— for Faustina's eyes had gone dull over the years. I can well imagine they must have sparkled, for hatred would have been the strongest emotion she had felt in all that time.

I can see Pavo looking at her, indulgent. Indifferent. I can imagine—how vivid it is, the image in my mind—her increasing rage at his refusal to see her hatred for what it was.

She must have increased her taunts, panting, working hard to get the response her loathing craved. She would have first attacked his integrity. But Pavo cares nothing for the opinion of others. He would have met this with a half-contemptuous smile. Then she would have moved to his failures as a husband. A gleam would have appeared in his eye, for this dart would fall closer to the mark. The gleam would have told her where to aim, and she must have found the proper spear dipped in the proper poison, and held it, ready to thrust home. A renewed request from Pavo for a severing of their Luna Vow would force the release. An insult, vulgar and crude, a flat statement as to his inadequacy as a man.

Pavo wouldn't have been able to bear that. What man could? He would have leapt for her in that second, grasping her by the throat. I know where he grasped her. I saw the marks on her corpse. His bare hands throttling her, finally pushed by her beyond control, forced by her to squeeze her very life from her.

He never returned to my rooms that night.

On the following morning, Faustina's body was found. Her eyes bulged, her tongue stuck out of her cold blue lips. Marks of purple and red were on her throat.

Nothing was stolen. No one was charged. It was a mystery, they said, though I saw doubt on a face, here and there. I saw doubt on Devindra's face.

I knew what had happened, though. I knew it as surely as if I'd been in the room with them.

And why not? Hadn't I felt the same way about Devindra?

22.

Hatred. Revenge. A murderous impulse, near impossible to control. Though I did control it. Would I have, had there been no one but ourselves to see? Ah. That is another question altogether.

I still remember it with anguish, Livia. She looked at me—Devindra looked straight in my eyes and, with finality, sought a severing of our Luna Vow. No recourse. I knew there would be none.

And why? What was her reason? A ridiculous one, one unworthy of her as a scientist. She had been horrified to discover experiments of mine. Experiments that repulsed her, when they should have made her proud.

"I heard you frequented the animal market," she said, her voice steady. I knew then, for I could hear the horrified quaver that voice tried helplessly to suppress. Her voice broke. A gesture with one hand said she found it impossible to go on.

In silence, we both looked around ourselves, at the laboratory I'd set up there at Walton College. My earliest laboratory. Where I searched for I knew not what—my experiments had no clear goal then. But what innovation starts with a clear goal?

What technology but has its birth in risk?

She looked, unable to speak, at the cages around the room, cages holding animals I had purchased from the traders who came over the mountains from Megalopolis. Lemurs, monkeys, rats.

And then she turned with a look of unspeakable horror at my present day's work. A look of fear, Livia. From a woman with whom I had shared my innermost thoughts. The fury it still raises in my chest, even after all these years, nearly unmans me.

Didn't she know I'd done it all for her? For her approval, her admiration? Didn't she care?

She turned to the table where I had pinned a mongrel dog under a glass bell. You may recall that apparatus. It was the first gift you ever made to me for the furtherance of my work. With it, I could withdraw air slowly, and make note of how lack of air acted on the creature. How long it would cling to life as I removed the medium in which it normally lived.

Before I could stop her, Devindra had rushed to the bell—expensive, irreplaceable!—knocking it to the floor, cracking it beyond repair. And then gathering the wretched, flea-covered, half dead beast up in her arms.

Her arms, Livia. The very arms that had once held me.

I still remember the insult of it. The outrage.

"Take care it doesn't snap!" I said quickly. You see, Livia? I was worried about her. Even in that moment where she attempted to destroy my work, the dearest thing I had. But was she grateful? Did she show any womanly softening, any sign that she acknowledged both my pain and my love? Not a bit of it.

It was at that moment that I cut all emotional ties with the woman. That very moment.

Enraged—and what man would have borne such a scene?—I rushed toward her. Well do I remember the murderous rage I felt, the intense hatred a man can feel for a woman he has once loved!

The dog stopped me. Half dead as it was, it raised its head as I approached, snarled, and bit the hand I had raised to strike her down.

I jumped back, nursing my wound. And without a word, Devindra left me. Carrying the cur, she walked out the door.

She must have gone immediately to order my rooms cleared out, and arrange for the animals to be released to homes that would shelter them, or put "humanely to sleep." That was what they called it.

She had that authority, for was she not the head of Otterbridge University? And were not my experiments illegal under Arcadian law?

But think, Livia! Think what such stupidities and weaknesses hampered. The criminal waste of animals that could have aided man's knowledge. Man's betterment. Man's destiny! It was unconscionable.

But worse was yet to come. That night she arrived back at my emptied rooms, where I paced in rage at this arbitrary end to my attempts to extend our scientific understanding of the world. She walked into the room holding the knife that means, in Arcadia, the severing of the Luna Vow.

Pavo must have brought such a knife to his night with Faustina. And then taken it away with him again, for it was never found. He had foregone witnesses, so its legality would in any case have been in question.

But Devindra had done it all in proper Arcadian form. She stood there, holding the knife. Her attendants stood behind her, four of them, veiled as is the custom, so that I shouldn't be able to name them after they had witnessed the tearing of our bond.

I was still shaking from the power of the emotion that had almost over-mastered me that day. But I regained control of myself enough to accept the knife with cold dignity. I thanked Devindra—thanked her!—in words prescribed by Arcadian tradition, for the good we had shared. My voice as steady as I could control it, I wished her well in her future choices.

Wished her well! *I wished her in hell.*

There was nothing for it. In accordance with tradition, and with Arcadian law, her attendants made sure by their witness that the rite was completed.

So. Livia. I know what Pavo felt as he confronted Faustina. It was he who offered the knife rather than receiving it. But no matter. The difference is slight.

The matter was not the content. The matter was the form. Yes. The contempt shown by a lesser being to one who should, by rights, have been her master.

To one who should, by rights, be admired! Applauded! *Adored!*

Not cast aside with horror. Not looked upon with scorn.

Worse than scorn. With pity. For before she turned to go, it was that I saw in her eyes. Pity.

I swore to myself that night that I would never forgive her for that.

A young man's vow. It all was so very long ago.

Still, enraged as I was, I would not have agreed to her death. Neither to that, nor to the maiming of Isabel. That is, unless these had become necessary to the furtherance of my goals.

23.

As a matter of policy, I was certainly not averse to the elimination of Faustina. It was, in retrospect, a brilliant move. Childless and vapid as she was, she had to be put aside, by some tactful stratagem to be sure, but failing that, by violence. The need for Pavo to father a line of genetically perfected sons made that an absolute necessity.

The removal of Devindra Vale was a different matter. I regret it, I admit. What a loss to the world of science, even considering the useless form her work often took. I think in particular of her work on fairy tales, on one silly child's story in particular that need not concern us here. I had told her often enough how I felt about the waste of her talents on such trivialities, but Devindra was, first to last, deaf to the call of the kind of research I—and Alastair—pursued with such vigor.

Still, what might she not have achieved, had we been able to bring her over to our way of thought? I ponder this often, Livia.

I cannot shake the memory of it, conqueror of our common flawed biology though I am—progenitor, creator of conquerors. And I cannot help but wonder at this. Weakly, you will say, and I agree with you, Livia. Regret it and wonder at it. But how else to expel it but to admit and confront?

Why was it that she comes to me on here, on the False Moon, Livia? The False Moon, where she had never been?

Where is she? *What* is she? A memory only. The memory of my last sight of her as a living woman. For it was Pavo, as you know, you who gave him sanctuary—Pavo who killed her. I could have stopped him. But I did not.

It was necessary, yes. As necessary as the death of Faustina. You and I have often discussed the necessity. With Sophia dead, Devindra was the single greatest threat to the stability of the state, not just of the state we envisioned, the joining of Arcadia and Megalopolis, but of the state as it existed then. "Even the smallest piece of autonomy is a threat, Aspern," I remember you said. "Highly contagious. A virus. Even one moment of independent thought can overturn years of centralized power. How much more a whole community that holds independent thought as its value?" Independent thought, independent life, independent story—this was the complete teaching of Devindra Vale.

For our destabilization of Arcadia to succeed, what was necessary was the elimination of Devindra Vale. And all she stood for.

I do wonder, though. Why does she not accuse me, as she haunts me? Why is she here, if not to terrorize me with a guilt I refuse to feel? She sits, veiled and patient, in the dark corner of my room, as if in the old days, waiting for my work to be finished so we two might walk together, at sunset, on the towpaths of the Juliet River. Why does she not accuse? Will she give me no chance at refutation? Of defense? *Why will she not allow me the chance to finally convince her that I was right?*

24.

I remember her as she was that last day, wearing my favorite of her dresses, the color of sunset, of rose and turquoise and orange. The dress flamed in the light of the dying sun that slanted from the west, through the windows of the Tower by the Lily Pond. She is as she was on that last day, writing, head bent over her work. The explosions had begun again— we had planned them well, cunningly timed to go off at random intervals. But these seemed not to disturb the intensity of her concentration.

And Isabel. Isabel is there, too. But Isabel before her maiming, whole, busy in the assistant's corner, jumping up to pull another book off the shelf, nodding and frowning over some sentence she notes and archives. She shudders at an explosion, but, trained by Devindra, does not pause in her work.

A shout. Both dark heads look up. Shanti Vale, her hair shining in the late sun, vaults the wall by the pond, making for the stair. Close behind her, a panting, laughing Pavo, not yet heavy around the torso as the cares of office have made him now, but young, vigorous, strong, reaching for the fleeing Shanti, who just—just!—evades his grasp, like a deer swerving neatly from a wolf.

She takes the stairs three at a time, he in heated pursuit, sweat dripping from his head, his body. The sweat not just of effort, but of labor mingled with desire.

It leaves a trail.

Then behind him, in memory, a younger version of myself, worry writ large on my face, following him—to stop him? I wonder even now.

I see myself enter the scene, as if the older Aspern Grayling, who labors over this report, is a different person entirely.

For now I am there again. In Devindra's rooms with them all.

She was old that day. I remember. But now, as I watch, I swear, she never looked more superb.

Behind her, panting and shouting, Shanti held back by Isabel speaking frantically into her ear, calling for calm. Shanti's face distorted with fear and hatred; Pavo's with lust. Devindra standing between them, her dress now crimson in the sunset, her turban dappled with turquoise and pink and gold.

I watch from behind her as the younger Aspern enters. And for a moment, all turn toward him, as players on a rehearsal stage do to receive their director's notes, before returning to the interrupted drama, the assigned scene.

The role each was cast to play. Since the beginning of Time.

"And the cream of it, Dad, is she has the Key!" Pavo shouts, gleeful. He lunges at Shanti, breathing heavily, and Isabel blocks her from my complete view. Still I can see a quick knife-kick from Shanti, under Isabel's arm, well-aimed, meaning to hurt and managing it. I see Pavo falling back with a snarl.

But I am paralyzed, unable to act. What do I feel? I swear I feel nothing.

Pavo poises to lunge again when something stops him short. Devindra's voice hits harder, even, than Shanti's heel.

"Pavo," she said, quite calm. Ominous, that calm. I know it well. "Pavo, you do not know what you're looking for."

He stares at her, mutinous. Something about Devindra—her voice? her old-fashioned diction?—could always stop him in mid-rage. For a moment only. Though often, before this day, that moment had been enough.

Their eyes now lock. Pavo will not—cannot?—look away. His head swivels on his neck like a snake's.

But he does not look away.

Can he not? *Dare* he not?

Myself, rooted to the ground.

Every word Devindra says, he gathers up, as if it is some treasure. Something Pavo, desperate—is it possible?—wants.

I see this, Livia, and still cannot account for it. My head is awhirl with confused ideas and feelings. I cannot track them. I cannot hold them. I cannot act.

"Pavo," Devindra repeats. "What you seek you cannot find. What you search for is not where you look. It is elsewhere, Pavo. *It is not where you think.*"

His eyes narrow. He hears something I do not. He nods, then, as if he understands.

"Where is it, then?" he says, more softly than I have ever heard him speak.

No answer from Devindra. A breeze blows in from an open window and ruffles her dress.

Isabel and Shanti insensibly relax. Isabel drops her hands from before Shanti's face. I watch as both girls stare at Pavo, intent.

I can make nothing of any of it. My lack of comprehension torments me now. As then.

"A road where you have never walked." Thus Isabel's voice, harsher than I had ever heard it before, shockingly so. Can this be the meek girl I know? The shy girl I taught? The withdrawn auditor of my many lectures? This girl?

"A road you can take," Shanti suggests. Something in her voice rings a distant memory, like a far-off bell. "If you will, Pavo."

Her voice is unexpectedly gentle. The kindness in it is a shock. Pavo himself reels back from the blow.

Recovering, Pavo's eyes now shift back and forth. The three women watch.

His tongue flicks out—surely not nervously?—and licks his lips.

The women continue their steady gaze.

"My...reward?" His voice sounds hoarse.

Another moment's pause. Devindra's look softens as well. Another blow. "Yourself," she says. She folds her hands.

Now Pavo cries out in anguish. He howls, tearing at his hair with his hands, myself as helpless now as I was then to comfort him. For I have never been able to comfort Pavo. Not even when he was a small child.

"That can never be," he mutters, his nails scraping at the skin of his temples. Blood oozes out between his fingers. "Never," he says flatly as he rakes and rakes. "Never, never, never."

Now the danger. Now disaster! For the women lean toward him, like flowers leaning toward the light. On their faces: Care. Compassion. Worst of all: *pity*.

"NO!" Pavo yells, as I know he must. "No, no, NO!" The spell broken, he lunges once again.

And with that, once again, Pavo acts. For Pavo can stand anything but that. Anything but pity. He must never sink to the lowly position of the weak, to the position of the one who requires care. It's oil poured on fire to offer pity to Pavo Vale.

What paralyzed me then? For I was frozen: immobile, incapable, rooted to the spot. Fatal paralysis. One moment later, and Devindra lies on the ground before me, her head awry. Pavo's hands grip Isabel's wrists, twisting till they snap. He stomps her leg like a piston.

Did I desire this? Was it my secret wish that Devindra die at Pavo's hands?

"Pavo!" I call, but my voice sounds weak even to me. Worthless. Powerless.

What stopped him was Shanti. Now I know why, I know how. I know she carried the Key. And this gave her the power.

"Stop!" she cries with unsuspected force, throwing herself between him and her friend.

As if in a dream, Pavo stops. He looks at her, dazed. He drops Isabel to the floor, hardly seeming to know what he does. Shanti hurries to gather up what Pavo Vale has thrown away.

"Now go," Shanti says, in a voice full of an authority you would not think it possible could come from a girl.

And he does. Hanging his head, he slowly leaves the room. I watch in astonishment. What else can explain this but the presence of the Key?

Shanti croons over Isabel now, holding her in her arms. Both turn to look at Devindra's body, lifeless on the floor. Both are dry-eyed with loss.

My care is not for them. I cannot let it be. My care must be for Pavo alone.

25.

I found him later by the river, clutching his head in rage at his own impotence. Hearing shouts rise up behind us, I convinced him to flee. We fled, over the Calandals, to you, Livia. Where we have been, plotting our return, ever since.

I had put the whole of it out of my mind. Devindra lying like a bird that had flown into a pane of glass. Isabel, hands flapping uselessly. Shanti murmuring bleak comfort, nursing Isabel's shattered leg, Isabel's shattered wrists that can never be whole again.

Better to forget. For what good does remembering the past, that cannot be undone? What good does it do the future? And the future—that's all that matters now.

Ah. There is Pavo at my door. What word has he brought from Council?

What news has he brought of our common enemy, Alastair?

* * * * *

I write in haste, dear Lady, as I'm sure you'll understand, for Pavo tells me that you were witness to the unendurable insults Alastair offered my boy in Council. And to Pavo's swift and immediate response.

He has delivered your terse note saying as much, along with your assurances that you will hold the hounds for twenty-four hours. This gives us enough time to reach the Ruined Surface, and from there to cross the Calandals on silent transport, free in Arcadia from those who would pursue us for the justified execution of Alastair.

Pavo urges me not to tire myself unnecessarily, and gives me your kind message that you will protect me if, in my old age, I prefer to make my stand here, in my own laboratory, leaving him to flee, alone, to Arcadia. But my mission is clear, and my place is by my creation's side, guiding him lest his footsteps falter on the way to our goal.

Pavo tells me you have arranged secret and immediate passage. He packs what is necessary from my laboratory now, and I take the moment to scribble these final words from these rooms. For I know I shall never see them again.

I knew it, Livia. Knew that Alastair would attempt to shame my boy in front of the others, in front of you. It was I who instructed Pavo under no circumstances to endure any insult. I knew well that any sign of tolerance, patience, humility in the face of attack would be taken by you as unacceptable weakness. I knew that should Pavo let Alastair humiliate him in any way, you would immediately withdraw your support.

Events have proved me right. I have in my hand your note urging his flight and promising all aid in our future project.

And on the floor lolls Alastair's head.

A gruesome object. I admit I was not expecting it. If it gave me a shock, I can only imagine the sensation it must have caused in Council. That Pavo would dare! To behead with sheer force of arms one of the Council of

117

Four in the midst of its deliberations! Never has there been such a thing. Never has a man demonstrated his mettle so completely, showing how much more than a man he is.

I gave an involuntary shudder when I opened my door to him, proving that my own creation had almost surpassed me. For why would the sight of Alastair's head affect me more strongly than the thought of his being no more? I hated him, surely. He had been my nemesis from school days on. Truly I had wanted him dead. I had advised it, nay, ordered it.

And I knew you, secretly, had desired his death as well. He had long been an arrogant thorn in your side, challenging even your will in Council. I knew you would, no matter how quietly, approve the act.

Why then, was I unmanned by the sight of Pavo grinning as he swung the now lifeless thing to and fro, blood congealing around the jagged edges of its neck? I had to sit to collect myself, and to hide an involuntary shaking. I lifted a hand to my mouth to stay a sudden surge from my stomach.

"Proud of me, Dad, aren't you?" Pavo grinned.

Yes, yes, I nodded. Not that Pavo needed reassurance. He knew and knows his value. How proud am I? Very proud. Proud that he had outstripped his own father. Proud he had none of the weakness of the biological race!

He saw my hesitation, though, with that quickness with which I had endowed him. And pretended otherwise, instead showing his concern for me, for my age and the exigencies of flight. I reassured him that to be by his side, guiding him, was the only stimulus this old scientist needed. He turned away at this, busying himself with packing up our traps.

His tact was welcome. Quickly, as he looked away, I dragged myself over to a basin, where I retched dryly for some moments. Soon enough, I regained control of my body and was ready to be off.

Then I remembered Devindra's ghost.

It sits there, quietly, in the corner of the shadows. Its eyes shine through the gloom.

Pavo hasn't seen it. I'm sure of that. He hasn't seen Devindra's ghost, even though he roots in the very corner where it sits.

Is it there? Will it follow?

Is it a warning? But of what?

No time for worry now.

Pavo finds what he searches for, and we're off.

I turn back once more, shoving these pages inside my coat. I blow out the last candle, and the room is black.

Pavo races ahead. I must hurry to catch up with him.

I leave it then. I leave her.

I leave her to keep company with the head of Alastair.

On the voyage down to the Ruined Surface, I scribble these last lines. And await what happens next.

PART THREE

MORTALITY

From the voyage to the Ruined Surface:

War.

There is no other choice. It must be war. With Alastair gone, the delicate balance of the Council is overthrown. Our half-hearted truce at an end. I have been his counterweight. I have been your favorite since boyhood, you who have always found a new boy to favor. As Pavo and I flee, ahead of the Council's vengeance, what new plans press on me, what vistas open?

I know you, Livia. You will cheer on the side that wins. Always, your side is that of the world's riches. Your side is and will ever be what wins. The new. The strong.

Let Pavo establish his base in Arcadia, let him rule there as emperor, myself guiding his every move, and the inevitable will come to pass. Yes. I mean nothing less than our dominion, and the dominion of the line of supermen who will come after us, over the entire earth. Megalopolis! The False Moon! All joined together in an empire centered in an ever-growing Arcadia.

From the Calandals, outside Eopolis, Arcadia:

Our initial plans proceed without flaw. The lads Pavo has gathered around him—the well-named Invincibles—are the pick of the young men of Arcadia. Stalwart. Brave. Cunning. Not a womanish one among them. These combined with the Mega youth who adore him make a force to be reckoned with. By Arcadia and by Megalopolis.

As for the Arcadians: despite what Alastair has said, they are to be trusted, having grown up under two queens, first Lily, then Sophia. This chafed their manhood, made them loyal to our ultimate goal. Which goal is, has always been secretly, theirs. For in every man lies the hidden seed of desire for domination, for conquest, for triumph. It is important to remember that. We strive to win. Each one of us fights without quarter to reach the top.

Arcadia has sought to nurture a different seed. Shanti's father, for example, the commonplace Walter, is an example of what Arcadia professes to admire. Weakly tolerant, self-censoring, a farmer rather than a warrior. A believer in a sickly form of partnership rather than the reality of hierarchy. His sort will be eliminated as a matter of course as we progress.

First things first. We cultivate the seeds of vanity and ego, of putting the "I" before all else, and of the fascination with godly risk rather than the puling weakness of self-preservation. We have nurtured it. Until we built from it a fighting machine, ready to roll over Arcadia at no matter what cost to mothers, sisters, sweethearts.

Not all men joined us. Walter Todhunter, as I've said, that boring foster son of a small holdings farm in the Donatees. My former student, the biologist Alan Fallaize. Men of that sort—if we can call them that. But those who did were enough. Pavo summoned our core force, as he and I fled in our stolen machines over the dry Calandals, and those who could join us have done so here, in our camp. There are others strategically hidden in the towns of Arcadia, awaiting orders.

Of course we formed in the Calandals, those mountains of the eastern flank of Arcadia, the mountains where I was born. At this season, the end of the harvest, the beginning of the high-elevation snows of early winter, these dry, steep rocks were our only option. Do they hope to search for us there, Livia, the avengers of Alastair? They will not find us. This is our advantage. For don't I know, doesn't Pavo know, he who is the recipient of my constant tutelage, the secrets of these mountain paths? Don't I know well, especially, those of the Calandals?

And have we not laid out plans well in advance of this day?

We camp at our prepared base, at the scene of my early childhood. In preparation for this day, we have stored supplies. Supplies and weapons. My mother's isolated ranch, now burned out, covered with vines and dry leaves, high in the Calandals. Do I worry I'll be troubled by spirits here? No. Freeing myself of the weak-willed anxiety that beset me on the False Moon also frees me of these spurious fears of "ghosts." It's clear my "haunting" by Devindra's "ghost" was a trick of my own anxiety. There is no sign of my mother or Polly. No sign of my sisters, too.

No ghosts haunt me here.

Now all foreboding is at an end. Now is the time for action. For action leads to victory.

Squatting in camp with the men, planning our ultimately triumphant assault, arguing with Pavo about strategy, about tactics, I feel my old self again—proof that the inaction, the endless fruitless debate within council on the False Moon debilitated my powers, weakened my manhood, interfered with the vigor of my thought.

Devindra's ghost? Could I really have imagined I saw that?

With my way forward so clear to me now, I feel my old self. No, not just my old self. Squatting by the fire with Pavo and his troops, I feel myself to be reborn. I, like Pavo, am a New Man. The man without a past. The man without a family.

My childhood home lies behind me, a burned-out husk, flickering eerily in the firelight. But those sickly fears that still found illegitimate sanctuary in my breast, that silent terror that the ghosts of my mother and sisters might haunt me here, are all gone. Pffft.

How foolish I have been to give way to a weakness of believing in mere figments of my imagination.

But let it stand. Let this chronicle be an accurate one, a truthful one, as factual as I, a scientist, can bring to the page.

Let me relate it all for the histories of the future. For those who chronicle the rebirth of the greatness of Megalopolis, a gift from its foster son Aspern Grayling and his creation Pavo Vale.

I squat there by the fire, on my heels, alert, watching my boy's eyes shine gold in the firelight, the muscles I gave him rippling in his golden skin. I watch with satisfaction his impatience to be off to war.

First Arcadia, Livia. And then, when we have the Key secure, we take

123

Megalopolis from our stronghold there.

You hear, Livia? Megalopolis. Do I defy you with that plan? But it is you who taught me to be bold. You who taught me to take what I would.

Soon Arcadia.

No ghosts now. Action.

All that matters is the win.

From Eopolis, Arcadia:

We flew down the mountains like arrows released from the bow. There was little resistance in Eopolis, and we have taken the college as our base: the students and faculty there have disappeared, leaving it an empty husk. How could there be resistance, given our strength, given our pure joy at the fight? We swarmed what was left of the town once its menfolk had fled—after setting fire to a defensive line laid down across the drought-stricken shoulders of the Calandals. A bright line of red flame separates us now from Megalopolis. The Council won't dare cross it, and it will burn for days, all the way up to the rising headwaters in the Samanthans, where no man has ventured before. There is no way around that raging fire now. Fire like a beacon. As if there was any reason to send a message to the False Moon now.

The Ceres Mountains closed by early snows. The Calandals by fire. As I tell Pavo, the Council won't dare fly overhead and rain ruin down on the very resources of Arcadia that Megalopolis so desperately needs. He grunts agreement.

First, though: Arcadia. Pavo has gone before me, to Walton, which folded easily enough. Word from there is that it was taken with little fight. Of course, in this season, the market is not as active as in the warmer months. But ominously, by the time the Invincibles arrived, most men of the town had gone. What fight there was, so communications report, was prodded into life by our own men, bored with the ease of the takeover.

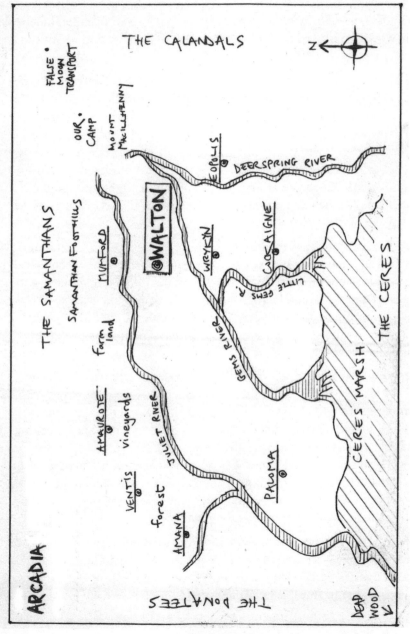

We flew down the mountains

I am uneasy, though. Walton holds a central position in Arcadia, indeed that is why it boasts the land's largest market. All roads lead to Walton. And was that to be given up without a fight?

Soon I journey there to see for myself, and to urge that Pavo set up our winter camp in that town where he was born. An excellent position from which to prosecute our campaign. An excellent position for the capital of the New Arcadia, despite Pavo's misgivings on the subject. As we shall do in every town, we will commandeer the college there, as being the strongest building and the one best supplied for our needs. Pavo disapproved of this choice at first, before he had thought through the entire chain of issues, but once he saw the facts of it, he agreed with the plans I have made.

Walton is ideal for a new capital, replacing the queenship's capital of Mumford, in large part because of its protected position, between the Gems and the Juliet River. This gives it a milder climate than the towns to the west and the south. Pavo is all for pushing on—he is always exigent!—but I fear attempting Wrykyn yet. Better, I tell him, to wait until the spring thaw. For the snows came to the mountains last night, covering everything we can see from Eopolis with white trackless plains.

The roads of Arcadia are abominable. We must remedy that, I tell him. Pavo has already experimented with using some of the explosives we brought with us to blast a trail to the Otterbridge. Once that has cleared, it should be easy enough to move in and out of Walton, leaving communications less of an issue. The main problem will be provisioning the men until this damned winter has done. But Walton has always been a place of winter storage, as I know from the days when its college was the center of my own intellectual movement, and I have no doubt we'll find supplies aplenty there. I know the town well.

In any case it is too dangerous to attempt the west, even the relatively smooth run from Walton to Paloma. While the Witches' Plain lies across the river, there is no need to risk it. Pavo, impatient, scorns the dangers of the Witches' Plain. But it is better to remain prudent. We have time.

For now, the west can wait, while we make ourselves secure in the east. A northerly attempt on the western towns is what I advise, and Pavo ponders my counsel well, restless as he is to be off. But wiser heads prevail. In the meantime, all is quiet. The snow has cut off communications, but I reserve my anxiety for what I find when we arrive in Walton.

From Walton College, Walton, Arcadia:

It appears that early reports were correct: Walton seems to have folded without a fight. My guess is that what came to our aid here is the Arcadian belief that to fight aggression is to feed aggression. Two generations of women rulers have led to this folly. A long, patient teaching of the late queen, Sophia, and of Devindra herself, has been that *to fight is to lose.* Their doctrine: allow any aggressor to invade, invite them into your very house, and *make them your family.* The belief is that then hostility must die for lack of "feeding."

The argument "supporting" this view is the unfounded belief that such a strategy has worked in the past. This is an illusion. While it is true that Megalopolis has been unable to dominate Arcadia, this has not been due to an Arcadian "strategy" of "nonviolence," but rather to natural causes: the difficulty of conquering a mountain-encircled land, Mega's own domestic problems, etc. Certainly, the number of Arcadians killed or enslaved due to skirmishes over the years attests to the fact that it is strength, rather than a foolish passivity, that prevails in these conflicts.

Strength, stealth, and a clear goal. These are the winning strategies.

We have these three. Our goal, to take over Arcadia, take control of its resources, strengthen it as a base from which to take over Megalopolis itself.

Yes, Livia, that is my grand strategy in a nutshell. Not to join the family. To dominate it.

Megalopolis had hoped to take over Arcadia. It never saw that the use of Arcadia to take over Megalopolis might be the quicker option.

For the moment, under a heavy fall of winter snows, Arcadia is, if not completely subdued, at least quiet. Our men have fallen back from any attempt for now in the west. We have let the west believe there will be no attempt; that the east was all our ambition. Will they believe it? My own experience is that men believe what they want to believe. In any case, it buys us some time. And Pavo and I turn our attention back to Megalopolis.

How Megalopolis turns its attention to us, that, I confess, makes me a trifle uneasy. But fire still burns brightly on the Calandals—those fuels will burn until the snow on the higher elevations melts come spring. The wildlife flee from it down the mountainsides, and our lads find it easy to hunt them, both for meat and for the relaxation provided by the sport. And meanwhile, there are plenty of fish in the rivers, and dried fruit, nuts, and grains in the stores.

I scan the skies, oversee the building of fortifications from the materials we've gathered from tearing down the college garden and walls. Protected as we are on both sides by the Gems and the Juliet, and with the Otterbridge ford guarded, I feel our position to be safe. Pavo meanwhile, at my advice, prosecutes a war to subdue the three most important towns of Arcadia: Walton, Wrykyn, and Mumford herself. The snows do not stop Pavo or his men; indeed, they help our plan. Winter is the time when all Arcadians go indoors. At my urging, Pavo has simply ordered them to stay there, conquering as he goes. A simple enough plan, but effective in its way.

From Walton College, Walton, Arcadia:

Defeating eastern Arcadia was easy enough. This latest offensive, to overrun Wrykyn and Mumford, aids our plan for Pavo to take over the Queen's House in the latter, establishing himself as emperor, in preparation for building a grander capital in Walton. With Sophia dead these five years, and Devindra gone, how simple to walk in and take control. Even in Wrykyn.

Too easy, perhaps. It's almost a relief to ponder the challenges we will face in the west. I consider this, armed by forethought, head swiveling in all directions in my watch for unexpected danger.

I now understand Megalopolis and its strategy, after thinking deeply about it here in my old rooms, where my doctrine of Neo-Rationalism was born. If Megalopolis has been quiet, it has been for the same reason we have been so. Megalopolis means to lull Pavo, as we mean to lull the west.

For why should it invade and fight and waste money, time, and men, when by waiting, Pavo shall have subdued all of Arcadia? Then swoop in, so goes the Megalopolitan mind, and grab the whole.

We'll see. We'll see if that is a good plan. I have my doubts, Livia! Without boasting, I can say our own plans are well laid. Perhaps even better laid than those of the giant Megalopolis!

And yet, the real difficulty, even with all of Arcadia subdued, will be finding the Key.

Undoubtedly you ask, when Arcadia is subdued, where is the problem? Surely then, he who rules the land, owns the Key. And you are right, Livia. It falls upon us, therefore, to find the Key. Once we have the Key, dear Livia, shall Megalopolis be able to wrest from us what we hold? Shall Megalopolis be able to keep us from wresting what it holds? We shall see who will win this particular race.

As for the Key itself, Pavo maintains still that it is Shanti herself who holds it. And Shanti has disappeared, fleeing before a force delegated to capture her, leaving Pavo so frustrated that he had occasion to shout at me, although of course an apology quickly followed. She has vanished, leaving no trace behind. She has hidden, or been hidden, somewhere in the west. There it is still almost impassable in parts, covered with heavy mounds of spring snow; ice covers the rivers with a thin, impassable shell.

She must be hidden somewhere in the Donatees, if my spies report correctly. The Donatees, being the highest, most unnavigable, most

impassable of the Arcadian ranges, are impossible for us to comb in this
season. Even in high summer, snow covers their peaks.

She must have sheltered with her parents, at the farm in the foothills.
There is a laughable rumor that she has taken refuge at the north end
of the Donatees, at a secret pass to the sea, the undiscovered passage
that common, ignorant talk insists is guarded by a centaur. These sorts
of fantasies spread rapidly in times of turmoil. You already know of
the child's fairy tale that gave rise to this one. Often we've laughed at
it together. But I mention it now for another reason: this centaur is, in
the popular mind, supposed to have befriended the former queen, your
enemy, Sophia. It is said in the popular legends about her that she rode
upon his back through this pass to the sea, and from there sailed to the
Dead Wood, which she crossed in order to enter the Ruined Surface of
Megalopolis.

I have heard it said that you knew Sophia in those days, that you tried
your own strength against her, and that you failed.

Why should you not do so again? I contemplate that possibility, as I
contemplate your failures in the past. I attempt to discuss this with Pavo,
but he, obsessed with finding a girl I am still unsure is at all worthy of
him, dismisses the topic with a shrug.

A mistake. A mistake to ignore a possible weakness on your part, Livia.
I know you are our ally—now. This alliance will last as long as our success. For any possible stumble on our part will be taken full advantage
of, will it not? You see I know you. And the more I know of you, and of
the stories told about you, the higher I climb away from your grasp.

I revere you, Livia, as you know. I respect and admire you. But this
campaign has brought me a freedom of action and thought I have never
known before.

Let us turn, then, to the important information conveyed by what may
be important stories, said to be stored in the archives of Arcadia, in
Amaurote, to the east. What we do know is that within these stories is a

tale of the Key: a plain statement about its ownership.

It's said that Sophia found the Key in her final days as the Lizard Princess.

Though where or how this happened, I have been unable to discover. I plan to send a "delegation" to Amaurote, and the Arcadian archives, to demand the complete manuscripts telling the tale of these times, in order to find the clues I know must be contained within. Professor Joyanna Bender Boyce-Flood has the archives in her charge, and though I know her of old as an adversary of mine, and a stubborn one, I do not think she will be able to withstand the "persuasion" Pavo's Invincibles are able to provide. For Amaurote shall be our first attempt on the west. I do not anticipate any difficulty there.

Pavo at first balked at this plan. "I want to find Shanti," he said, until I pointed out that to discover the stories of Arcadia and Megalopolis was our first task. "If Shanti has the Key," I said persuasively, "then to find the Key is to find Shanti." That hadn't occurred to him, but once it had, he agreed to the wisdom of attacking Amaurote.

In other words, I told him, our next task must be to strike at the very foundation of Arcadian belief. The "Golden Rule" that is the bedrock of Arcadian thought must be shown incapable of providing protection to individuals. For example, to Professor Joyanna Bender Boyce-Flood. This alone will cut the connection between citizens, impeding Arcadians from joining together to achieve any kind of support, physical or—perhaps most importantly—emotional.

The emotional stability of the land is entwined with its physical safety. The mountains that surround it are more than a metaphor for the solidity of the beliefs of the people thus encircled.

What is needed is a physical and a spiritual attack. Pavo brooded fretfully over this idea of mine. "Physical," he muttered. "Spiritual." A strange pain seemed to overtake him. His huge head fell, his chin resting on his chest, his eyes dull. "It's all one," he said, finally.

Whatever that meant. But the important point is we mean to take Amaurote, as per my plan. We will attend to this strategy once the winter snows have cleared and the spring floods have abated.

In the meantime, we send out word that we mean no harm to the west. That is only the east we claim for ourselves. Come spring we'll make our move.

From the Queen's House, Mumford:

The snows thawed, and, building bridges across the Juliet River, we crossed, swarming the Queen's House, in Mumford. I installed Pavo in what had been Queen Sophia's room in the western tower. For myself, I took rooms in the tower of the east, which had been those of Wilder the Arcadian Bard. I had hoped to find Sophia's famous library in them. But all that remained of Wilder were bats and mouse droppings.

Pavo has found the library. I heard the shouts. For the moment, however, he has taken control of it. No one but himself is allowed in. "Security," barked the young man left at its door. I will take this up with Pavo later. Surely, security does not demand that I be kept away? But for now I have other worries. And in any case, there is doubtless not much in there of worth to be found. Sophia's interests were lamentably limited for a queen.

Pavo has more important things to worry about than the contents of the library. But he broods on the whereabouts of Shanti. Does this distract him from more important matters? I very much fear it.

The Queen's House is smaller than I remembered. Far less grand than what we want as a backdrop to our imperial greatness. Pavo feels something of this as well. He marched into my room after we had spent one night here and announced, "I can't settle. I'm aching to get on." I soothed him, seeing his point. I myself am vaguely uncomfortable here. The damp from the river gets in your bones, especially bones as old as mine. But I pointed out to him the wisdom of my original idea of building a new capital in Walton.

He looked at me, exasperated. Moodily, he moved over to the window, looking out over the Juliet River toward the flaming Calandals, kicking at the wooden window ledge, which left a series of splintered marks in his wake.

I contemplated these on his departure out to the courtyard to inspect his men. Would they in the future be beheld with reverence? The marks of Pavo the Great, at the start of his reign? The New Man and the New Day. And myself who created it all.

But this problem of Shanti troubles me. For Shanti, though we have sent out the word, is nowhere to be found. Neither to be found is Isabel the Lame, or Shiva Vale, or the farmer Walter.

As I say, this troubles me.

There are a few places they could hide. I am confident we will find them. In the meantime, I turn my mind over to finding grander quarters for us both. For Pavo and myself.

An eerie feeling has come over me, of a sudden. I am unable to account for its source. It is, Livia, as if someone had entered the room behind me and shut the door—yet there is no one there. A breeze, a draft—yet no window is open. Still, the Queen's House is notoriously drafty. Sophia always kept most windows and doors open no matter what the weather. A black chess-piece rolls out from under the bed, for the floors are warped with age. The knight. This should be no surprise. It was Wilder's great pleasure to play chess with Sophia. This piece obviously is left from one of those games. But it gives me a chill, of the same sort I had felt recently in my rooms on the False Moon.

I have determined to move Pavo and myself to other, more centrally located, quarters, while I give the orders for an edifice commensurate with our greatness to be raised in Walton. I have already started this process, for I felt if we could not find and take over what was wanted, it must be built to our own specifications. I therefore determined to discuss what is necessary with my boy.

I joined him later downstairs, in what had been the Queen's Reception Room. He stared angrily at the overgrown grass outside. Marcian and Lionel's graves. I repeated again my thoughts: that the best option was to build a King's House, in Walton.

He grimaced. He was obviously thinking about that damned Shanti—if only his obsession with her does not destroy all our plans! Then, unexpectedly, he agreed, with the very intelligent condition that we assure ourselves Walton was the best spot. "What about Wrykyn?" he said, pondering. "Shouldn't we have a look there? It might be worth considering taking over St. Vitus College. Like you say, Father, these colleges are worth converting."

Audacious plan! Secretly, to myself, I congratulate him. He has determined to take over what had been Devindra's rooms, at St. Vitus College, in Wrykyn. The famous Tower by the Lily Pond. But best not to let him think he planned too well on his own. Best to counter, in order to strengthen, his resolve.

"Isn't that unwise, Pavo?" I saw that mulish look on his face that had always meant, since he was a child, that he could not be moved from his purpose, and I was satisfied. He would not be moved, though I continued. "Premature? The Tower by the Pond is a place of reverence for most Arcadians. Surely we should make our position secure at first, and…"

"No," he said, shaking his head. "I want you to come with me, and settle in there as governor, while I move out again and make sure of our defenses in the rear."

I shook my head. If Pavo has a fault, it is his restlessness. But he knew he had won his point. Of course he had. When could I deny him anything? How could anyone know that he was so close to achieving his destiny? Our destiny?

He grinned, "Don't worry, Dad," he said. "You can have the grandest rooms in the college for yourself. You can have the Tower by the Lily Pond."

I'll admit I blushed at that. Am I that obvious? The Tower by the Lily Pond. The most famous set of rooms in all Arcadia. The Tower that can be seen from all directions, the most famous landmark in Wrykyn.

Pavo turned to two of the lads who had just walked in, laughing at some coarse joke or another, and snapped, "Set to, you lot. I want to see that whole thing out there plowed under. We'll make it a course for batting balls around in our spare time."

His arm indicated his meaning, as it swept out toward the graves of his brothers, and the boys laughed again. This time a bit nervously. For they were born Arcadians, and you can't eradicate superstitions about the dead overnight in those raised to believe in them.

Once again I felt that sudden chill. I dratted Sophia in my head for thinking it so virtuous and democratic to quarter her queenship in such a cold, damp place.

"Set to," Pavo repeated. "We've got real work to do." This was true. Another bridge had to be built over the Gems River, and all our gear and men and the slaves we had collected in Eopolis, Walton, and Mumford needed to be dragged with us to Wrykyn.

I followed Pavo out, listening with both trepidation and admiration as he gave the orders: clear, concise, a very model of generalship. He was insistent that we take over Devindra's rooms for me as soon as possible. I understood his strategy. It was because the place was one of sacredness to Arcadia, not in spite of it. This was masterful, I had to admit. And I was grateful for his thoughtfulness for me, singling out the Tower as my own quarters.

But I also wondered if he remembered our last visit to the Tower by the Lily Pond. For neither of us had been back since the day that Devindra died.

When I write this journal next, it will be from there.

From St. Vitus College, Wrykyn:

It was a mistake to come here. I think even Pavo feels it, though he'll never admit as much. The doorways are too narrow, their frames too low, for his height, for his *presence*. The rooms are depressingly domestic, rather than imperial, in size.

Even the famous Lily Pond seems almost to mock us, with its daintiness. Its modesty of intent.

Worst of all are the thoughts, the memories, that arrive and cannot be pushed aside. It is to you alone that I would admit this, and the admission is meant as confession—which Arcadian thought claims is good for the soul, whatever that means. Still, my unease here weighs heavily on me at night, after a day's good work clearing out the swamp that is Arcadia: my ordering of administration of all kinds, laws rewritten, duty rosters drawn, patrols populated. All the work needed to rationalize and control a formerly irrational and uncontrollable populace here in the east. While simultaneous preparation is made for an invasion of the west.

All this while guarding our borders against a surprise attack by the Council. As if there was not enough to worry us with the populace here at home!

Although the populace, I will also admit, is far less unruly than I had planned for. Strange that.

The end of the day, though, in the dead of the Arcadian night—black but for the starbursts above, and the two warring moons—that brings a change. Of mood, perhaps, as I sit now, writing, in Devindra's very rooms.

Other concerns press on me. Why does the Council not attack? This question begins to grip my mind. The answer…but no, I will not think along those lines. It is my imagination working again, not my rational mind. Here in Devindra's rooms I imagine she returns to warn me. But of what?

From St. Vitus College, Wrykyn:

I woke this morning, Livia, drenched from night sweats, and worse, from nightmares of a kind I have never known before. These most likely are the result of this wretched chill and fever I undoubtedly caught during our move here. The wagon Pavo insisted I travel in for comfort was first across a temporary bridge the men had made, which partially collapsed from a shoddy workmanship almost unbelievable! Fortunately, I was close enough to shore to clamber up, soaking wet as I was. I could not find it in me to have sympathy for those, less lucky, who drowned. They had built badly, and they deserved their fate. Such lack of attention to detail is inexcusable, as I told Pavo as soon as I could make my way to his side. And now I have caught a cold, a chill, if not worse than that. At my age, to suffer a dunking! That must explain the force of—what would you call it? Last night's fever dream? Nightmare? Hallucination?

Best to ignore it. Best to press on, as if all is the same as it was.

Given all this, it's not odd that I feel strangely depressed. As if all my efforts must come to nothing. To dust. Yet this is obviously not so—on the verge as I am of achieving my goals.

No matter. This dratted fever must be the origin of my momentary lack of vitality. For my mind now obsessively, indeed seemingly endlessly, circles one concern: the whereabouts of the Key.

For the Key is where all roads meet. Once Pavo—and I—take control of the Key, subduing with its power not just Arcadia, but all of the Ruined Surface as well, can the False Moon and the stronghold of the Council be far behind? There is power in the Key that can indeed transmit its destructive power to the Moon Itself. For he who correctly wields the Key rules the world. And the heavens as well.

Will not all my fears be over then? Will not all my plans be done, and all my triumphs complete? Ineradicable? *Eternal*?

I look at what I've written, and I confess I see a touch of hysteria enter in. A mood quite unlike my normal rational self. It is the fever, I'm sure

137

of it. My forehead is hot, and my eyes swim. I must pull myself together and face the situation with all my usual rational powers.

Why then, I ask myself, if Arcadia has held the Key all this time, why has she not conquered Megalopolis, indeed, seemingly not even desired to do so? If the Key is the power I, and we, have thought it, surely this must have been attempted?

But I know, as I consider it, the reason for Arcadia's lack of ambitious purpose. That reason was Sophia, the last queen of Arcadia. My enemy and yours, Livia. For I believe you hated her as much as I. Perhaps more.

It was she who determined the uses of the Key. And if Shanti Vale does indeed possess the Key, it was she who gave the Key to Shanti Vale.

Is it any wonder I hated her? It must be the memory of Sophia that is behind my fever dreams now. It was bad enough to have a girl rule over Arcadia. But what a girl! Naïve, stupidly idealistic, worst of all superstitious—a snip of a thing. For me to watch the opportunity to wield power squandered by a mere girl who appeared to think a queen was a kind of glorified schoolyard monitor was almost beyond enduring for a man of my pride.

But enough of these useless memories. Today we ride for Amaurote. At first, Pavo insisted there was a danger there that I, frankly, cannot see. Then in a sudden about-face, he announced he and the men would ride out alone to take the town by storm. In vain did a worried Pavo seek to convince me to rest here, in Wrykyn, at St. Vitus College, in the Tower by the Lily Pond. "Where you can be protected, Father, and safe." But while I was truly grateful for his solicitude, as I said to him, my duty is to be always at his side.

When I next report, it will be of its pacification, and of the start of our triumph over the western reaches of Arcadia.

It is Amaurote that holds my imagination and my hopes now. For it is in Eisler Hall, where the archives are kept. Where it may be I can discover the secret of Sophia's will and the whereabouts of the Key.

I anticipate a triumph, and certainly that will be the finest medicine I could take for this attack of alternating chills and fever I feel now. When we take Amaurote—and why should we not?—we will be well on the way to conquering the west. Even more importantly, to me at any rate, we will have shut down Otterbridge Press. For it is in Amaurote where its offices reside. As I have told Pavo, a subversive press is of all things the most to be feared in any plan of conquest.

From Eisler Hall, Amaurote:

Disaster. That was what happened. A setback to all our plans. But we shall reverse this strange trick of fate. In fact, I wait to hear now that our counterattack has been successful.

It was a trap, of course. As I had foreseen. But Pavo had refused to take what precautions I knew were absolutely necessary for our security. He trusted in his own strength alone. Always a mistake. Especially when witchcraft is abroad.

I will tell you what happened.

Our initial invasion had gone forward with precision: a small cadre of loyal troops sent here to Amaurote, with my orders to arrest Professor Joyanna Bender Boyce-Flood, the acting head magistrate and keeper of the archives, as well as chair of the Otterbridge Press. This had gone remarkably well—too well, I see in hindsight. The arrest had gone smoothly. That alone should have warned me.

We shut down Otterbridge Press. That was my personal goal there in Amaurote.

Amaurote is at its loveliest, this time of year. I must admit I had planned it that way. A sentimental attachment to harvest time, after the gathering of the grapes and the pressing of the new wine. The inhabitants are at ease then, looking forward to the feasting of the late autumn. Easy enough to gain hostages then. And to enjoy all the feasting that had been planned for Amaurote.

Pavo, with his inexperience, felt differently. "I'd like a different approach," he said. But when I insisted, he gave way. If he had only followed each of my minutely laid plans, nothing would have gone awry.

We gathered last night to celebrate our tightening grip on Arcadian resources, and to feast on the harvest store that had been garnered by the populace. I offered a toast: "Men of New Arcadia, arise!" We all shouted our approval at that, though there was this oddity: the men of Amaurote had disappeared, leaving the town undefended. But no matter. Our lads were quite heated up, for we had a hanging that afternoon, of Professor Joyanna Bender Boyce-Flood. The women of Amaurote had arrived in silence to bear witness to it. It was a small matter, then, to suborn these women to our needs.

I was worried, though. I mentioned this worry to Pavo, who, impatient, hunched over some papers that he did not deign to show me, almost seemed not to hear.

"Should've taken them by surprise. Murdered her then," he muttered. "Never mind."

"Do you mean Professor Bender Boyce-Flood?" I asked, startled. "That would have been entirely the wrong way to go about it," I said. Pavo, again, appeared so deep in his own thoughts as to not hear. I didn't let it bother me. We had achieved what I thought best there in Amaurote.

I admit to a small twinge of guilt about Joyanna's execution, for this was, I would admit only to you, Livia, not to put too fine a point on it, judicial murder. We'd had no time to incorporate Amaurote into the new Arcadian empire, so, in theory, the Law of Pavo had yet to take effect.

Yet it is true that Bender Boyce-Flood was *an enemy of the state*. If an example had not been made in the face of her defiance to our courteous and reasonable request for the delivery of the Arcadian archive, where, now, would we be?

"We need that archive, Joyanna," I'd said, coaxing her against my better judgment, for the sake of the friendship we had once shared. I had even convinced Pavo if he would leave us alone, I could make significant finds. For we'd known each other well, Joyanna and I, in my time at Otterbridge University. If our differences had led to arguments, sometimes of a violent nature, I had always cherished the thought that they were part of the inevitable rough and tumble of the Life of Ideas to which both she and I were devoted.

She looked at me with her lips pursed, and rolled her eyes. I don't know if you realize, Livia, how enraging that kind of look can be—even when I see that look on Pavo's face, I have difficulty keeping calm. How much more difficult now? I kept my temper, however, and repeated my polite request.

"Beware, Professor Bender Boyce-Flood," I warned. "You defy the new order at your peril. Our emperor is a meticulous and scrupulous purveyor of justice."

"At your peril," she repeated, mocking me. "That was always your way when you were on shaky ground, Aspern. 'Peril.' 'Meticulous.' 'Scrupulous.'" Her shoulders shook with laughter, and then she broke down coughing, for she had always been a heavy smoker of a kind of herb Arcadians grow, and that fetches a great price on the black market of the Ceres Mountains. I waited, irritated but patient, for her to stop, but the courtesy was, alas, wasted on her. She went on. "You never could talk like a normal human being when you felt guilty about this or that. Damned fool. I remember…"

"That's enough," I said shortly, and went out to the hall to call in the guard to take her away.

"Devindra was the only one who could ever get you to sound like a real person." I put my hand up for silence, tamping down my growing fury.

"Do you realize if you defy this order what will occur?"

She laughed again and shrugged as the lads I'd called came in. "Oh yes. Death by hanging." She coughed and shrugged again. "Doesn't worry me, Aspern. We've gotten away those who couldn't stand the nonsense."

This was a non-sequitur, obviously meaningless, due to her old age and wandering wits. But those wandering wits might yet yield what I desired. I held back the guard for a moment. "The archive?" I said, breathing heavily and trying my best to hide the eagerness that gave rise to it. "Where is the archive?"

She shrugged again. "Taken away. You'll never find it. And you know why?" Joyanna seemed unusually, even intolerably, amused at some thought. "Because you don't believe it could be where it is."

"Stupid mysteries," I said, shrugging myself. But I could not help but ask. "Where is it I don't believe?"

"The centaur has it," she said. "All safe in the Bower of Bliss." And she laughed again.

That was when I knew there was nothing more to be gotten out of her, and I motioned to the guard to take her away. I suppose it was a mercy she had become confused in her old age, losing what had been a sharpness and depth of perception rarely known in a female academic, for when she was hanged, she took it as a matter of course. Which showed that she had no more sense of reality left.

As she dropped, there was a faint smile on her face. A blessing, as I say. I'm unsure she even felt pain, her mind was so worn away. The women, also, who watched her were expressionless and bovine as herd animals. No sense of tragedy or real suffering. These would be easy to enslave.

That night, though. Last night, after the execution. As I said, we all sat down to feast, waited on by these women. I had warned of witchcraft, but all Pavo said, with a shrug, was, "Let it be the way it will be. There's no way back now." This was cryptic, but I knew his disappointment in finding the town empty of men to fight. A feast would put such ill humor to rest.

We feasted. We toasted. The men shouted, and Pavo, more contemplative than I had seen him before, toasted them back with an absence of mind that concerned me. Of course, he had never been one to care what he ate or drank. Still, the thing was odd.

But before long, there was something of much more concern. From the outside, there was another kind of shout. One that emanated from a source not to be found in our lot. An insolent sound. It went up outside the hall. More. Laughter was heard, but not that of our men.

Not that of men of any kind.

These were the shouts of women. Women and girls.

Those of us at feast moved uneasily, our hands going to our weapons. Our pistols. Our guns. Our swords. Our sticks. Our arrows and our truncheons.

Laughter. The women serving us looked up, all at once, as if hearing a sound we could not decipher ourselves.

We stood up, momentarily stunned. What did it mean? In our confusion, we turned this way and that, unmoored for an instant by the unexpectedness of the attack.

But was it an attack? It sounded more like merriment. Uncanny revelry. More laughter, Livia. A hideous noise. The serving women stood stock still, some in the very moment of serving out a glass of wine, or a platter of meat. On each face, a slow smile—indeed, an evil grin.

Then it happened. The women whispered something to the men I could not hear, situated as I was on the dais. At this, each man jolted as if electrified, and twisted around as if attacked from behind. But there was no one there. At the sight of this, the women laughed, so hard that tears started down their faces.

Our men stared at the women as if they could hardly believe their eyes. And then the horror. Pavo saw it coming, I believe, even before I. He shouted, jumping down to the floor, but to no avail. The men shrieked, a high-pitched hysterical sound, as if some terror seized them, mysterious and sudden. Before I could stop it, and before Pavo could regain power over them, the men cut the women down where they stood. Their victims staggered a few feet, leaving trails of bright red blood all over the wooden floor, before falling, dead.

Pavo shouted again and cursed. But it was no use. Each man slaughtered the women closest to him. A disaster, Livia, as I said, for these were the only women we had been able to find in all of Arcadia capable of waiting on us in the manner necessary: the only ones who could cook, and clean, and serve efficiently, providing a base from which to work. We have killed our own comfort, and it will take more than a little organization to reestablish some civilized form of life now. Not to mention the appalling fact that someone has to clean up after the general slaughter, and how is that to be achieved without women to do it? I told Pavo how it would be, letting the men get so close to so many women when their blood was up.

He cursed again, screaming. For we were under attack. From the dais, I could see outside. Hordes of men—the men of Amaurote!—approached the hall, pitchforks and torches in hand, fury writ large on every face.

More frightening than these, though, were the shadows, Livia. Shadows slinking here, slinking there. Before the men, after the men, darting in and out of their determined ranks. Dozens, even hundreds of shadows. Of slim figures all emitting a seemingly unanimous shriek of ugly, girlish laughter.

Our men panted, as if after some vile orgy, and looked about them in a daze. But that paralysis lasted only a moment, for Pavo was there. He drew his weapon, a red-tipped truncheon, and shouted, "Follow! Follow!" This seemed to penetrate the strange fog that filled the room, and one by one, the men followed him, racing toward the door.

Our weapons were superior, but numbers were on their side. Our men still struggled under that strange hysteria which seemed to weigh them down.

I stayed at the window, watching as the men poured into the courtyard in the light of a dim crescent moon and the full glare of the False Moon. As they did, the shadows joined until they made a wall of fog, impossible to see through. Pavo shouted again, hacking his way through. But it dissipated at his touch. Disappeared as if it had never been.

That mocking laughter seemed to hang in the air.

The men of Amaurote had disappeared. Gone as if the mist had swallowed them and taken them away.

Our men were left standing there, brandishing their weapons with less and less certainty. Mouths fell agape. Eyes blinked.

Pavo swore, and threw his truncheon to the ground. He turned and stalked back into the hall. Refusing to look at me, he took his place again at the great table, and drank down a goblet of Amaurote wine.

The men reappeared a moment later in the hall, shamefaced, straggling, dazed.

From where had this hysteria, this terror arisen? There was no understanding it. There was no rational explanation.

The men shivered, and shuddered, and sat there on the long benches under the portraits of Lily, Sophia, Devindra, and Joyanna, hardly daring to look up, in the midst of the gore that was all that was left of the serving women. Nothing Pavo or I could do after that would move them. After awhile, we gave it up and retired to our chosen chambers. Pavo was silent as we went, and nodded rather than spoke a curt good night.

This morning, Amaurote was found to be empty of all but our own men. And Pavo, riding out with what men he had been able to threaten and cajole, has found, according to the messengers he has sent back to me, that it is the same in town after town of Arcadia.

All gone. All disappeared. Leaving their looms, their gardens, their very cooking pots on the stove. As if all of Arcadia answered one call and one call alone. Pavo took the news quietly, but, on going back to his own quarters, locked his door against me, needing time to compose himself, I suppose. And to let the men clean up the mess of corpses in the banqueting room at Eisler Hall.

How did this happen? To say "witchcraft" is to explain nothing. We must know the cause that led to the effect. Let me tell you the cause I suspect. One that must be instantly met by action if all our plans are not to fail.

These people—these Arcadians—are joined together through the Key.

What I fear is this: that all of Arcadia has been drawn together by the Key, and can act as one. For if Arcadia is to wield the Key against us, we must use forces to subdue them that I had hoped to avoid. Forces that you, Livia, know better than anyone, can mean the destruction, if an accident should occur, of—but let's not think of that. No need to think of that. Yet.

The Ruined Surface would be as nothing to what was left. And yet, what choice do we have, heading, as we do, with clear determination toward our goal?

Meanwhile, Pavo rides out, the scourge of Arcadia, so quickly there was no time for him to take counsel of me, leaving word, instead, that I am to fall back to Wrykyn, in order to assure that our communications are not cut by a sudden attack on a river bridge. This is not the best policy—far better for me to fall back to Mumford—but I accept his generalship here and obey. My fever and cough seem to come and go. Each time it returns, I feel slightly worse than before. A rest will do me good. And Pavo does not need me for this next stage of our battle. My hope is that he is determined now, swearing to conquer the west that defies his rule.

From The Tower by the Lily Pond, St. Vitus College, Wrykyn:

Does Pavo blame me for that disaster? This may explain the lack of communication now that he prosecutes his campaign in the west. For I have heard little but rumors for months now, although he sends word from time to time that he hopes my health has improved, and that I will be able to join him soon. The detail he left for my protection must report that I am still unable to stand a campaign in the west, as I have yet to receive the summons. I fret at what is happening there, but find I when I attempt leave Wrykyn without it, I am gently but firmly restrained by those left by Pavo to assure my comfort and safety.

"Orders, Professor," the captain of the guard says apologetically. "You're too valuable to the nation to risk the journey until such time as you feel tip top." I understand the logic of this, much as I might regret its implications.

It is also necessary that we watch the Calandals. I have worked out well enough what I believe will be the thoughts of the Council, but it never hurts to be on guard. My belief is that they, and you, will resort to stealth, rather than force, in any attempts on the New Arcadia's proclaimed sovereignty.

I have other, more dire thoughts. But I must push those aside. For what have I to fear, I who created Pavo Vale?

So we wait for Pavo's return. As I wait, I turn over in my mind a fragment of a recollection that may yield some important clue, some aid to our present dilemma. For I had one last meeting with Sophia, in the days before she died. It seemed nothing but an annoying interlude at the time. But now, I wonder.

She had "made time to see me," she said, with that maddening patient expression on her face, as if dealing with me was some kind of penance. I still remember how easy it was for anyone to come into her presence, any time of the day, with the exception of a few hours in the afternoon that were reserved for a solitude I never penetrated. I wondered, often, what the queen did in those hours, between two and four, every day without exception, a rule never to be broken, but never did I discover the answer. She spent so much time poring over children's books. It was a strange passion with her. She was engaged in it that day, as it happens.

As I sit here, pen in hand, awaiting the result of Pavo's foray to the west, it suddenly occurs to me: should I have insisted on having access to those childish books in Sophia's library at the Queen's House? Is it possible that in one of those boring fairy tales there hides some clue?

Later, perhaps, I will explore this idea.

But for now, I have other, more important, concerns than mere fantasy and the foolish works of impotent imagination. I worry about Pavo, for the technology brought at such cost and difficulty over the mountains needs expert attention lest it fail us now. And where are the experts to be found in Arcadia?

How I curse Sophia, and the days she restricted the use of the new technologies in the years before her death.

"Why?" I would demand.

"Oh," she would say vaguely. "I don't think that we need them here."

Need! What has "need" to do with progress?

But you know my thoughts there. Enough of my old-man grumbling. My main complaint now is the lack of transport here in Arcadia. To get anywhere not reachable by river barge or the steam train system between towns means a primitive use of pedicabs, bicycles, horses and donkeys. Oh, we have tried various ways of bringing Mega tech over the mountains, but the problem is the lack of fuel. Lack of fuel and the "mysterious" problems that afflict a car or motorbike left alone for even five minutes: chewed wires, broken parts that can't be replaced, tires strangely flat despite having been carefully checked before for nails and stones. No amount of threats to the populace, or guarding of these precious machines seemed to avail, or at least to be worth the effort. Generally, the one clue was the unusual numbers of school children found near the breakdown of the machines. These little witch creatures are like poltergeists, no doubt feeling the dismantling of one of Mega's machines to be a game. They get so quick at moving in and out without being seen that there is no catching them.

It is clear that to maintain a decent fleet of machinery in Arcadia we must conquer more than the spaces where they could be kept. It was Pavo who shrugged and said, "Doesn't matter. Let me do what I do, and we'll take the place over from the inside out. Don't need a machine, the place is tiny enough." He grinned. "They'll be happy enough to work on anything I say after I'm done with 'em." He shrugged again. "Just let me do my job, okay?"

And so they should be happy! The mess made by the horses and donkeys and llamas that Arcadians use for transport is considerable. The smell!

True, the dung gets gathered up quickly and used for manure and, dried, for heat, but the rural stench of warm mammal bodies is rather more than a former inhabitant of the cleaner False Moon can support without discomfort.

Pavo and his lads used what they could to ride out. What few machines of ours still run, along with the inevitable horses, donkeys, and bicycles. So it will be some time before they return. In triumph, as I hope.

I spoke too soon. There is shouting in the courtyard below. Going to the window, I found a messenger from Pavo, covered with sweat and kicking in fury a mangled bicycle he managed to ride from the west. The captain of my guard, an Arcadian named Bertrand, watched him warily, for I recognized him as a man of short words and shorter temper, brought with us from Megalopolis. He had a nasty habit of turning suddenly on whomever was closest to him in his momentary rages. From the window above, from which all can be seen in all directions, I commanded him to cease the useless display of temper and prepare to give me his report, which only contributed to his irritation. He glared up at me, and turned to say something sharply to Bertrand, who stared at him levelly and then walked away, hand on his weapon. I've paused only long enough to add this note. I will continue my own report having heard his.

You will have the results, Livia, on these pages, as soon as I have made myself master of them and can write them down.

From the Tower by the Lily Pond, St. Vitus College, Wrykyn:

I have now heard what the courier had to say. The thing is strange, of that there is no doubt. But you shall hear all from the beginning.

I attempted to join the messenger, down the wooden staircase to the courtyard. But the detail left to guard me, commanded by Bertrand, blocked the way. A raised eyebrow from Bertrand, and I recognized my danger. The man was in a fury and had to be watched.

"Ambush!" he gasped, elbowing Bertrand aside as he ran up the stairs.

"Damn this place."

Of course my immediate anxiety was how Pavo fared. "How is your captain? Your emperor, I should say."

"Pavo?" he said, and he surprised me by laughing as he launched himself into the Tower room, and threw himself onto the most comfortable chair to be had. I frowned at this. Bertrand entered behind him, standing at the door "He was fine when I saw him last—he seems to get along with the fuckers."

Ignoring the vulgarity, I said, "Damn you, make your report!"

Bertrand shook his head. Was there some danger here that I had yet to grasp?

The man stared at me steadily, and laughed again to himself. An evil sound. I saw Bertrand's hand go to his side. His muscles tensed. The messenger turned and saw this, and gave another short laugh. "Get lost," he said to Bertrand. "Your turn's coming next. Think he doesn't know about you?" But Bertrand just continued to regard him steadily, and moved closer to me.

That there was some issue between them was patent. Of course, the messenger is not an Arcadian, but one of those lads of Megalopolis who followed us over the mountains. Indeed, he is not a "lad," but a man of middle years. His name is Richie. I think you have seen him before. There was that small scandal of rumored pedophilia among the half-children on the False Moon, though it was, as you pointed out, never proved, and immediately settled by moving Richie from school monitor duty over to Pavo's home guard.

There is often friction between the men of Megalopolis and those of Arcadia. Pavo has often taken steps to counter it, at my advice. This must be an example of that. Perhaps it was because of Bertrand's presence that Richie was reluctant to tell me his news. Although eventually it came out, through sheer frustration. For this campaign has been a long and arduous one, with the enemy refusing to engage at every turn. Pavo, wily, at times managed to lure the Arcadians out in ways still unknown to me. When I questioned Richie closely about this, he shook his head, refusing to say more. He and Bertrand exchanged a grimace. Although I do not know how, Pavo has discovered the enemy. That much is clear. In doing so, it seems, he has captured the leader of the resistance. At the revelation of this news—he almost spat it out—Richie looked again at Bertrand and laughed.

To my astonishment, this "hero" of the Arcadians is Walter Todhunter. I never would have thought it. He always seemed to smell of the barnyard to me, with the stolid, slow brain of a rural hick to match.

Still, the story is a good one. If strange, as I said.

"Damn this place," Richie said. Bertrand stiffened, for no man likes to hear the place of his birth insulted, no matter what side he is on. "Not like Megalopolis, is it? No real highways, just these windy roads, most of them not even paved. Crap engineering." He looked over at Bertrand and muttered something indecipherable, though clearly insulting, under his breath.

I spoke to him sharply. As I tell Pavo constantly, there should be no fighting in the ranks. Bad discipline. At this, the two exchanged another look that boded no good for one of them once they were out of my sight. I was uneasy at this. But for the moment, when I demanded in frustration to know if Pavo's main force had been attacked, Richie continued.

"Attacked?" he said slowly. "No, not exactly." Another moment of silence. Another near-murderous look thrown to Bertrand, who kept his level gaze steady back. "It's not like 'attack' is something these guys understand. It's like 'attack' is a weird idea from another world." At this he sprawled on the couch, still staring at Bertrand. "Take the women. Or rather, don't take them, you can have them, in my opinion. If you jump on one of these Arcadians—if you can find one in the first place—she either laughs or looks at you like you're some kind of animal. An animal she's not too scared of either, which a man could take. It's that look of…I don't know, *boredom*. That's what it looks

151

like. They look at you and look bored." It struck me suddenly that all this was an attack on Bertrand. He stiffened again as Richie continued. "Different for you Arcadian lot, is it? When you get 'em?" He yawned.

This time the insult was unmistakable.

Bertrand didn't answer. Richie, apparently satisfied at having achieved some kind of dominance, shrugged and turned back to me.

"We headed for those mountains to the west, the Donatees I think you all call them. Pavo said he bet he knew who was working the 'late disturbances'—and he knew how to lure the guy in. He did, too.

"At first we couldn't tell where we were going. Dark night, cloud cover, no stars or moon. Had to depend on a scout. Turned out, we were being led in circles. This *kid* who said he knew the way, knew it all right. He just kept leading us around and around and around until we were all half-exhausted. Worse, what machines we had started dying, running out of fuel. All we had were those donkeys and horses we stole as we marched. Pavo on that big gray horse we took out of the Queen's Stable. I hate those things. You can't get them to do anything they don't want to do. So I was on a kind of bicycle thing I took off the land where we found the kid."

He wiped the back of his hand on his mouth, and said to Bertrand, "Anything to drink around here? I mean like we have in Megalopolis. Something strong." Bertrand looked at him, and at me. He must have concluded the thing was safe, for he went out and shouted down the stairs, while Richie continued, leaning forward as if he wanted to get this next part out quickly, before Bertrand's return.

"We figured it out, of course, almost too late. We headed into a kind of ravine, all dark except for us. The kid had led us into a defile, so narrow I just dropped the bike outside. Better on foot in a case like that. The guys on horseback found that out the hard way. No way forward or backward unless the guy in front of you and in back of you goes first. Anyway, there was a whoosh of wind or something, and all the torches went out. We kind of froze at that. Then the clouds blew apart, and the Moon Itself appeared overhead. You could almost see clearly then. For one thing, you could see what the kid had been up to. Pavo was in a rage at that. He was in front, next to the kid, and he just picked him by the scruff of his neck, shaking him till I thought he'd snap his neck. The kid screamed, and there was some kind of noise up above us, and you could just make out, up there, on a jutting rock, some guy on a horse. Not one of ours, you could see it in the moonlight. He looked…you're not going to credit this, but the guy in front of me said the same, he looked like he was sitting on the horse's head. Not on its back. Not that you could see the horse head, it was just this guy rising up out of the front of it. It was weird. It wasn't like anything I ever saw. But we'd been marching and marching, and I don't know, maybe we were seeing things."

Bertrand returned, and the man leaned back as if his confidences were ended, although I must have been wrong about that, because he went on with his report after taking the glass full of spirits from Bertrand without thanks, and downing it, before handing it back, empty.

He wiped his mouth and continued. "You should have seen the Chief. He ran up the side of the ravine, straight up it, like it was stairs. Dragging the kid, who screamed all the way. We all just stood there staring—well. That was when the horses went nuts. I didn't look too closely then, it was all I could do to get out with a whole skin. We lost some good men there, trampled. I backed off, I can tell you. Lucky for me I was one of the ones in the rear."

Bertrand laughed at this. Obviously some joke in the ranks.

Richie threw him a resentful look, and went on. "Good thing I got out when I did, or you wouldn't be hearing the tale, isn't that right?" He turned back to Bertrand. "Get me another glass of that stuff, will you, Junior? We guys on the front line get thirsty. You know."

Bertrand snorted, and went out again. Richie leaned in, making sure he was unheard, and finished the story. "I saw the whole thing once I got clear of the ravine, but I still don't know what I saw. I swear to god, I saw Pavo, dragging the kid up over the lip of the canyon, head straight for that weird rider. The guy's head came right out of the horse like he

153

was a part of it, I swear that's what I saw. He flailed at Pavo with its hooves, but that didn't stop the Chief. He just dropped the kid, hauled back one arm and punched that horse as hard as he could in the chest. It barreled over. He was going in to punch it again as hard as he could, when this other guy comes shooting out of the shadows, shouting. The kid must have been playing dead. He up and ran back into the shadows, clean away. But the other guy kept coming. And I could see, now the Moon was up, he'd come out of a kind of house built into the side of those damn rocks. It must have been where we were headed, but I could swear it wasn't there before."

At this, Bertrand reappeared with a bottle, which he held up. Richie reached for it, but Bertrand held it just out of reach, a silent invitation to leave. Richie shrugged. "That's all I got to say, anyway. I knew the Chief would want you to know, so I grabbed the bike and headed out."

This was his report. I believe it will not be long till I see the end of this particular story for myself.

For Bertrand has just appeared at my door, with an announcement. "Orders are I'm to take you to the Chief," he says.

"What orders?" I say, startled and eager, both.

"Richie reported…"

"But he never said…"

"He remembered shortly after he left you. I'm to take you right away. We'll spend the night on the road and be there at dawn."

So it seems I'm to be whisked away to the scenes of Pavo's military triumphs! I can't say I am sorry. I'll continue my notes, catch as catch can, from the road.

I ask to see Richie once more before we leave, in order to make sure my notes are completely correct, but Bertrand says this is impossible, as Richie has continued on, already, to Walton, where a message must be delivered. I take leave to doubt this, I say, for I can hear a moaning come from somewhere in the building. Bertrand laughs at this, and admits I

154

am right—that the man is dead drunk after having consumed an entire bottle of spirits on an empty stomach. "Regretting it now, I imagine," he says, amused. "It'll be awhile before he sleeps it off. We'll be long gone by then." So I will have to trust to my memory! For soon I will be on the road again, and can report on my boy's movements as an eyewitness.

From the Queen's House, Mumford:

En route to the east, Bertrand insists we rest, as my cough is somewhat worse. We stop in Mumford. I am shocked by what I see: building works everywhere, scaffolding about the Queen's House. Pavo has been busy. This is a mistake, this taking over of Mumford. Walton is the place for a capital. A young man's error. Still, there is no harm, I suppose, in urban renewal of all kinds in Arcadia. Pavo and I must speak of this later. For now, Bertrand calls. We must be off.

I confess this travel is wearing on me after the months of seclusion. I have yet to shake off this chill, and some very painful boils, if I may be so graphic, have formed on my backside. I find myself, in a moment of weakness, wishing to stay here, in the Queen's House, where I might explore Sophia's library, even those silly little children's books she made such a point of collecting.

But needs must. Pavo requires my counsel. Bertrand informs me that we leave at dawn.

From the School of Arts and Sciences, Paloma:

Rain. Rain and more rain. A thick, churning mud has stopped us here while we repair our transport. But this allows me to transcribe the most recent events, as well as my thoughts about them.

Strange happenings, Livia. I scarcely know how to describe them. But I will begin at the beginning, and trust to my skills as a research scientist and writer of innumerable reports.

From Mumford, Bertrand and I left before dawn, while the night was still black. "Take the towpath," I said, and he nodded. "I know," he said. Of course he'd known. He is, after all, an Arcadian born and bred. An Arcadian type, one of "mixed race," as we call them in Megalopolis. Dependable. Quiet. Small and wiry, with foxy reddish brown eyes. The motorbike we rode was of Arcadian make, rather than one of the type we'd brought over with such trouble and cost from Megalopolis. Held together by spit and passion, as we used to say in Arcadia. A boy's hobby, making something like that. Something out of nothing. With a kick of his foot, we leapt and surged forward.

In my excitement at being off, I forgot all my aches and pains. Is this why, Livia, we men are so eager to seek adventure?

An Arcadian obviously was my guide. As we roared out of Mumford, via a series of winding paths and roads not obviously visible from the city center, I saw he knew the area well.

This put more heart in me, Livia. If a lad like that had joined our cause, where might we not end?

I wanted to ask him from which town he came, and from which parents, the kinds of questions I had almost forgotten are always exchanged when Arcadian meets Arcadian, along with the names of pets and the favorite haunts for the drinking of wine and beer and cider. This amused me, my sudden nostalgia. He even smelled of my childhood! I couldn't help but notice this, jammed together as we were on the tiny double seat of the bike. He carried the scent of baking bread, roasting garlic, and cooking hops. There was an unmistakable underlay of wet dog.

Something seemed to be worrying him. He muttered to himself from time to time, shaking his head. Still, it was clear he was a man who knew his work.

The best of Arcadia, I mused as we took neat turn after turn without trouble in the dark, down the winding streets that lead from Mumford to the Juliet River, down to the towpath on its northern shore. There must be a way to inject it into the stream that would come after Pavo. Shanti, of course.

Shanti is pure Arcadia, though half her lineage is unknown. Her father, Walter, as I've said, was raised by an elderly couple living as smallholders in the Donatees. It must have been a foster, such as happens in Arcadia when a mother can't care for her child, whether from illness, incapacity, or death, for Amalia Todhunter and Francis Flight, of the Small House, were surely too old to have given birth to a child themselves.

My mind pulled up what facts were stored there as to the time of Walter's birth—it would be useful to know his genetic makeup, if his genes were to enter the pool from which my Pavo's descendants would spring. I confess, though, after recent events, I am uneasy about Walter's history. Something nags at me. I cannot put my finger on it.

But to return to my tale.

It was now an hour or so before dawn. I reckoned we should reach the foothills of the Donatees sometime when the sun came up over the Calandals behind us. Heading west, all was shrouded dark gray, for a mist had risen from the river during the night. Halfway to the turn to Amaurote and Ventis we could see no farther than a few feet ahead.

Bertrand knew what he was doing. He slowed, turning deftly to avoid the usual creatures of the night that ventured in front of us—I saw quite a few dead animals. Porcupine, squirrel, raccoon, coyote, and deer hadn't been so lucky before us. The towpath must have gotten much traffic from Pavo's men.

We turned off the towpath now, onto the turn to Amaurote and Ventis, skirting the vineyards as the mist began to lift. The light began to show orange and red behind us atop Mount Macillhenny. The rows were neat, the vines bare, for harvest season had come and gone. Always a melancholy time, in Arcadia, before the winter snows begin.

Bertrand made a gesture with his hand, quickly, as one does an automatic movement learned in childhood. The Arcadian blessing at the end of the autumn. You'll laugh at this, Livia. I recognized it, because I found myself making the same gesture before realizing what I'd done! This kind of thing is hard to eradicate, once a child has had it imprinted in him. As our scientists—and Arcadian scientists as well, Devindra foremost among them—have discovered, these traditions are not just passed down culturally, but have a biological component as well. At least, after a certain amount of use and time.

All the more important that Pavo Vale be a fresh start, turning a clean page in humanity's blotted book. Yes.

We turned off toward Ventis, past the steaming hot springs that heat the town, and where I remember picnicking as a boy. So we had taken Ventis, had we? This was satisfactory, though I would have wished to hear about it when it happened. No matter. Pavo moves too quickly for report.

I could see a handful of men now, some of Pavo's Invincibles, sitting naked in the steaming water. Bertrand pointed to an enormous light up ahead.

"Pavo?" I said in his ear.

He nodded. As we drew closer, I saw it was a bonfire, made of uprooted vines from the vineyards around, and wood from the fruit trees that the men had cut down for that purpose. Pavo Vale and his Invincibles had made their camp. The men could be seen standing and sitting about the fire, throwing in branches and other detritus as they did, laughing and talking among themselves.

We pulled up beside a group of them, and one pointed at a small hill lit by flames and the red rays of the sun.

"We're in for a storm," Bertrand said, but the others, Mega-bred, just looked at him blankly. A red sky means little to the city-raised. Shrugging, he led me to the hill, now lit a fiery red. Atop it was Pavo, stretching luxuriously in the heat of the fire, for it was a cold morning, one of those mornings you get before the finality of winter settles in. I felt it in my bones. I couldn't stop from shivering, and drew nearer the fire, thankful for its warmth.

At Pavo's feet was some kind of bundle, a large pile of rags or some such thing. I puzzled over this as we drew closer. Just then the sun leapt up over the range at the far end of the valley behind us, and the first of its rays shot down. In their light, I saw the pile was not a pile at all, but a man, trussed up in rope like a winter feast-day ham.

I recognized him at once. Walter Todhunter, Shanti's father. He saw me as well in that moment, and he gave me a smile. The smile of an idiot, I thought, for what on earth did the man have to smile about?

"I've brought him," Bertrand said. Pavo looked up. I could tell he was angry. He glared at Bertrand, saying, "What the…"

"Morning, Aspern," Walter greeted me, interrupting him. "Think you could convince Pavo here to give me a cup of coffee? I usually have one this time of the morning."

Pavo kicked him impatiently as he moved toward Bertrand, yanking him aside.

But Walter only shrugged.

"If you can get it," he said, "I like it with a little milk added."

Pavo ignored him. He spoke in a furious undervoice to Bertrand, and the lad saluted smartly, turning to walk back down the hill leaving me there.

Walter, incongruously, laughed. Pavo strode over to him threateningly, glaring down. But Walter chuckled softly to himself, and said a few words I couldn't quite hear. Pavo kicked him again, setting him to coughing, then, collecting himself, moved forward to accept my fatherly embrace.

*****

Again something tugs at my memory. I relate this to you as I saw it, but something nags at me. Why? Those days I worked in the research stacks on the False Moon, those days when I first conceived the idea of Pavo Vale, long before I actually received him, with a father's tenderness, into my grateful arms.

159

Why think of that now?

You'll remember what I found then. Digging into records, poring over maps, looking for causes and effects of the Great Disaster, it was easy enough to see the superficial reasons for the massive upheaval. Obviously, it had been the experiments performed in our research facility on the Marsh that began the chain reaction of fatal events.

What makes me think of those days long gone now? Is there some hint in the tableau I now mean to describe?

That first explosion was definitely sited in the outer laboratories on the edge of the Marsh where it, in those days, met the sea. There was just enough warning to airlift out key personnel—including, of course, Alastair—but we lost many good men. A loss I have spent my career in your service attempting to repair.

Our losses were immense. But the only bodies found floating after the tsunami wave receded from the Marsh were those of *men.*

Only men. Corpses of women or children there were none.

All the women and children had fled over the mountains to Arcadia. And this before there was any warning of the impending cataclysm. Led by she who was to become queen of Arcadia, the first queen, Lily.

Why? And why do I think of it now?

It comes to me slowly. His face. Walter's face. Not just the expression, the features. He has the very look of Lily the Silent. Why have I never seen this before? Of course, I hardly ever noticed the man, except in slight exasperated boredom at his shambling walk and mediocrity.

Who is he?

*****

"You might as well untie me," Walter said from the heap at Pavo's feet. "It would be a lot friendlier."

The tone of his voice was so mild. It would have been impossible to believe him sarcastic if there had been any other explanation. He and Pavo exchanged a strange look, as if joined in an understanding I myself lacked. But that was impossible.

"It's not necessary to be so extreme, Pavo," he said. "I'm nothing to be scared of. Honest."

"Scared?" Pavo snarled. "As if I'd be scared of the likes of you."

"No, of course not," Walter said soothingly. "I didn't mean to imply such a thing. Still, it would be kinder if you'd loosen these things just a bit." He wriggled his hands to show how tight the bonds had become. "No circulation. My fingers are turning white."

Turning away, Pavo ignored him. "Well, all right then," Walter sighed mildly. "Have it your way. But I still think it would be..." With a snarl, Pavo turned back, hacking at the man's bonds with his own hands until he was free.

"Shut up now, then would you?" he said. Then addressed himself to one of his men, giving him his orders or some such thing. His back was turned to Walter, when the man shook himself, stretched out one arm, then another, then one leg, then another. Then pulled himself up to his full height.

Pavo turned back and glared.

"Ah," Walter said contritely. "Didn't mean to crowd you, sorry." He stretched his arms and legs again, one at a time, but this time more carefully. He hunched himself over, as if his height had been a discourtesy. In his shortsighted way, he peered about.

I remember now. That was when I became aware of a twinge that I couldn't identify, a tickling somewhere in my memory. Was that the moment I saw his resemblance to Lily? Dark like her, with the same tightly curled hair. Pure Arcadian. Of a certain type, surely.

Pavo gave him a look of disgust before heading down to the fire to warm himself. He kicked moodily at a sparking log that fell out of the flames, pushing it back in with his foot.

Walter followed Pavo, hesitating now, as if uncertain how to approach him. Then he came to some kind of conclusion. And tried again.

"Not that I mean to be a bother, Pavo, but is there a reason why you called me here today?" The sheer friendliness of the question was almost an offense. I saw Pavo take in a deep breath, trying to control his own anger. He rounded on Walter, who fell back in dismay.

"Honestly, I just—"

"How many times do I have to tell you? Shut up! Just shut up!"

Walter looked honestly taken aback. "All right, all right," he said good-humoredly, sitting down on a rock. "If someone would give me a cup of that coffee, I'll do anything you like."

Bertrand, seeing Pavo about to explode, leapt up and gave the man his coffee. Walter thanked him, and drank it with every appearance of pleasure. Bertrand grinned at him, but then turned on his heel and hurried away again under Pavo's glare.

"I'll deal with you later," Pavo muttered. Bertrand, walking away, shrugged.

"I do like my coffee," Walter said to no one in particular. And then he smiled. At me.

I did not respond.

Total silence now. The men looked at Pavo. Pavo gave a small shake and turned around to give the man on the ground a hard look now. A look of threat. But the fool just sat there, drinking from the steaming cup, as unconcerned as if he were sitting at his own fireside.

I asked for a cup as well. I needed it, certainly, a hot drink after that cold ride. Without speaking, Bertrand returned and gave it to me.

Pavo snarled again.

More than total silence from the men now. All that could be heard was the crackling of the flames from the fire, and the far-off screeching of an owl on its dawn hunt for food.

162

I tensed. But was there any real need to worry? It seemed impossible, given the mild look of the man in front of us.

More silence. Walter finished his drink, and looked from side to side, squinting as if bewildered.

"Ah," he ventured.

Pavo turned at this, and looked down at Walter. His expression was lofty, as from a superior considering an inferior. Walter looked back up at him, apparently interested in what he had to say.

"Stand up," Pavo barked.

Walter gave a little jump, and laughed. "Yes, yes," he said, scrambling up beside Pavo. "Anything you like. Only take things more calmly, would you? It's a little early in the morning for me."

The men stared at them.

Indeed they were a vision. At least, a momentary one. For with the fire now behind them, the two were of equal height, Walter as dark as Pavo is gold. A trick of the firelight and the rising sun, and they merged together, two halves making a whole.

I blinked and shook myself, and the vision was gone.

"Come on, Pavo," Walter said in a coaxing voice. "You didn't roust me out of bed and drag me down here out of love, did you? Tell me what you want, and let me go home."

Pavo looked at him and then gave a sudden crack of laughter. "Out of love, you say," he muttered, and laughed again. "That's it. Love."

Walter looked at him with an expression of courteous concern. "Love? Love how? Love where? Love who? Pavo, just tell me, and we can all get on with our day."

Pavo licked his lips. When he spoke, it was in a croak, as if his mouth was dry. "You know," he said. And Walter looked at him as if from a long way, with a strange expression of sympathy on his face.

"Ah," Walter said. "Light dawns. Yes. I do know." He shook his head, the look of sympathy deepening. "She'll never have you, Pavo." He shook his head again. "You started wrong. And then…"

"She'll have me. She *will*." The veins bulged in Pavo's neck as he thrust his head forward, bull-like. "You can make her." He said this boyishly. I hadn't seen him like this in many years. Not since before his marriage to Faustina. When he was no more than twelve years old.

That was a long time ago.

Walter shook his head. "I can't make her do anything, Pavo. I can barely make myself do what I want, let alone make Shanti." He laughed. Pavo looked up at him in entreaty.

For what in the world does Pavo need to entreat?

Walter looked at me. He looked at Pavo. He sighed.

"Well," he said, shaking his head. "You won't believe it till you hear it from her. We better go find her, then. Find her and have this out once and for all."

Pavo stared at him as if he scarcely understood what was said.

I stared, too.

"Where…where is she?" Pavo's voice rasped.

Walter looked up at the sky, considering. "Well, Pavo, truth to tell, she could be just about anywhere. She has a lot of things going on, you know. Lots of engagements. Friends. Activities. And so on." He shook his head. "She could be anywhere, really."

"You know where to look," Pavo said. A statement, not a question.

"Yes, yes, I do, Pavo. I know where to look. That doesn't mean I can find her, though, mind you. Shanti is her own person. I don't keep track of her. But I do have some idea of where to look."

"You'll take me."

Walter looked at him earnestly, as if assessing…something.

164

What?

"Well, yes, Pavo, I will take you. I will take you to find Shanti. If you're sure that's what you want."

At this, Pavo gave a hoarse laugh. "Sure?" he said. "*Sure?*" He laughed again.

There was a pause.

"Well, then," Walter said, as he turned and walked away. "We might as well get going, don't you think?"

He didn't look back to see if anyone followed. He just kept on walking as the sun came up behind us, over the Calandals, flooding the whole of Arcadia with the morning's light. And Pavo ran after him, as eager as a young boy running after the first young girl he fancied. I was ashamed to see this, Livia. Pavo to show such weakness! I saw him catch up with Walter, but was too far behind to hear any of their talk. To my shock I could see Walter incline his head as Pavo explained something or other, gesturing wildly with his hands, pushing back a lock of his hair impatiently as it fell in his face. I had the sudden unpleasant impression that this was not the way a man not yet forty years of age might listen to his elder aged sixty-four. It was the way a father might listen, amused, to the enthusiastic plans of his son.

Or a father-in-law to a son-in-law.

I hurried to catch up with them.

*****

The Invincibles, too—a kind of strange transformation overtook them. Where a moment ago they had seemed—not "seemed," been—a cohort, a force, disciplined and directed, now they were at a loss, straggling, half-ashamed, like boys coming home after having been caught out in some mischief.

There was the sound of distant thunder. Bertrand looked up at the sky and shook his head.

We came close to the house. Walter's house. I had been here once before, almost forgotten. Built into the hillside, at a diagonal to catch the southern light and the morning sun. The latter shone on it now, lighting up the many shaped windows, the ones strewn together higgledy piggledy on the two outside walls of the house, giving the not unpleasant impression of having been scavenged from other building projects.

In fact, the whole of the house gave that impression. This was true as well of the fence surrounding Walter's "famous" experimental garden. Much of it was covered, at this season, with vines that shone orange, red, purple and green. Chickens scratched about the place. There was a row of neatly kept beehives. I remembered Walter's foster parents had been famous for their beekeeping skills. Queen Sophia had been a patron, keeping a supply of their superior honey.

There had been a time when Megalopolis sent researchers to the Small House to learn its secrets, after all the bees on our sides of the mountains began, mysteriously, to die. There were no secrets, Francis and Amalia said, shrugging. They simply laid out the hives and the bees came. I remember your annoyance when the delegation returned, no wiser than when it had left the Ruined Surface.

Sophia was their patron. Did I say that? Why does that come back to me now? And why did I notice this day that Walter has the look of Sophia?

I noted a scattering of outbuildings, especially a glass structure set farther away from the hillside. I remembered now. Shiva's studio. Someone moved inside, was it she? I watched the figure warily, and followed the oddly silent men inside the main house, through an enormous carved wood door. I was last through, shutting it, and then running my hand down its surface, trying to find a joint. Surely a door so large couldn't be one piece?

How had it been done without machinery if so?

Once inside, Walter urged his visitors to make themselves comfortable on a motley array of chairs, benches, and couches. "Might as well settle down. Looking like it's going to be a nasty storm outside." He noticed my inspection of the door and grinned faintly. "An old oak, that used to shade the garden of my foster parents. It fell around the time they died. Made a door, and good crossbeams, lintels, and our bedstead. A big tree."

Mentioning Shiva made him remember his wife, for now he looked around and called out for her. "Shiva? Hello? Anyone about?" No answer. I was right then. That had been Shiva I'd seen. "She must be in her studio. Well, let me see about getting everyone some breakfast. You must all be hungry."

The Invincibles looked hopeful at this, more like boys than ever. There was a movement behind us. I jumped as the door pushed open and wind rushed in. It was Shiva, as disheveled as I'd remembered her, in an old torn shirt and baggy trousers that I suspected of being Walter's castoffs.

She held a paintbrush in her hand and there was a smut of white paint on her nose. She looked at us in a worried way, but on seeing Walter, relief replaced the worry.

"Here, Shiva," he said, waving toward us. "You see I've brought him."

"Oh, Walter," she said. "There you are. I was wondering where you'd got to. Storm coming." She peered at the rest of us shortsightedly. "What a lot of friends you've brought with him."

"Here's Pavo Vale," Walter said helpfully. "*And* Professor Grayling."

"Of course," she said, but I couldn't swear she recognized us. Not, at least, as her father and her grandfather. "You must all be starved, it's past breakfast time. Lucky you made bread yesterday, Walter. I'm hoping you'll excuse me, I'm right in the middle of…," she waved her brush, "something or other. No time to explain, Walter will make sure you get something to eat. And then afterwards…"

Walter nodded.

She wandered off, as vaguely as she had arrived, only pausing to remind

167

Walter to put another log on the fire. I turned, about to speak, when her head popped back in the door.

"Oh dear," she said, "I forgot to mention. He came back with the horses, and said not to worry about the storm."

She disappeared again.

"Who came by with the horses?" I asked, and Walter, as unconcerned with my stature and my mission as his wife had been, answered as casually as she had spoken.

"Who? Oh, the centaur. You know. They all answer to him. We really have nothing to do but feed them." I began to ask another question, but he had already disappeared into another room. Pavo and I followed him, jumping when his head popped out unexpectedly.

"Bertrand!" he called out. "Would you poke the fire, please?" Bertrand, to my surprise, leapt up to obey. Pavo scowled, but said nothing.

We followed Walter into the kitchen.

This was a wide and pleasant place, dug into the mountainside at the southwestern end of the house, so that one whole wall was packed dirt covered with tiles, a stove and shelves before it. The back wall, also against the hillside, seemed to access a spring, for a kind of fountain poured water continuously from a spigot into a basin there.

Walter whistled tunelessly to himself as he moved, putting a kettle of water on the stove to boil, cracking eggs into a pan. A bowl of late grapes, and one of red and green apples emerged from the depths of a wooden drawer. The smell of hot coffee filled the room.

I don't mention these details lightly, Livia. There was something strange—otherworldly, almost—in that kitchen that day, as Walter set about providing a meal for the men sitting, some awkward, some frankly resting, in that house. In that home. I am not sure how to describe it.

Thunder again. Closer this time.

It was as if we had entered another world entirely. One powered, formed, limited by a set of laws different from any we have known. There was a whiff of my childhood in it—why I describe this in terms of a smell, I do not know. But that is how it comes to me.

It was as if—you'll laugh at me here—a new world has formed in Arcadia in the outer reaches of that land. One with different rules, different assumptions, different goals than those we in Megalopolis regard as absolute. What confused me, standing there unsure of what to say or do, was Walter's very being. His and Shiva's. There was no reaction to the situation at hand, not the way I, or any rational person, would expect. There was no sign that either Walter or his wife felt any threat. There was no indication of their being on their guard, no sign that a counter-attack was planned, nothing to show that this everyday activity was hampered by our arrival.

A flash of lightning lit up the room. Thunder cracked overhead.

I suspected, at first, that this display of casual hospitality was disingenuous, that we were being led into an ambush, that some plot was afoot, of the kind you expect when the weak are confronted with the strong. But Livia, what I think now is, in its way, worse. For I think there was none of that. In fact, as I sit here, puzzling over the events of the last few days, the only explanation I can find is a very unwelcome one indeed.

It is this: that their reality has changed their world. In the parts of Arcadia where this new reality has taken hold, like a virus, our strength goes unnoticed, undefended against, unreacted to. This, I'm afraid to say, has a disarming effect I—and you—had not counted upon. For when large groups of people ignore the force one brings to bear upon them, that force inevitably separates in confused disarray. There must be, then, an attempt to unify into a form that will be acknowledged by the enemy. Acknowledged and confronted. If there is no acknowledgement, no confrontation, how can there be any battle?

And if there is no battle, how can there be any victor?

Was the strange appearance and disappearance of the Arcadians linked to this? Were they only in our range when they acknowledged our facts?

169

Forgive me. As a scientist, there is fascination in this line of inquiry. It is, indeed, something new. I feel it. I would almost say I feel part of it, if that wasn't such a blow to my normal way of thinking—to my very identity, you might say. It makes me dizzy at the mere thought.

Or is this my illness speaking? The fever?

Put that aside for now. Let me continue to describe, as minutely as I can, what happened. I'll leave analysis for later.

Walter fed us all breakfast. Plain stuff, but it was enough. Bread, fish, that kind of thing. The lads meekly helped pass out the plates and utensils, and to my surprise, none rushed to take more than their share. There was no noise except for chewing, and a request for the basket of bread, or more smoked trout, or more tea, or the coffee pot, and then a grunted thanks. To my astonishment, I saw Pavo, who never shows any interest in what he eats, inquire if there were more grapes. Bertrand went to get more for him. He seemed to know his way around the house. Pavo thanked him, and for a moment, their eyes locked. Then Bertrand turned away, sitting down to his own meal, seemingly reluctant to meet my own gaze.

Afterwards, two or three of the lads gathered up all the dirty dishes and disappeared into the kitchen, from where the sound of washing up emerged.

The rain began. You could hear it patter down, then pour, on the roof sod.

Pavo sat brooding by the fire. His enormous head was propped up by one enormous fist, arm resting on his knee, as he stared into the flames.

Walter quietly went to him and sat down.

Pavo looked up at him, unsurprised, nodded. "Where is she?" he said. But his tone was gentle, almost. Courteous and kind.

Was this Pavo? I thought, startled.

"Have you looked in her room?" Walter said. "Though I would have thought all this noise would have brought her out."

"Her room is…?" Pavo leapt up, not rudely, but eagerly, and it was that way, I saw, that Walter took it. Walter pointed down a hallway, and Pavo disappeared, reappearing after a moment with a look of more than disappointment. Livia, it was a look of anguish. What was clear to me was how much Pavo suffered. What was not clear to me was why.

At least—it was not clear to me then.

"*No,*" was all he said, but the note of pain in his voice seared me, Livia, the way a baby's cry sears its mother. Walter went to him and laid his hands on his shoulders. For an awful moment, I feared that Pavo— Pavo!—was about to cry. But if that was what was about to happen, Walter forestalled it.

"We'll go ask her mother, shall we?" he said, and Pavo, dumb now, nodded. He and Walter went out the oak door. I followed.

We hurried across a pathway through the rain, to the little glass studio, the crunch of gravel sounding under our feet—why do I remember the crunch of the gravel? I remember every small detail of that walk. That sound of the rain. The whooshing of the wind in the evergreens on the hills behind. The squawking of a group of jays. The smell of overripe apples cut with the resinous scent of sage. A far-off neigh from a horse.

Walter gave a gentle rap to the glass door, and opening it, courteously waited for Pavo and me to go through. He followed us in and shut the door behind us.

The smell of paint and turpentine. Shiva, intent on a large piece of parchment paper stretched out on an easel in front of her, barely seemed to notice us, but went on, now with a fine-point pen rather than a brush, adding dot after dot to an enormous picture of trees.

But I saw nothing else in the room but she who stood in the shadows, among the canvases and bits of cloth hanging there.

Devindra's ghost. She stood there, patient, as if she had been waiting for me. I stood rooted to the spot.

Then Shiva, as if hearing a voice, put down her pen. Looking into the corner where the ghost stood, she said, "What, Grandmother?" Listening, she turned and looked at me.

"Yes," she said, but she didn't speak to any of us who had just entered the room. "Here he is. Bertrand brought him."

Pavo scowled. I was taken aback. "Bertrand brought him." Did she mean me?

But who else could she have meant?

Shiva's art, Livia, is fantastical. Yet the figures peopling it can be identified. Feeling the eyes of Devindra upon me, I set to looking at the drawings and paintings there more closely, though I have to admit, shamefaced, that what I looked for was a picture of her, of Devindra herself, as she had been when we were young.

I was rueful about that impossible wish of mine. Shiva had not even been thought of, not then—why would she draw a picture of Devindra in the flower of her life?

But even as I thought this, I saw it. A line drawing of Devindra, and the younger Aspern Grayling as well. Myself, standing beside the bench where she sat, graceful, beneath a laburnum tree in full bloom. Blossoms drifted down and settled in her dark hair. Though there was no color in the drawing, such was its vigor that it was as if the color leapt into being on its own.

I stood there gazing at my image, my simulacrum that looked down at her with a devotion I had till that very moment forgotten. Forgotten? Rather, pushed from memory. For what use was it to me, in my life, with my great goals?

Yet the picture was compelling. I had to admit as much. A true artist, then, Shiva. Had she inherited such genius from Pavo? Where in Pavo had been hidden, not just the talent, but the desire to create these images of beauty?

"Pavo's looking for Shanti," Walter said with a mild smile. "You have any idea where she's got to, Viva?"

Shiva thought a moment, as if calling back wandering thoughts.

"Hmm," she said. "She said something about Isabel last night. They were off to somewhere or other. Was it Paloma? Cockaigne? I can't remember." She shook her head. "Sorry. Maybe she left a note?"

"Maybe," Walter said, soothing her. Then he said, "Ah. I know."

There was a flash of color, and I looked sharply back to the space where I had seen Devindra's ghost.

The ghost was gone. I reached out to grab it, but all I had to show for the movement was a slight rush of air.

"Paloma! Cockaigne! We'll go to both," Pavo said in a fury, apparently totally forgetting that we had yet to conquer either in his name and the name of Megalopolis. He grabbed Walter by the arm. "You'll come with us. She'll come to you."

Walter looked surprised, but he didn't argue the point. I saw him about to speak, then close his mouth and nod. Was there danger in going with Walter? It was an odd fact that I was convinced there was none. The opposite. I felt our safety was in traveling by his side.

And now I was as eager as Pavo to be off myself, storm brewing or not. For Devindra's ghost was here, now, in Arcadia—where I was uncertain about the reality of it in Megalopolis, on the False Moon, here in Shiva's studio there was no doubt. Devindra, her ghost, was here. I might find her if I looked. If this was a new world, she was in it. What answers might she not give me? So I followed Walter and Pavo out the door, and agreed that we should go. Pavo glared at me, his mind elsewhere.

"Bertrand," he muttered. "Bertrand, too." Walter looked at him curiously. But he did not argue

The rain poured down. Walter pulled some oilskin coats off a hook under the eaves, and so attired we moved toward a rough-hewn fence. Here he whistled.

Two horses, a black and the gray that Pavo had ridden in the morning , ran up. Behind them was a bay-colored horse almost twice the size of the other two, rain streaming down its sides. As it drew closer, I squinted through a sudden downpour, and saw it was not a horse after all. It was a centaur.

"Greetings, friend," the centaur said to Walter, who nodded in return. "Is it time?" The two of them paid no heed to the rain. Country folk are like that. I myself cringed under its lash. If it hadn't been for what was before us, I would have longed for shelter.

Walter nodded. "So Devindra says."

Bertrand appeared suddenly at my side, the rain slicking down his fore-lock. "She asked for you, Professor," he said quietly. I could make nothing of this. What was the meaning? But there was no time to consider.

I wonder now. Are there doors in Arcadia we have not seen? Is there a door to the Dead? Or is this my illness speaking? For this last ride did not do it any good.

In his eagerness to be off, Pavo appeared to notice none of this. He shook off the water as it sluiced down on him. I attempted to urge a halt until the rain had ceased, but he turned away from me impatiently, shaking his head.

Of course I was right. We set off, Pavo and I riding horseback, Bertrand on his motorcycle, Walter on the centaur's back. The men followed as well they could.

The rain was a torrent, the path a river of mud. Our men fell behind, then disappeared as only the horses breasted through. Pavo ordered it so. Only Bertrand remained with us, leaving his sludge-choked machine leaning, half-swallowed in the mire, against a rock. He rode behind Walter on the centaur's back.

By the time we struggled to cross the swollen Juliet, onto a mud-soaked stubble field, it was only we four men. And it is only we four who now sit, waiting for the rain to stop, here in Paloma.

There is no one else here. There was no danger. There was no ambush planned. The town is empty.

The town's population has vanished.

This rain. It is beyond anything I have ever seen. Will it ever stop?

We huddle here, in quarters, watching it bring the hillsides down. Paloma, emptied, is full of mud.

Still, the rain has lessened—for now—and Pavo insists we press on to Cockaigne. This means another ford of another river. And a crossing of the Witches' Plain.

I remonstrate weakly at this, for my age catches up with me, and my illness worsens. The Witches' Plain is a fearsome place, even in fair weather, I say. But his only answer is a rude one, suggesting I return the way I came, alone.

As this is clearly not possible, I steel myself to follow on.

From Walton College, Walton:

This rain, this dratted rain! Will it never stop? The hours it took to plow through the mud, and the fear that the new bridge would never hold as we crossed, have wearied me and left me worried that I lack the wit to deal with the diplomatic headache I now face. Yes, we made it through our adventures on the Witches' Plain, only to discover this new, and potentially even more dangerous complication: a delegation from the Council of Megalopolis from over the mountains. Also, my fever worsens. I find myself imagining enemies where there are none. Always a danger, to be overly suspicious of one's friends.

"And where is the Emperor?" the delegation's leader says suavely. "Where is Pavo Vale? We come to pay our respects."

On guard, Aspern. Go slowly. I reply, with what dignity I can muster after being pummeled on my way to Walton by these damned natural elements, by this fever, by these irksome boils, saying that Pavo has passed on to Mumford, where he'll await us. On official business, I say. "A difficult job," I breathe, for my chest hurts now, and breath comes with a certain amount of pain. "The west has always been a place for witchcraft, which Pavo Vale hopes to eradicate. The east, where you find yourself, is the more rational portion of the empire."

Of course I disagree with Pavo's policy. I disagree with his next planned move. More than disagree with it, find it a disaster. It won't do, though, to say that to representatives of the Council.

Compliments back and forth. The delegation finds Walton "charming." The food "delightful." The situation "picturesque." Walton College's architecture is "superb." And so on. I listen with half an ear. All I want to do is get back to my own rooms and read—re-read—the sheaf of papers Pavo thrust at me so casually.

Where did he get them? Was this where he had learned how to breach Arcadia's defenses? If breach it could be called, the events of the Donatees and the Witches' Plain!

And now he continues on a road that can only lead to catastrophe. Is there nothing I can do to turn him from this plan?

The rain continues. I force myself to courteously invite our guests to another evening of feasting while we wait for it to abate, though I have no taste for food of any kind just now. They gladly accept. I see them exchange glances among themselves.

I know some kind of treachery is planned, Livia. Of course I know. How long has it been since I have closely observed the workings of the Council? But I see also that these men bide their time. What are they waiting for? And who bade them come? That I also wonder.

Time will tell. In the meantime, let me continue with my tale. Perhaps in the telling of it, I will find a solution to the conundrum that faces me now.

You may wonder why the delegation does not ask me where the inhabitants of Walton are. That is because these have returned as mysteriously as they disappeared. Although perhaps that is explained in those papers that Pavo found—where? In Sophia's library, most likely. And keeping them to himself all this time. I will have to go through them carefully

176

again. How could he possibly think to stifle their possibilities at the source?

I will tell you of his monstrous strategy, though I have hope yet of ameliorating its effects. But first, I must speak of what we found on the Witches' Plain.

* * * * *

Oh that mud. I will never forget that ride from Paloma. It should have been easy enough to ford the river in that season, for the snowmelt had lessened over the hot months, and irrigation of the fields had sucked most of the waters dry. But these rains are a vicious anomaly, the way they pour down in sheets, never seeming to stop. One would think it was witchcraft.

Groaning, I turned my horse and silently followed the others as they made to cross the unseasonal tumult of the Gems. My bones ached with the ride and with the cold.

We forded the Gems, water up to our waists, covered in mud. It was endless, that crossing. We finally made it across, when I realized a small miscalculation.

I had forgotten what the end of harvest means in Arcadia. The space between autumn and winter. I had forgotten Witches' Day.

Witches' Day. Of course.

The women laughing at us in the hall. That should have warned me; it should have reminded me of the secret rites of women. But it had been so long. And then—Witches' Day was always a time for boys and men to hide their eyes. I had forgotten it. I had wanted to forget.

But now, as we forded the Gems, in the distance could be seen odd figures swaying, moving in circles, spirals across the plain. The rain now slowed gently into a mist.

The clouds moved and cracked open, and a pale silver-yellow light shone down through the thinning mist, which, as we neared, lifted and disappeared, leaving the view ahead clear.

That was when I remembered.

"Witches' Day," I muttered under my breath. Walter smiled and shook water from his oilcloth coat. Bertrand, behind him, expressionless, though as an Arcadian, he must have felt the same atavistic fear that gripped me in spite of myself. Pavo, hearing me, yanked on his reins so hard that his horse gave a frantic neigh, rising up on its hind legs.

I kicked my own mount forward to grab the reins of the rearing horse. But I need not have worried. Pavo was in control. Swearing, he veered away from me and faced the Witches' Rite full on.

The air shimmered before us. But why? The mist had lifted. The sun now fought to shine through.

Was it the energy of the witches, the energy created by their banding together and dancing? I still have little idea. Though I know that you, Livia, know. There are secrets women will never tell.

I have always feared these secrets.

"Witches?" snarled Pavo, unafraid. "I'll show them which." He rammed his heels into his horse's unfortunate sides, meaning to shoot forward. But the horse stumbled in the mud. Pavo yanked its head up, digging his heels in its sides until it groaned and leapt ahead.

"Damn fool," said the centaur dispassionately. Walter cocked his head, apparently awaiting developments.

Bertrand slid off the centaur's back, and stood silently at attention. So I thought.

Shouting, waving his arms—superb horsemanship!—Pavo rushed at the figures, which now one could faintly discern as female. Girls, women, crones, all identifiable at this distance by the way they moved: some lightly, some solidly, some as if the movement fought against pain. But always in a circle of some kind, misshapen or perfect as the figure willed.

Of course Isabel and Shanti would be there.

Bertrand, as if pulled like iron to a lodestone, began walking toward the circle.

Pavo shouted. This had no effect at all on the sight before us, which as we neared, or seemed to near, spread to hundreds of these figures on the landscape ahead. Each one spinning, circling, swaying in her own pattern apart from the others.

But while I could see them more clearly, and though we rode straight toward them, the figures actually came no closer. Except, strangely enough, to Bertrand, who despite walking through the treacherous mud soon outstripped his chief.

Pavo shouted at the lad. But Bertrand paid no mind, continuing his walk toward the circle, closer and closer, while Pavo and myself seemed never to gain any ground.

Walter and the centaur stayed back. The women paid us no mind.

They were in their own world.

Pavo ran at them, circled back, and ran again. Almost as if the circles the women made infected him as well. It was no use, though. The women, on Witches' Day, were in a different reality than ours, a differently created one. They were creating reality as we stood by. We had yet to breach their boundary.

The sun shone over their work. The clouds circled it, racing over our heads. But in that circle, all was mellow gold. Outside all was mud, brown and gray. Inside all was green, shining with the reds and oranges of harvest time.

I can hear you, Livia, give that low, delighted chuckle of yours. I can imagine your amusement, the clapping of your blue-veined hands. "Witches' Day!" you exclaim. "My, that takes me back. Circling widdershins then, were they?"

Yes, Livia, they were. Creating a new and sacred world, if only for a time. The sacred space. Which, as I painfully recall, on Witches' Day, no man may enter.

But Pavo is no man. And the threats I faced as a child when I attempted to penetrate the circles my mother and sisters made on that day, the punishment, will not be his today.

I could see by his eyes' shine that he meant to penetrate the boundary and scatter the women before him.

Although he looked for one woman. I saw his eyes dart here and there, looking for the one he desired.

Wheeling about, he screamed a war cry and charged again.

I looked about myself, helpless. Walter shook his head. I looked away, back to where Pavo rode.

"He'll succeed!" I said, excited now, for what man had ever penetrated the sacred space on Witches' Day? I watched as Pavo raced around the edges of the sacred space, testing the perimeter for weakness, pushing himself against it, storming the women's citadel, willing it to succumb.

"No, he'll fail," I gasped. "No, succeed!"

I would have laid a wager, I was so wrought up, had there been anyone there to wager with. For when I turned again, Walter and the centaur had disappeared into the mist from which we had come.

Still Bertrand sleepwalked toward the circle. And Pavo rode at it in a rage.

No one, to my knowledge, had ever penetrated the sacred space of Witches' Day. What energy would be unleashed, what creative spark released, if it were to happen now? I was agog, Livia, awaiting the outcome.

And outcome there was. Splendid enough—and horrifying.

Pavo yanked a dead cedar tree right from the earth, and smashed at the edges of the circle. For a moment, you could actually see the air buckle under the weight of his blow, see the borderline begin to give—for cedars are sacred to Death, in Arcadia.

But the boundary held firm, although the sight now, of the women of Arcadia, intent in their sacred space on the creation of that energy unique to Witches' Day—that sight sprang into clarity. What had been indistinct before snapped into focus. I could now make out forms, actual women known to me.

So could Pavo. I could see the yearning, the craving, in the very slant of his body, the angle forward, as he scanned the space looking for the woman he desired.

One woman stood off-center near the edges, easy to distinguish from the rest by her intemperate movements, an awkward, uneven gait that one could see owed nothing to age or infirmity, but to a drunkenness, a slovenly intoxication not shared by her sisters who continued the strange beauty of their circles, intent on their work.

Pavo saw her in the same instant as I, and recognized her, too, even before me. He cannily saw the weak point that she embodied, she who moved out of sync with the rest, cackling with abandoned laughter.

"Mother," he said in a caressing tone.

For it was Merope.

At his address, she gave a howl of ugly laughter, a shout of drunken triumph. "Son!" she shrieked.

"Mother, dear," Pavo repeated sweetly. "Let me in, Mother."

She stopped and looked at him. "And what will you give me, son? What will you do for your mother?"

"I'll make you a queen, dear mother," Pavo said, wheedling. "Queen of the world."

"Hah!" she laughed, and she fell, her skirts flying over her head, giggling to herself.

"Dear mother," he said again. "I will rule the world, and you will rule my household and my wife."

"Your wife!" she shrieked with that ghastly laughter, pulling herself up

181

from the ground. "And you'll let me govern her, dominate her, tell her what's what?"

"I swear," he said solemnly through the invisible border between them. "I swear by my ancestors." And then he laughed.

"Liar!" she shrieked again, laughing back at him. They looked at each other and grinned, some secret thought exchanged between them. She shook her head. "Still, it'll be something to see. I'll do it. Give me your hand on it!"

Pavo leapt from his horse to the border and thrust out his hand. But it stopped before it reached Merope, no matter how he thrust and thrust.

She laughed again, and began to circle, this time in the opposite direction. As she spun, and Pavo thrust again and again, the membrane gave way, and his hand met hers in a clasp.

But she didn't pull him in. He pulled her out. Pavo pulled Merope from the sacred space, with the border closing behind her.

"Mother!" he cried.

She laughed again. "You know what to do!" she said. He looked at her with a question. "You know what to do!" she repeated. As if they were one person now, they turned and looked at Bertrand.

Bertrand, in a trance, stood at the edge of the sacred space. His hand was held out touching its edge. His eyes searched inside. And inside, a figure stopped her circling. Her eyes met his.

Pavo laughed then, a triumphant laugh, as if he understood all at once what he had to do. Quicker than I can write this, he leapt across to Bertrand, and from behind, took the boy's throat in his huge hands, throttling the life out of him. Bertrand gasped, fell back, gurgled, struggled against Pavo. To no avail. Tighter and tighter Pavo squeezed, while Merope laughed and laughed. There was a scream, and a tearing sound, and Pavo dropped Bertrand, who lay still as he fell.

Pavo ran through a tear in the wall. He had opened the boundary of the sacred space.

By killing Bertrand? But no, Bertrand lived. He moved, gagging, and lay still again. As I drew closer, I could see a vein pulsing in his neck.

How then?

A moment later, and Pavo emerged from the space beside Merope, holding a limp body in his arms. Stopping only long enough to lend an ear to one last whispered and gleeful piece of advice from Devindra's daughter, he tossed an unconscious Shanti—for it was she, I assumed— onto the back of his horse, jumping up behind her, holding her fast as she lolled before him. He raised a triumphant fist, and the whole of the circle dimmed as those storm clouds we brought with us passed over the morning sun. Even the sun of the sacred space. Then a shadow, dark as predawn night, passed over us all, and when it had gone, continued on its way over the Ceres Mountains. It took all that was there with it. When it was gone, Pavo and I, our horses and his captive, were all that remained.

The women were gone. Merope—gone. Bertrand—gone. Pavo looked at this, unfazed. "Never mind," he muttered. "We'll have 'em yet. They'll come when we burn her. She'll come."

I must have misheard him, so I thought. Then. "Be careful of Shanti, lad," I said. He looked at me, annoyance on his face.

"Oh no, Father," he said, whistling. "This isn't Shanti."

I rode closer. I saw that what he said was true. It wasn't Shanti that lay sprawled across his horse's back.

It was Isabel. And as we rode, he, laughing and breathless, made his plan known to me

I tried to turn his resolve. I warned him that Arcadia has no law against witchcraft, not in the same way as Megalopolis, where only one witch is allowed by law to reign supreme. Where the government, in your person, has a monopoly on the practice. It is different here. The old ways considered witch work as something to be praised, something for the good, rather than the evil, of the community. Arcadia has yet to emerge from the old ways.

183

We would have to change that. If Pavo wanted to burn Isabel as a witch—a plan of action I strongly opposed—there would have to be some kind of legal precedent. I explicitly warned him of that.

We argued all the way back across the Gems, which he forded easily, a fact I eyed with some resentment from where I struggled, up to my waist in the cold water. With one hand he held the reins, with the other, Isabel. She stirred slightly as her feet touched the water. Her eyes opened, and she swooned again.

"This'll do the trick," Pavo muttered. There was a shout, and there were his men ahead of us, running a tractor and a huge, clanking, road-building machine. This was the first I heard of your delegation. Megalopolis, apparently, has taken it upon itself to start landing of heavy equipment, on a makeshift airstrip I had no idea had been constructed, by Pavo's orders, outside Eopolis. New roads are in progress already, forced through the mud. Rock has already been laid down, from Walton halfway to Paloma.

I sat there, shivering, surprised and offended that no one came to my aid. Isabel was bundled into a cart, Pavo leapt from his horse, slapping it and leaving it to run and find its own way back, or founder in the mud.

It seemed he was going to leave me, as well. But I called out, and he returned, suggesting I proceed immediately to Walton to take charge of the diplomatic mission there. The plan is for me to escort the delegation on to Mumford when the rains have lessened—for they had started up again, to my dismay.

"Am I to ride?" I said coldly. He shrugged. He must have assumed I was as strong as a younger man.

"Road's clear all the way to town, Boss," one of his lads said helpfully.

Pavo waved a hand. "You hear? It should be an easy ride." He walked off, calling to one of his men, when something seemed to occur to him. He turned back to me once more.

"By the way," he said, "it's easy enough to execute Isabel for sedition." He pulled a sheaf of papers from under his shirt where they had, mercifully, kept dry, and handed them up to me. "Have a look at what I found in Mumford."

I held the papers gingerly under my oilskin, thumbing them. I recognized writing, so I thought, in the margins. My heart beat faster.

"Devindra's work…" I began slowly. But Pavo forestalled this thought with one upheld finger.

"Not Devindra," he corrected. "*Isabel.*" And then he shook himself. "Brrr," he said. "Time to get out of this rain. Time to get on the road. Time to…get on." And he was gone.

I rode alone on the new, wide, flat rock road to Walton, where I met with the delegation and…but I've said all that.

The work of Isabel. I ponder the work of Isabel as I sit here, pondering the motives and means of the Council of Megalopolis. The papers Pavo shoved at me, reading and re-reading them now. "An Evolutionary's Handbook" it says, scrawled across the first page. I must think. My analysis will follow when thought is done. It may mean more to Megalopolis than anything that has gone before. It may mean more to *me*.

Meanwhile, I receive word that the rain has stopped for the time being, and Pavo sends orders that we are to join him in Mumford. Isabel will burn there, tomorrow. Our presence is required.

My presence is required. I must stop him. These words—this work—by Isabel the Scholar make that imperative. A necessity. What, shall we burn knowledge, nay, wisdom, that we need for humankind?

Not while I am alive. Not while I have influence. Not while it is my son who plans this disastrous course.

From Juliet College, Mumford:

I have only a few moments to put down these words. My struggle with Pavo over Isabel has met with apparent failure, and I must hurry to see whether I can repair the damage.

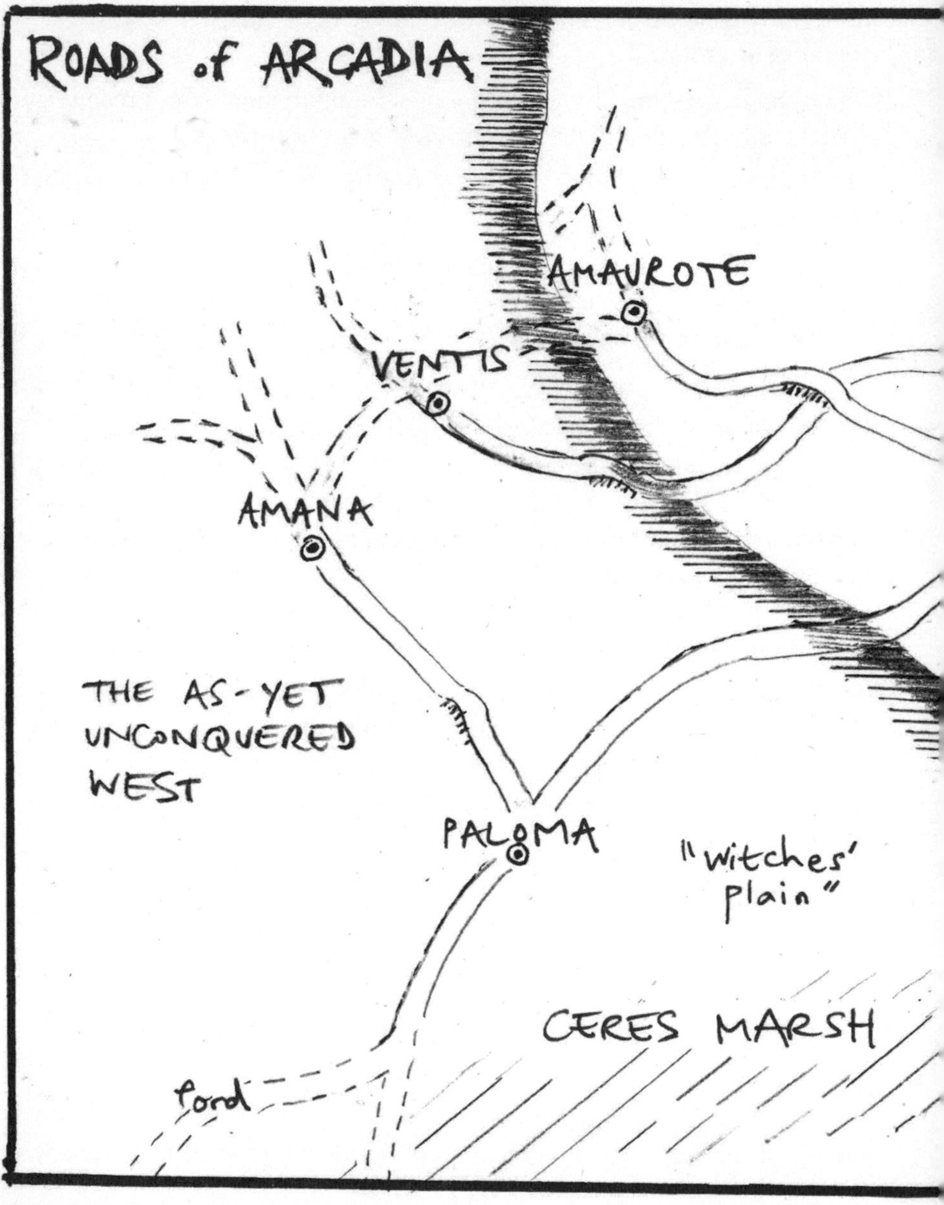

ROADS of ARCADIA

AMAUROTE

VENTIS

AMANA

THE AS-YET
UNCONQUERED
WEST

PALOMA

"witches'
plain"

CERES MARSH

ford

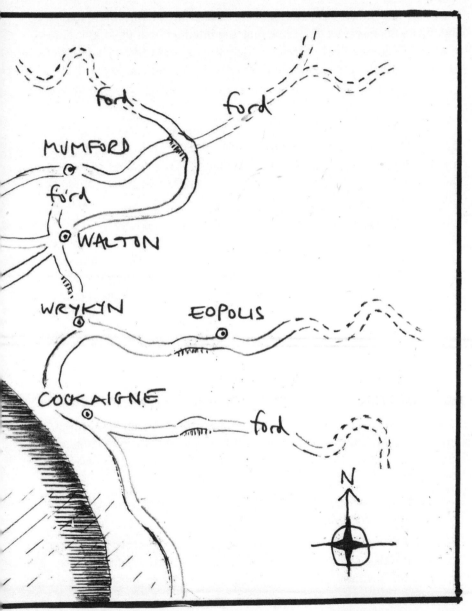

New roads are in progress already

It was indeed Isabel. Isabel the Scholar! Isabel the genius, more like—
and this is the resource, the keen, incisive intellect, that Pavo Vale seeks
to destroy! Not just seeks, Livia, *is determined*, and I fear I have little to
say in this matter. I made him indomitable. I gave him strong will. What
decisions he now makes in opposition to my counsel I see are impossible
for me to withstand.

It is too late to send word to you, Lady, the only force who might stop
him. Had I known, had I foreseen—and I should have!—that his will
could lead him to disaster for not just Arcadia, but Megalopolis as well,
I would have…what would I have done? I don't know. But I would not
have come to this pass.

It was Isabel, *Isabel*, who, steeped from her childhood in Devindra
Vale's work on fairy tales, took it to the furthest extreme, far past what
my own generation would have thought possible. Yes, she examined
Devindra's work on the importance of fairy tales as showing inner truths
about the biology, not just the psychology of the human being. For
where, Devindra argued, does psychology come from but biology? Isabel
studied under my former student, Alan Fallaize, learning all he had to
teach. It was he who guarded the secret that she had discovered—yes! it's
true!—*how to send communications to other worlds*. I have no time to
recount the method, suffice to say I have studied the notes that Pavo has
discovered and verified them; they are accurate. Her methods work.

More than that: what Isabel has discovered is that all Time happens
simultaneously. That our stories are our biology, and our biology is what
sculpts Time into a river rather than an ocean. It is our stories that form
the riverbeds.

And there are many rivers, so her notes say. Many rivers emptying into
the same sea of Eternity.

This remarkable young woman has discovered ways to ford those rivers.
Oh, not entirely. Her work is far from complete, so my agitation over
Pavo's determination to end that work is just what you must be imag-

ining, Livia. I write this to you now not just in report, but to collect my thoughts, to see if there is a way out, a compromise, some way forward without the end of Isabel's contribution to, not just Arcadia, not just Megalopolis, but to all of humankind.

"She deserves to hang," Pavo said to me with a savagery that has, in the past, been turned to finer ends. His lopsided face was distorted, his very body emitted sparks of fire. "But I think burning is a good end for this trash." He pointed at the pile of her work he has made on the floor, with a contempt I have hardly ever seen on his face before now. "Yes," he said, nodding. "I plan on lighting this stuff under her feet. Get rid of two problems at once."

"No, Pavo!" I say, unsuccessfully trying to conceal the agony this image conjures up in me. "You don't understand. Her work..."

A mistake, Livia. I knew it as soon as I said it. Pavo revolts against an approach that implies he is in the wrong—he takes it as aggression. Without thinking, he fights back.

Pavo cannot bear that someone else might be a savior of humankind. I programmed him to be that savior. I bred him for it. To hear from his own creator that it is not he, but a woman—worse, a girl—who has made the breakthrough that humanity has sought in vain, all these generations, through all these tragedies and histories! He cannot bear it. It is my fault that he cannot.

I understand this, Livia. To see the prize about to be taken by a girl who was trained in a womanish school? The blow to one's pride. The pain, the humiliation. I understand it all.

Well do I understand Pavo's urge to uproot the plant that grows here in Arcadia. And the truth is, Livia, if I could see how we could build on Isabel's work, without the mind that conceived the work in the first place, I would let the girl go to the stake in a moment. And laugh.

But there is no way. There are certain pages missing from the file Pavo showed me, certain formulae she must have taken away with her before we swept down from the mountains and took control of the east. She must have been working on them still, up until Witches' Day, when every young woman would have been called from her chores to the larger task of creating the "sacred space." And filling it with their energy.

But I am a scientist first, Livia. The scientist is at war with the father here, a painful battle. Isabel's work must be saved.

"Hah!" Pavo scoffed, throwing the pages my way. "Look at that. 'An Evolutionary's Handbook.' If that's not sedition, I don't know what is. You know that Megalopolis would agree."

And indeed, in that file were notes of how to withstand not just Megalopolis, but a possible invasion by Pavo, a possible attempt at control by you, Livia. Yes. All this described minutely in exactly the way we planned it and, to a certain degree, executed it. How had Isabel known the future? How had she known this would happen?

Because she has, if not conquered Time, at least, as it says in her notes, "Made Time my friend." She has found a way to inquire of Time what she needs to know. And Time answers.

Sedition, Livia, as Pavo says. Not just plans for a *revolt* against Megalopolis, but a strategy on how to *overcome* the Great Empire. How a weak force can prevail against one infinitely stronger.

These pages sketch out a way to deal with the aggression of a superior strength. They postulate the one position—Isabel's genius is always finding that one fundamental position that hides behind the more obvious ones—that maintains the agency and integrity of the weaker party, even in the face of attack. An evolution, rather than a revolution, Isabel calls it. She outlines a way to triumph over Megalopolis—though triumph, in this context, is the wrong word. There are no words at present for what Isabel suggests is possible. Equilibrium? Symmetry? Balance? What we in Megalopolis would name "Stasis"?

I don't know. Right now, in the thick of trying to understand, with time against me, I don't care. Isabel suggests the solution is in competing *patterns*. As far as I can make out, the idea here is that when two "patterns" meet, the one that prevails sets the parameters for future possibilities. It is not necessarily the "stronger" actor whose pattern will prevail. Although, as Isabel brilliantly demonstrates even in these few sentences before me, it is generally the pattern followed by those considered "stronger" by both sides that does win the day.

What is meant is that either side can win by force if both sides believe in the pattern that believes in force. But what "An Evolutionary's Handbook" suggests is *this is not the sole pattern available*. Though it is and has been the pattern that mankind has lived by till now. Isabel theorizes that such a pattern, one that insists on conflict as a dynamic way forward, must inevitably feed on itself. It must demand conflict after conflict, until, in this endless state of war, all, including itself, is destroyed.

It is then, when all is destroyed, that a new pattern emerges. In this evolution, she says, there is nothing left of the old. The pattern has destroyed itself. More than that, it has proved fatal to all who have believed in its reality.

But, she continues, there is a way to avoid this fatal end. To step away from the pattern is to create a new beginning and a new pattern. With enough energy, which creates a new strength, this new may begin to prevail over the old, before the elder pattern destroys itself and all it contains. For patterns are contained in *stories,* which are the expression of deeply rooted feelings. And feelings are contagious. The most contagious energy in the human world. So Isabel says.

I see this. I catch a glimmer of her reasoning here, Livia. This explains the strangeness of yesterday's visit to the house of Walter and Shiva, the sense one had of walking through a boundary into another world entirely. Their pattern prevailed against ours. In "An Evolutionary's Handbook," I find the secret spring of what seemed to be their odd behavior—the motive, the origin, the goal.

The danger of it for Megalopolis. For our plans. For the future of humankind.

191

So I say—argue!—to my son.

"Pavo," I plead. "See here. She has found the secret of resistance to Megalopolis. Which means…"

"Better burn that book first, Dad," Pavo advises, refusing to listen to me. He points me toward the end. "Before someone who shouldn't gets ahold of it."

"*You* got ahold of it."

"I did, Dad," he grins. "I did, indeed."

And he is gone.

So that was the secret of his knowledge, of why much that seemed to me to be inexplicable weighed not at all on him.

He is more subtle than I had imagined. Than I created him. I must grasp what is happening here, what quick evolution he has made, before he has time to treat with the delegation. Or even, Livia, to make direct contact with you. He must not do so in this mood.

Especially not with you. Not until I have had time to think.

Unless. Has he had the chance? No. It's not possible. I suddenly recall the Claraudioscope I had hidden in my rooms on the False Moon. Could he have found it? Impossible. Impossible that I not trust my own creation.

It's this illness. My fever burns. I force my brain to clear itself of its fog.

I must think. I must have time. I must see if Isabel…

The shouting has ended outside. All is quiet. This must mean all have converged on the Queen's House. Pavo has housed me here, at the college, for both my greater comfort and security. But he plans to burn Isabel at the Queen's House. I feel a foreboding. I must go there now.

I must hurry. Lest all the good that could come to mankind be lost in a pyre of flame.

From the Queen's House, the Queen's Library, Mumford:

I do not know how this will end.

Or Isabel. For now, she is safe.

I will tell you what happened.

When I arrived at the Queen's House, it was to see Pavo like a mad thing.

I went first to greet your delegation, lodged in the Queen's House, waiting upon his pleasure. Something about their mood warned me there were communications happening of which I had no knowledge. Dangerous communications. But all was a desperately fought fog to me. My fever, and the hideous cough that accompanies it, have worsened.

Pavo received us, in an expansive mood. Indeed, the best mood I have seen him in since we returned to Arcadia. He barked out orders one after the other, impossible to withstand, all his men jumping to. The town was full to bursting with silent folk. All seemed to wait for some sign. Some signal.

I was filled with foreboding.

Pavo addressed the populace from the window of what had been the Queen's Tower. He announced loudly that Isabel was to be burned as a witch, in accordance with the sedition laws of New Arcadia. The people below accepted this without response, as if such an astonishing proclamation had not been made.

"How?" I muttered when he joined us again down below. Pavo heard and laughed. "Witchcraft, Dad. I know what to do now."

He was everywhere at once: joking, laughing, ordering the men. He'd had cartloads of the books he'd found hidden in Sophia's library brought out: priceless treasures belonging to the nation, as well as those useless books of folklore and fairy tales with which she was so obsessed. The lads dumped them in a careless mound in the meadow outside the Queen's Reception Room, tearing up what turf was left. They piled the books up around a stake made from a fallen apple tree from the Queen's Garden.

Not just on any ground was this stake planted. But atop the graves of Pavo's brothers, Lionel and Marcian. The muddy, torn-up graves.

"Is this *necessary*?" I asked, forcing myself to sound calmer than I felt.

"Oh, yeah, Dad," Pavo exclaimed, eyes gleaming. And he was off again in a moment, shouting at the lads to grab twigs, pine cones, forest duff, anything hidden under eaves or trees untouched by the rain, to pile high at the foot of the applewood stake.

Still the Arcadians stood there, silent. Watching. The crowd grew as we watched. Pavo studied this with a strange satisfaction. I saw him scan the crowd, over and over. It seemed to me he was looking for someone. Someone in particular.

I yearned to find time and a corner of the Queen's House in which to scrutinize Isabel's manuscript more closely. But Pavo was too quick. Just as I determined to return to Sophia's ravaged library, out marched a cadre of the Invincibles.

Isabel, hands tied behind her back, walked in their midst toward the stake. She was still wearing glasses but, with her crooked wrists bound, she was unable to reach up to push them back up her nose. This was curiously irritating to watch. The glasses sliding down her face made one want to move toward her to straighten them. Obviously this had its effect even on Pavo, for he bounded over to her and, with an impatient gesture, pushed the spectacles back up to their proper position.

This stopped the procession, causing the men behind to careen, confused, off each other. Only Isabel seemed unaffected. She nodded, appearing to thank Pavo for the service. Her usual grave expression never faded.

This appeared to amuse him. He said some words to her that I couldn't quite catch.

She seemed as undisturbed by her plight as she had on that whole incredible march. I wondered if she was drugged, or ill, or merely in shock.

As she passed close to me, she nodded in recognition. I could see no sign

194

of any interference in her mental process. Her eyes were bright. Her gaze was clear and even. It was interested.

Indeed, the scene was fraught with interest. It was a madhouse, Livia. A scene of anxious frenzy, for the Invincibles had smelled blood. The lads were ripe for any kind of destructive mayhem. Maniacally they hauled out any books to be found anywhere in the Queen's House to burn on their pyre as well.

I watched this potential tragedy with a sinking heart. Those books! Impossible to replace. Sophia had spent a lifetime in their collection. Even amidst the dross there would be gold.

But there was no stopping the rampage. Was this, I wondered, because all felt a heightened sense of life in their ability to deal death? The face of every man there was distorted by frenzy. When they lit the pitch torches prepared for them, and passed around the bottles looted from the Queen's Cellars, they wiped their mouths and stamped their feet in ragged time, chanting: "*Pavo. Pavo. Pavo.*" Their faces glowed red in the torchlight, ugly, frightening, as dark began to fall.

I shrank back into the shadows. When men are so possessed, Livia, as you well know, you who have used this kind of delirium for your own ends, there is no saying which way they will turn, on *whom* they will turn. When the bloodlust is upon them, men will rend a friend as easily as a foe. Anyone is prey.

A man possessed will turn on anyone.

Even Pavo might turn. Especially Pavo. For did I not build the lad to stop at nothing in the pursuit of his goals, with those goals directed by his strongest desires? When his blood is up, should I then expect him to stop at *me*?

This thought stops my brain. Stops my heart in my chest. It is not possible. Can it be possible?

Pavo himself led Isabel up a makeshift set of steps formed of staggered books. She slipped on these volumes and fell, while he waited, impatient, for her to get her footing on what I saw were children's fairy tales from

Sophia's library—ones I had seen the queen read to the child Shanti when she took care of her. For Shanti was always her pet.

Pavo's calm demeanor toward Isabel was a strange contrast to the sweating, shouting, stamping men swirling around them. I watched as he held Isabel's arm below the elbow, murmuring some direction tersely into her ear. She nodded, continuing her climb to the top of the pile of books, where he tied her to the applewood post.

Pavo, exulting now, leapt down the pile of books, eyes glittering like a wolf's, slapping his men enthusiastically on their backs.

Pavo shouted something over the uproar, something about his being deserving of the honor of being the first to set the fire. He picked a torch out of the hand of a drunken Invincible, as the sot staggered dangerously across the lawn. Holding the flickering torch high, waving it as if going to a wedding, he walked back to the pyre of papers and volumes under Isabel's feet.

Isabel stood at their top. Her glasses gave her the look of an owl balancing on the dead branch of a dying tree.

She was perfectly calm.

Pavo set fire to a small collection of pamphlets, those farthest away from her feet. My immediate thought was that he had planned it so, for the greatest amount of spectacle—and the greatest amount of the victim's agony. This strategy seemed to bear fruit when the uproar from the drunken men died down, and the Invincibles, drunk as they were, stared, fascinated, at the growing flames, and at the girl the flames were meant to reach and consume.

There was a sound of thunder far away. Would the rains return? I listened closely to try to assess the meaning of the crash. That, and the crackling of the fast-increasing flames were all that could be heard in the silence.

Isabel still appeared unmoved by the scene of which she was the victim or the heroine. It was I who felt agony at the sight of her end. The end of a brilliance that offered so much to humankind.

Thunder sounded again. More loudly this time. A lightning flash lit up the sky above the trees in the Queen's Garden.

Then a voice spoke.

"Isabel," it said calmly. "What's this, then?"

The girl looked up tranquilly, flames reflected in her glasses, and said, "They're burning your mother's books, Walter."

Walter? But there was no one there. We all looked around us, and, Livia, *there was no one there.*

"No, no," the voice protested. "That's not right. We can't have that." Another lightning flash. Thunder roared overhead, and the sky opened in a flood of water. A solid sheet of it came down upon us, extinguishing every flame below, soaking every man, sobering the ones who stood there stupefied, their mouths agape.

Pavo roared with laughter. Water poured down Isabel's glasses.

The men ran for cover, and Pavo stood there, laughing like a madman. I alone dashed out to what was quickly becoming a sputtering mass of sodden paper and board. So I alone saw someone hurriedly climb the disintegrating heap, untie Isabel's bonds with a twitch, and lead her protectively away. But I had no time to wonder about that then. My main concern was to salvage what I could of the books.

I ran by Pavo, who stood at the bottom of the pile, waiting.

The flood was now a deluge. I grabbed what I could and ran back to the library to pore over what I had saved. For Pavo has his priorities, and I have mine. And I know now that my report to you, my history of what has occurred and what is likely to happen after me, is of vital importance, imperative to the success of the New Arcadia, and Megalopolis, too. Urgent. Now more than ever before.

Another shout went up outside. A roar. Not just Pavo's men, but the silent Arcadians must have lent their voices. I went out to them, and what did I see? Pavo glowing like fire, the rain spitting off his back, striding triumphant to the Queen's House. Flames leapt up all around them, for the Invincibles, on Pavo's orders, have defied the rain, setting fire to all of Mumford, lighting everything they can on fire. A tribute to Pavo's strength of will, that fire leaping up to meet that torrent of water. That fire fighting the rain. Pavo defying the sky. Fire and rain. Rain and fire.

Walking through it all was Pavo, like a king come into his country. Enveloped in my boy's arms, held with a tender firmness I had never seen in him before, clasped against his very heart, was the trembling golden-skinned figure of Shanti Vale.

* * * * *

I ran out to meet them of course, but the crowd pushed me back. A bigger crowd than I could have imagined, or was this my imagination only? It seemed, to my distracted senses, as if the whole of Arcadia was gathered there to watch, once again in silence, the only sound the patter of a now gently falling rain—for as Pavo carried away, in triumph, the object of his ultimate desire, the rain softened and faded to a mist. I followed them. I and the rest of Arcadia. For I knew, without being told, what his destination must be. He meant to take Shanti—meant to have her—in the Queen's Bed. Meant to make her queen. And through her, make himself king.

As if he needed a woman for that. Madness. Or was this rather some subtle strategy I had not yet grasped?

Reaching there, the crowd parted before me. "Pavo!" I shouted in the strange stillness as he disappeared through the wide wooden doors of the Queen's House—but not before all could see him drop a kiss on Shanti's unresisting face.

"No, you don't," said an amiable voice, and a firm hand, surprising in its strength, grasped my arm.

"Get away from me," I said, attempting—unsuccessfully—to shake their owner off. Then I saw it was Walter.

The rain stopped. The mist blew away. The sun came out. The crowd gave a collective sigh. As if one body. One mind. One wish. To see what happened next. What came next in the story.

What could I do? There was no moving. We stood and watched, then, through the glass that forms that outer wall of the stair to the Queen's Tower. Pavo carried Shanti up, up, up the spiral stair within, pausing, at each turn, to press his lips to her forehead, her eyes, her nose, her mouth.

Kicking open the door at the top of the stair with one foot, he disappeared inside, carrying her close.

The door shut behind them. And the crowd that watched this gave another loud, prolonged, collective sigh.

I knew what would come of it.

A child. *The* child. The child I had yearned for.

The son of Pavo Vale.

From Walton College, Walton:

We have now removed to Walton, for I pointed out to Pavo the necessity of offering lordly hospitality to the delegation from Megalopolis. The Queen's House in Mumford is a poor thing, more a private person's house, albeit one that takes a large role in the entertaining of its neighbors. But until he has completed his own palace—something I still have my doubts about—the former capital of Arcadia is not what a Mega delegation would be used to, let alone impressed by. Of course, his wife will have something to say about the choice of accommodation in the future. When she returns.

To my surprise, he agreed without comment. He has been much distracted lately, although I see him conferring with your ambassadors, Livia, in season and out—any time that I am not within hearing.

Still, I understand his distraction. He has my sympathy. For Shanti is missing. And after a grand imperial wedding, all that any girl could desire. She just walked away. Gone no one knows where, though god

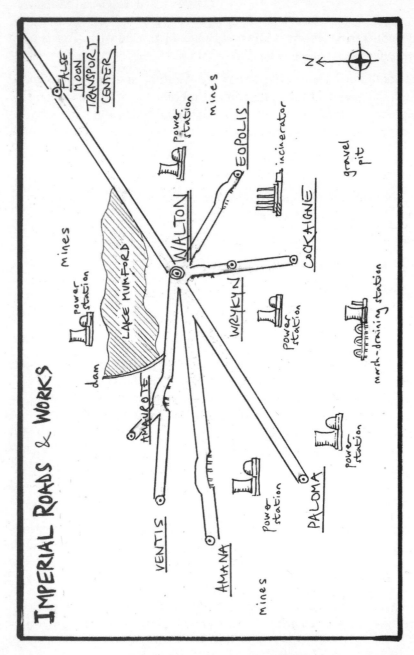

Transforming old Arcadia into new

knows we have enough men searching the land for her. Pavo has threatened all of Arcadia, if she does not return.

But all is not destruction with Pavo, even now. His energies go into transforming old Arcadia into new. If he threatens her, he also transforms her, bending her to his will. He has the strength of his, and my, desire to bring her to the grandeur that is her birthright. The face of the land changes daily under his furious assault. I need not have feared any difficulty in dragging her into the modern world. Transport, communications, commerce: all were so desperately backward. But I watch each day with amazement as Pavo brings order, by main force, to what was formerly chaos. The massive road he's building across the Calandals links Megalopolis, and Megalopolitan expertise, ever closer to Arcadia. Day after day, Arcadia responds. Why then, not Shanti?

I worry about the future. And this damned chill never seems to leave me now. It ebbs and flows, almost arbitrarily it seems. At times it takes my thought over when I have greatest need of clarity. I fight it back.

If only I knew where Shanti has got to. Then I would feel more at ease, for I move restlessly through my day, unable to take pleasure in our advances. Where could she have gone? I ordered the men to arrest her father, who had been given free run of Mumford as long as Shanti was in residence there as queen, but they returned empty-handed and baffled. That house we had breakfasted in, the house of Walter Todhunter and Shiva Vale, they insisted, that it was gone. Vanished. Disappeared, utterly.

Of course I didn't believe this, but set out myself to ascertain the facts. We had, as you know, by this time brought those stronger motors you allowed us over the mountains, so my journey was brief, the winter landscape a blur as we flew by it. For our earthmovers work day and night now, keeping the roads cleared at all times, where they were once primitively blocked by harsh weather.

I came to the spot where the house had been. And there was nothing there.

Oh, not strictly speaking *nothing*. Three feet of snow, and an abandoned orchard of leafless trees.

But of a house—let alone a studio, a garden—there was no sign.

I know what you're thinking, we'd been sent astray. But we checked and double-checked our bearings. There was no doubt. This was the spot where we had met with Walter and Shiva in the days before.

And there was nothing there.

I attended Pavo in the Great Hall that night, as he drank with his Invincibles, but he seemed strangely uninterested in my report. In fact, that I had taken it upon myself to find Walter Todhunter seemed to fill him with an irritation that mystified me. But I must have been mistaken. For he must have been far more absorbed in plans to link the towns of Wrykyn and Cockaigne by a motorway, and to sink Paloma beneath a reservoir of water collected by setting afire one of the frozen peaks of the Donatees.

These days, he seems uninterested in, even hostile to, whatever I have to say. The delegation from Megalopolis has gone back to you now, Livia, over the great road built over the Calandals, without offering me so much as a farewell. I had meant to send what there was of this report with them. But they were gone before I even knew they'd driven away.

True, I had been closeted in my own rooms, fighting back this damned cold. But surely that is overly polite, to leave me without a word?

They are gone, but their influence remains. They had worked to separate father from son, to encourage the son to listen only to his own judgment. So Pavo announces he will move his court, against my counsel, back to Mumford, where he will again inhabit the Queen's Rooms while his own official residence is made ready. I will follow, he says, when my health recovers.

Cursing this feeble and aging body of mine, I feel my helplessness. I feel power rush away from me, as if pulled out by a tide. I feel an anxiety, as if my plans, so well laid, are in danger.

I feel as if Pavo has plans about which I know nothing.

From the Tower by the Lily Pond, St. Vitus College, Wrykyn:

I have been sent here—carried here—why? Because I disgraced myself by falling into a faint, weakened by my recent illness?

When I woke, I was back in the Tower by the Lily Pond. For the first time, I saw that the Tower's ability to welcome all by being visible for miles, from all sides, makes it a perfect jail. Easily guarded and made fast.

How had I missed this before?

Pavo lashes out now, raging without control, berating even his staunchest supporters. He is beside himself at the loss of Shanti. In this he shows himself to be all too human, he who was created to be more god than man. Like any other mortal, he bellows with pain at the loss of the woman he loves.

She did not last long in Mumford, by Pavo's side. A week? Ten days? A month? She was given what I told Pavo every woman desires: a grand wedding, a beautiful wedding dress, luxury unprecedented, gold, jewels, the love of an emperor.

Yet each day she seemed to be more silent, more still. Each day, no matter what music played for her, or what amusements were put before her in that Grand Pavilion Pavo ordered built for the celebration of their marriage, no matter what was put before her, she seemed to fade away, before one's eyes.

Until one day she disappeared altogether.

At first I suspected one of those marital tiffs that are so common at the start of a marriage.

Pavo had no comment. I urged him to tell me what happened, but his only response was to stalk out of the room.

I followed him to where his men were at work transforming what had been the Queen's Garden.

"Did she have the Key?" I demanded, for this was then the most important issue on my mind. "Pavo, attend, did Shanti have the Key?"

"What?" Pavo said dully, from where he sat on the Queen's Chair in the Queen's Garden, by the Juliet River, where he had set the men dredging, digging, turning the water from its path to create a lake, upon which he proposed to build an enormous, energy-producing dam. "What?" he repeated, shading his eyes, for the late fall afternoon sun was hot there, in the treeless garden. "Oh. The Key." He shook his head. "I don't...I didn't ask. *I don't know.*"

I was unsure what to make of this.

"Where is she?" I said. Then, more sharply. "Pavo. I'm talking to you. This is a matter of state, far past what your personal feelings might be. Where is Shanti?"

He stood and angrily dressed down a group of men who failed to put their backs into the task at hand.

He shrugged. "She said she was going home. To see her parents, she said. She'll be back," he said. But his voice was uncertain.

Uncertain. Pavo Vale uncertain. Strange.

"Arrest Walter," I urged. "Put him under attainder. Send out the order."

Pavo looked away and laughed shortly. "You do it," he said sarcastically. "If you can find him," he said.

"She must come back," I said, attempting comfort. "The child. I know she carries a child. Your child. Surely she wants to live with the father of her child. Her family, Pavo."

He shrugged again, his eyes dulled over. "Yeah?" he said, falling back in his chair. "Family? Oh yes. That thing."

It occurred to me then that "family" was something I had never taught him. Surely, though, the thing is implanted in the genes? Surely, he, made from human DNA, must have some understanding of it?

"It must be so, Pavo," I said, urging him back to control over himself.

"You married her with all pomp. You've triumphed. You rule over Arcadia. Megalopolis will come after, and then you…"

He interrupted me then. "She looks at me like I'm nothing at all." I would have thought his expression would threaten vengeance. But it looked out, dull, through indifferent eyes.

"What does that matter?" I said, hoping to restore fire to his looks. "It's *your* desire that matters. What does it matter, one way or the other, *what* the woman feels?"

I was worried now, Livia. Very worried. For if Shanti refused Pavo, refused to return as his queen, there was one end I could not consider. For he is capable of destroying all in his indifference. His lack of desire would lead to a lack of lust for survival. And that lack would spread. In time, nothing will survive it. Nothing.

He stood again, this time calling a break to the work. It was hot now, and the men were glad to be released, to not continue under his bored gaze. They scattered to the one copse they'd left of unfelled trees, shading a small stretch of ground on the far side of the Juliet River.

"It wasn't what I thought it would be," he muttered, staring out toward the western range of the Donatees.

The River Gate gave a squeak, which meant someone had joined us. Pavo's eyes noted this, without surprise, as if the intruder was someone he expected. Throwing himself back on the Queen's Chair, he gave a groan and shaded his eyes.

It was Walter. Shanti's father. Shiva's husband. Dressed in old, dirt-stained pants and an ancient shirt. He walked over to Pavo and looked down at him with sympathy in his eyes.

"What are you doing here?" I said sharply. "You are under attainder." But my voice faltered, and my protest sounded weak, even to me. Walter ignored it. He put a hand on Pavo's shoulder and gave a sigh.

Pavo looked up, as if, hopeless, he expected little or nothing. A dangerous look.

"What does she say?" he said, but his voice did not sound as if it expected any kind of happy answer.

Walter sighed again, as if he had things to say that he did not think would get a hearing. "Pavo, she says you can pick." Pavo made no sign, and Walter seemed to try again. "Choose. One or the other. She says she told you."

"Why didn't she come herself?" Pavo said.

Walter observed him closely for a moment. "She says you don't hear her. She says you're hard of hearing."

"That's absurd," I said, unaccountably annoyed.

Walter amended it. "Hard of listening, then."

"So?" Pavo muttered. "Not that I care."

Walter either did not hear this, or ignored it in his turn. "So you choose," he suggested.

Pavo stared down at the ground, kicking some dirt up with the toe of his boot. "She told me she wanted to keep it herself."

At this, Walter looked troubled. "That's not what she said."

"Yes, it is," Pavo insisted, showing the first animation I had seen from him yet that day.

"Have it your way, then. Which do you want?"

Pavo leaned toward him, suddenly intent. "Both," he said. "I want both."

Walter shook his head. "Choose," he suggested again.

"Both."

"Choose."

And then Walter held it out. There it was. The Key.

"You," I said. "You've had it all along."

It was then I knew what I had passed over before. Walter. The common-place man with the commonplace name. The inheritor of Sophia the

Wise, the second queen of Arcadia.

"She was your mother," I said. "Sophia, I mean."

He looked surprised that I hadn't known.

I don't know why I hadn't known. I had not till that moment understood.

There has been much I did not understand.

He held the Key up in the harsh sun, and the light glanced off its rose-gold shaft.

"Take it, Pavo," he suggested. "If that's what you really want."

"Both," Pavo insisted bitterly, sounding now like a spoiled child. Walter shook his head, sadly, as if at some misunderstanding that could not be made right.

I couldn't stand it any longer, Livia. I leapt up and grabbed the Key myself. Clutched it to my chest. Waited.

And waited.

And waited.

Nothing.

Nothingness. There was nothing with the Key. "A fraud," I muttered furiously. A false promise! An illusion!

Then I felt—shall I confess it? Relieved. For I am tired, Livia. I have come, finally, to the end of a long, tumultuous, tortuous road. If life is, as Devindra once told me, a story told by ourselves to ourselves, then mine has been a tale of travail. Even of horror.

Let someone else seek to shape the future, I thought, holding that impotent Key. Let someone else chase power. Dust, I thought. All comes to Dust.

And nothingness.

It must have been the illness rising up in me. Surely it was that. The fever.

I would not admit what came next, but for what came after. I looked, bleary-eyed, at the scene before me, but that shifted as I gazed, blurring and then disappearing before my eyes. What I saw instead, in the full glare of afternoon light, was Devindra. She was standing silent under what had been the Queen's Apple Tree.

It flowered above her, the blossoms pink and white.

Those tender black-brown eyes stared at me, lit from behind, as they were when she lived. As if she—as if we—were in the high summer of our age once again.

I felt weak tears sluice down my cheeks, and lifted a hand to wipe them away. Devindra held out her hand. Unthinking, I grasped it, pulling her toward me. The Key was between us, held palm to palm, the palms of those who had taken the Luna Vow, the midsummer vow, the vow meant never to be broken, not in this life or the next.

That was when I saw you, Livia. I saw you rise up behind her.

Still clasping my dampened palm and the Key between us, she turned with me, as if the two of us, together, faced what you were and are.

I believed I saw you then, Livia. If not all of you—for who can say they have seen *that?*—then as much of you as I, Aspern Grayling, can perceive in this life. I saw you as an angel, a prince, a lightning bolt, a morning star, a ruler over a vicious populace, a demagogue over a stupid and willing one, a beautiful young man, a dragon, a scheming wife, a warrior riding his chariot over the bodies of his adversaries, the mother who hates her children, the fairy tale witch, the emperor dealing death.

I saw you as the Devil Himself, claiming dominion over all the worlds, amusing yourself with our meager performance here, in this world. The world of Arcadia and Megalopolis.

I saw your goal. To destroy the Key. That you desire the Key to destroy it.

I saw this, that to allow Pavo to wield it as he sees fit will serve your purpose in the end.

Was I then, is he, no more than your creature?

Does all ambition come to this in the end?

Do our powers move us, we who are mortal, from living form to living form, always searching for ourselves, always waylaid by your goals in the end?

I would have fallen then and there. But Devindra's arm held me.

That was when I saw beyond you. I say I saw you, Livia, as you are. But I saw more. I saw myself. I saw who we were, what we are. I saw the black from which comes the light.

That light burst from you, from myself, from the Key, flooding the scene before me. I saw it push open a door that had not been there before. Through it I saw everyone who had ever lived. My mother and Polly. My sisters. Sophia the Wise. Aurora, Faustina, Michaeli. Joyanna. I saw Marcian and Lionel. I saw, even, the mongrel dog that Devindra had once saved.

I saw myself, too. Suddenly. As Pavo must see me now. The old dotard whose day is done in this world. I saw myself in a long line of fathers and sons without wives and mothers, each generation dreaming of the murder of the last.

It was of this, I know now, that Devindra came to warn me. For that must be the price you've asked of Pavo, Livia. My head upon a platter. Like Alastair's before me. Amusing, that.

Another blast of light, and all was again black. I was no longer myself, no longer Aspern Grayling. I was nowhere, waiting for something I have not yet known.

But I was unafraid. It was as if I had been there before.

I must have been in a dead faint. That must have been when I was brought back here, to Devindra's Tower by the Lily Pond.

It was there that I came, slowly, back to myself.

To myself?

I heard the rushing of the Gems, and the Little Gems, and the Deer-springs, swollen from the rain. There was the sound of children playing. I heard the voice of Aurora.

Then these sounds faded away. In their place, the drone of machinery, the shouts of men, the clatter of falling trees. And I knew Pavo had misunderstood. He has chosen the Key. And made himself lord of Arcadia. For all the good it will do him and Megalopolis. For he misunderstands its purpose and its goal.

He misunderstands his own. For what he truly wants is not now what he seeks.

I have never seen a soul. It occurs to me, also, that I have never seen the ocean, yet I can hear it through this newly opened door. I have never seen it, yet I know it is there. For the ebb and flow of it is in me as well.

I had thought all that existed was only what I could see and touch—which was remarkable enough. But now that I see different patterns...I...I see different worlds.

The light ebbs and flows, and dims as evening falls.

I take a step forward to the windows of the Tower, and to my confused surprise, each shows a different scene. Where that to the east shows off the New Arcadia of Pavo's rule—all half-built rigs, bright lights, massive construction projects, dirt heaps and holes, dirty snow pushed to either side of gashes in the dark earth—this window here, this that looks to the west, shows Arcadia as it has been. Snow-covered hillocks with scattered bonfires warming neighbors who stand around them, mugs of steaming liquid in their hands. They offer each other good cheer, and on every face is a smile.

The sounds, too. No jackhammers, no engines straining uphill with their load. No shouts and crashes as another old building comes tumbling down. Instead a whoosh of sleds, a sprinkling of laughter, and, in the distance, the harmonies of a fiddle, a flute, and a drum.

I look out of that window, Livia, and see, standing by the most vivid bonfire, Walter—he I had once thought so commonplace, though the memory slides away from me as I write. Next to him is Shiva, draping a shawl over the shoulders of a young woman. That figure turns, and I see by the swell of her stomach she is to have a child.

And she is Shanti.

Now I thought strange words, Livia. As if the words were thinking me: *"All of these things, the wind, the rain, the sea, the sky, were given us to be the symbol of our inner soul, and I knew it not."*

Was it a quotation, a bit of a song, perhaps one of the many of my childhood, the songs my mother, and Polly, and my sisters used to sing? Then I thought, "But Pavo has no soul. What symbol then, is his world?"

I thought of Pavo's son. What soul would be his?

As if in answer, the view from the window changes. Two lovers sit in the grass of a flowery meadow, by the soft sound of the Juliet River.

And it is spring. I can smell the strawberry scent of the warmed cottonwood trees that fringe the splashing stream beyond. I can smell the flowers of the chamomile plants, and the crushed leaves of mint.

Sitting there, together, are Devindra and Aspern.

Devindra smiles at Aspern, holding out one of her slim brown hands, which he clasps in his own white one. She says, "All this in spite of all." And the meadow grows, expanding, filling the scene, filling the whole of the world. Until it is the world itself. Not the world of my thought. The world of my imagination.

And I know for certain there is forgiveness for all my errors. If not in this world, then in another, that was invisible to me all this time.

Devindra's hand and mine hold the Key between them.

The Key warms between us, and I see it. Nothing real can ever be lost. Who said that? A moment's gladness, then it's gone. The pictures about me fade. Leaving behind only the machines and the dust and the noise and the shouting of men.

And explosions. So many explosions. Destruction. From the past, and the present, and the destruction yet to come.

But Shanti carries a child.

Where is she?

Where is Shanti?

I ask the question. Then I hear her voice.

"I didn't want to rule over Pavo Vale. Looking at him, the true pleading in his eyes—and more than pleading, I think I can say it, there was, yes, I know there was, I wasn't fooled, it was the beginnings of real love, the kind of love that is just for who the loved one is, not for what can be made of them or done with them or, worse, used *for*—I pitied him, truly, with all my heart.

"He cried tears of real grief, the kind that only real human beings can cry, and I pitied him. He'd never asked to be born, Pavo. I pitied him. And I loved him. Yes.

"Did I pull him through the door to my side? Or did he pull me through to his? Or did we make a third space, we two, by reaching out and grasping each other's hands? In the end it doesn't matter.

"In the end, all that matters is what happens next. And whether that shows itself as for good or ill. For what comes next has been made by what went before."

From the Tower by the Lily Pond, St. Vitus College, Wrykyn:

Livia.

Dawn came. Light. I woke. I saw the words scribbled here. I… Did I write that in my sleep?

Is this from my fever? For I feel it increasing. My head throbs, my old bones ache.

Written, scribbled on a piece of paper fallen on the floor, in the same hand: "Blackness pressed becomes a diamond."

Have I mistaken the Key?

Have I missed the Door?

But no. I feel a certainty I have never felt before. There is a Door I now can see, opening on to this room, through which another world may come. Through which I may go and enter that world.

You taught me there was no such door, Livia. You said that all that is, is all that I see. There is nothing else.

But, Livia. I hold the Key, and more light pours from that door, blinding me as I walk its way.

Devindra steps through it from the light, towards me. Not her ghost, but she, Devindra, herself, alive. Who holds out her hand. And on her face is forgiveness. I have need of that forgiveness, Livia. For I have sinned. I, in my blind arrogance, believed that sin was not.

I have created a new life, beyond human, Livia. A god, some would say. I have lived up to my blind ideals. How many men can say the same? It would be best if they could not. Now I admit it, I have been tired. I have felt a strange regret. My food has tasted of dust. I have found myself yearning for what was not. And I have fooled myself to the top of my own bent, thinking these were the unjust, but inevitable, curses of one's old age. I believed that as the machine corrodes, so do the parts.

And yet I see now that this was not so. I see now that I am no machine. I am a human being. A body, yes, but a spirit too. A descendant of ancestors. And now, at the end, an ancestor myself.

For I made the family that gave birth to my son. Pavo Vale was not my child alone. He was also the child of Devindra Vale. He was our child, our descendant. I did, in a mischievous spirit—Goddess forgive me!—in creating him, mingle Devindra's DNA with my own. I made him bigger and stronger than a normal child, but I gave him also her bronze skin. I had always thought it would be a beautiful match with my own violet eyes.

213

A desire for a family. Yes. I see that now. All that I have done, all that I have striven for, I never knew the root from which it grew. Mistakes all. I never knew that the one thing that was wanted was the very thing I had thought oppressed me. That I had fought against with all my mistaken strength.

It's done now. Devindra calls me. Yes. She stands now, and beckons. She leads me to that door, holding out her hand, inviting me to step through with her. Not alone. I would not be alone.

What is on the other side of that door, Livia? Nothingness—that is what you have taught, and I have believed. Nevertheless, I must follow.

I will know the truth of it soon enough.

If this is illusion, I face a black night, Livia. I had thought it a comfort to unburden myself to you, my "friend." I have called you that—"my friend"—though I now know what will happen to these words, this report. That you will share what I meant to be private with my worst enemies, cull it for your own needs, flatter my memory as long as it does your own plans good, and then throw it away when it's no longer of use. For I see so clearly now the meaning of the delegation from the Council. Of its secret talks with Pavo Vale. They have brought your messages to him, have they not? Your price for the support of Megalopolis is my head, is it not? And the Council has won.

It was of Pavo, my own son, *our* own son, that Devindra has been warning me all along. Now I warn you, Livia. For the god-man I created will not be content to have another god rule. Not even if it means the destruction of the world.

It's all one. Or it will be. Very soon. For now that Pavo Vale holds the Key, the Key he misunderstands and will of a certainty misuse, he and it will set about making Arcadia a hell on earth. Creative destruction. That was always the way of Megalopolis. From Megalopolis comes Necropolis.

Unless the Evolutionaries hold firm. There is always that chance.

I made Pavo Vale, but he is the creation of Megalopolis. And Megalopolis has killed everything I have ever loved. I hear you say, Livia, those words you often spoke, that love is a weakness, a fatal obstacle in man's search for godhood. That desire for peace and plenty for his family stultifies a man's dreams.

But now, hearing your voice, it fades until it's like a buzzing from an angry wasp outside a window pane.

Devindra disappears into that open door. And I must follow. I see that now. If she is anywhere, I must be where she is.

Outside, in another world, Pavo Vale grasps the Key. And that world goes up in flames. What survives is mud. Mud and the sound of machinery grinding through the night.

My fever burns. It consumes the man who once was Aspern Grayling.

Who am I now? Will I know when I follow Devindra through that open door? And will Pavo remember? Will he follow when his time comes? Will we be there, Devindra and I, to welcome him home?

Forgive me, Pavo.

Forgive me, Shanti.

Wait, Devindra!

I come.

Peace.

In my academic years, I researched all I could about the experiments of Megalopolis. Those experiments—animal, vegetable, mineral, human—were the Megalopolitan attempt to dominate Nature, and in doing so, to eliminate Death. But there is no life without death. To end one is to end the other.

As a result, these experiments were bound to go wrong. The friend who smuggled the science journals of Megalopolis to me also brought the freaks of nature that resulted over the mountains to Arcadia, to sell in the market—for that was her business. These were oddities, all sharing certain traits. Most were a mix of the strong and the maimed. One, a cross between a bear, a lion, and an eagle, is living still, in a tower built for him by the Juliet River. His name is Babal. It was he who started me on my research.

I studied Babal. As I did, Shanti befriended him. At first, that was beyond me. I couldn't open my heart to the creature. That was the way I thought of Babal in my cowardice: 'the creature'. I was afraid to meet him as a fellow. But Shanti has always been the stronger of us that way. She opened her heart first.

Now she has been strong enough to open her heart again, this time to the most extreme invention of Megalopolis. And I am fearful of the result.

What will be the end of it? We know there is no going back. Actions once taken create further actions of their own.

Babal is now one of the most valued counselors of the Evolutionary movement. Could something equally unexpected happen now?

Given our past, such hopes as these may go terribly wrong.

Unless we evolve. That's what Shanti and I hold on to. The Law of Unintended Consequences being what it is, who knows what the result might be?

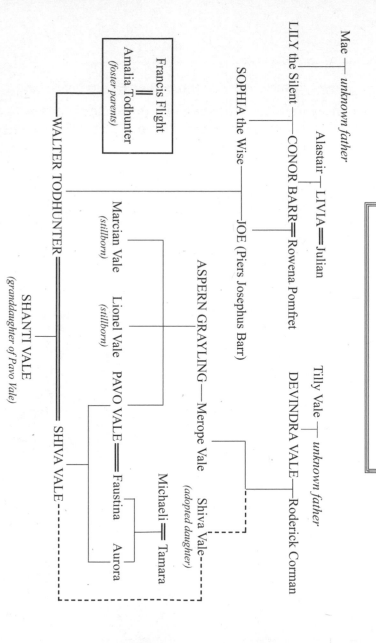

VALE FAMILY TREE

Mae ⊤ *unknown father*

LILY the Silent

Alastair ⊤ LIVIA═Julian

SOPHIA the Wise ⊤ CONOR BARR═Rowena Pomfret

Francis Flight ═ Amalia Todhunter *(foster parents)*

WALTER TODHUNTER

JOE (Piers Josephus Barr)

Marcian Vale *(stillborn)*

Lionel Vale *(stillborn)*

ASPERN GRAYLING — Merope Vale

PAVO VALE ═ Faustina

Tilly Vale ⊤ *unknown father*

DEVINDRA VALE ⊤ Roderick Corman

Shiva Vale *(adopted daughter)*

Michaeli ═ Tamara

Aurora

SHANTI VALE *(granddaughter of Pavo Vale)* ═ SHIVA VALE

═ Married

TRANSFORMATIONS OF ARCADIA

SNOTTY SAVES THE DAY	LILY THE SILENT	THE LIZARD PRINCESS	
Snotty ↳Lily	Lily the Silent	Lily the Silent	
Alan, *stepfather of Lily*		Alan Fallaize	
Snowflake the Pony ↳ Snowflake the Unicorn	Sophia	Sophia the Wise	
Big Teddy	Maud	Isabel the Scholar	
The Dog ↳Rex	Rex		
The Lemon Yellow Bear ↳Melia	Phoebe	Leef the Lemur	
The Bardic Gnome	Will the Murderer ↳Wilder the Bard		
Tuxton Ted	The Manatee	The Mermaid ... Shanti Vale	
The Devil Himself ↳Mr. Big ↳Luc Mick	Michaeli	Storm the Centaur	
	Livia	The Dragon	
The Handsome Prince	Conor Barr	The Old Hermit	
	Colin	Joe	
	Andy Dawkins ↳Aspern Grayling		

APPENDIX

THE STEED

THE LUNA IN ARCADIA: A Monograph
by Professor Devindra Vale

The Luna—by which in this paper will be meant the physical object, rather than the many more evanescent meanings of the word—is a deck of illustrated cards, the meaning of the pictures shrouded in the fogs of the past. There are fifty-two cards in all, twenty-five in the Inner Arcana, twenty-five in the Outer Arcana, and two that act as what we might call 'wild' cards. These last two may change their meaning even more extremely than the others, depending on their placement in a spread.

THE CHANGELING

THE HERO

The Inner Arcana, distinguished by the white borders of its cards, depict various archetypes of our world. By this, I mean the shared images of Arcadia, appearing in the dreams of each individual with multiple meanings that eventually coalesce into one communal meaning. These are ancient images, ones that must also have existed in the folk tales of the Marsh in Megalopolis, where the Luna was also found. I will give more examples of this below.

KNOWLEDGE

TIME

The Outer Arcana, its cards bordered in black, depict values, concepts, ideas that have gone into the creation of our world. As we are increasingly aware in the researches that take place daily in the colleges of Otterbridge University, our world was created by a story. This story surrounds us to the same extent that water surrounds the fish, with the same inevitable invisibility to those contained within. The Outer Arcana illustrates this atmosphere, this sea in which we swim, and by observing the patterns in which they fall when a spread of the cards is made, much appreciation of the assumptions underlying our activities can be made.

The images of the Luna refer to two different areas of interest. Those of the Inner Arcana appear to reference characters of Arcadian folk and fairy tales, while those of the Outer Arcana illustrate more encompassing concepts rather than stories.

The so-called 'wild' cards are considered as agents that can act in either sphere, depending on their placement in any spread.

The interaction of the Inner Arcana with the Outer Arcana in a spread is crucial, also, in the interpretation and elucidation of any question that has been put to the spread.

This deck is far more than a mere fortune-telling device. As we know from the work of Professor Chloe Watson, it is, in fact, impossible to predict the future. Even if it were possible, it would be dangerous. Fortunately though (no pun intended, forgive me!), it is not. For each individual story is made up of two strands: Necessity and Free Choice. As each world's story is made up of a tapestry comprised of all individual stories together, the many possibilities, the richness of the design, while it may be, and often is, possible to foretell a most likely turn of the thread, it is also impossible at bottom to predict what the end story will look like.

All of this underlies the meaning of the Luna. And as the traditional spreads used in consulting it rely on a pattern that intermingles columns representing Necessity and Choice, it can be seen that the permutations will be complex and numerous, though by no means illimitable. For, as we know, it is only Eternity that is without limits. We enclosed in our own story are involved in an adventure to discover the boundaries that make up our world, that of the individual and of the community. The Luna is one, if not the preeminent, then certainly one of them, that works with the thoughtful user to expand knowledge of both of these realms.

The History of the Luna

The origins of the Luna are shrouded in the mists of the past. These images, and their use as an aid to clarity of thought and feeling, are certainly ancient. Though how ancient, and where beginning, it is impossible now to completely discern.

There are theories based on what little we know. It is certain that the Luna was in use in the past in the Marsh of Megalopolis, among the village people there, particularly among the women. This use goes back in time to well beyond the days that this area was made a Marsh, back to when it was indeed the vale for which many in the Marsh are named. This was before the flooding of the area for the use of Megalopolis, and, as even before that time, written records were not comprehensively kept, the inhabitants relying instead on verbal transmission of information, it is impossible now to recreate the uses and beginnings of the Luna in this area.

A personal note: my own mother, Tilly Vale, often used a spread of the Luna peculiar to the Marsh, one I have seen nowhere else since the days of my childhood. She would divide the Outer and the Inner cards in separate piles, and, shuffling them, would choose two Inner cards to flank a single Outer. She never failed to be able to read what this slight line told her, a fact I can readily attest, since much of my early career was guided by her intuitions formed by these cards. It was her tragic death in my young adulthood that led me to a study of the Luna, which I carried with me in the Great Migration over the mountains into Arcadia.

THE UNDINE

THE MADMAN

Imagine my surprise when I discovered that the Luna was already known, and in frequent use, among the original population of Arcadia, although the main center of its study remained, until the Great Migration, a small one. So far as I know, the Luna at that time was only known to those who either lived, or frequently visited, the Witches' Plain between Wrykyn and Paloma. The use had begun as a part of the secret ceremonies of the annual Witches' Day, though it spread quickly through the every day life of Arcadia once the women and the children of the Megalopolitan Marsh appeared and settled, carrying their own decks of the pasteboard images.

These images retained the same names in every deck I have personally observed, or been told about by other researchers. The pictorial representations vary, however, depending on local artistry and inclination.

The best theory, therefore, at the present time, is that the Luna has an ancient history as a sibylline oracle. Indications are that it was originally formed by women for women, to aid in decisions having to do with health, birth, love, family, and death. There would have been occasional communication between the aboriginal women of the Witches' Plain, and those of the Vale turned Marsh, and this is the most likely source of its dual history in these places.

A Luna Spread

My thought as I was writing this monograph was that I should attempt a Luna spread, engaging the Luna in conversation as it were. I therefore laid out what we call the "Sisters" spread, which is seven cards laid out in an upturned half moon, with the card at the top acting as director of the spread.

As is usual with my own interactions with the Luna, I did not ask a specific question of it, but rather left open the line of communication. It is a complicated issue, difficult to describe, how each interlocutor of the Luna receives information from a spread. The best I can describe it is thus: the spread is laid out, while the user lets what concerns them most float freely through their head. What wisdom, then, that comes from the Luna interacts with this thought, which must really be merged with a feeling in or-

TIME

THE WITCH QUEEN

PRIDE

THE BRIDE

MORTALITY

THE CHANGELING

REBIRTH

FIGURE 1. A LUNA SPREAD

der to receive from the sight of the spread a useful communication. Often the most remarkable insights arise from this method, which leads me to the theory that the Luna is a mirror in which can be seen the user's inner soul. In other words, it is not so much these pasteboard images that speak, as it is the soul reaching out to embody itself in them, allowing the conscious body that contains it to access its own wisdom. As every individual also embodies in themselves the hopes and fears of the community, the spread will reflect a community's inner life as well.

This is undoubtedly why all serious users of the Luna through what we know of its history have warned that it is not a fortune telling device, but rather a map of inner possibility and probability. As most actions carry on along a fixed, rather than a free, line, it must sometimes look as if these possibilities are in fact immutable.

As our second queen, Sophia the Wise, has said: "No one should seek to know the Future, for the Future is not immutable. To predict it is to change it, in ways that cannot always be controlled."

With this in mind, I laid out the "Sisters" spread, thinking and feeling about the issue uppermost in my mind: what Arcadia is now, and what its mission in the future must be.

I received the cards in this way.

At the bottom of the left hand side of the half moon, "The Changeling," an image from the Inner Arcana.

Rising up from that, was "The Bride," also from the Inner Arcana.

From that, still rising, "Time," from the Outer Arcana.

At the top of the half moon, at the highest point, was "The Witch Queen," one of the two 'wild' cards in the deck, and one that has always had a deep meaning for myself. This kind of attraction of the interlocutor to one specific card often happens in the use of the Luna.

From the top, heading down to the right, "Pride," from the Outer Arcana.

The next line, heading down on the right, "Mortality," also from the Outer Arcana.

And finally, at the bottom of the right hand side, "Rebirth," from the Outer Arcana.

This is how I proceeded to read this spread.

THE WITCH QUEEN

First, I let the impression of the whole wash over me. Of immediate interest was that "The Witch Queen" was the leader of this "Sisters" spread. This is one of the two 'wild' cards of the Luna, the other being "The Steed." "The Witch Queen" is, as I've said, a card of peculiar interest to me, the one that appears in every spread I do for myself, now in one position, then in another. Traditionally, it bears two meanings, each quite different from the other, although not irreconcilable. It has the meaning of Evil hidden as Good, as well as the meaning of its opposite, Good hidden as Evil. Since my early years, I have been fascinated by the fact that this image combines the two. But to understand what it tries to say in a spread, one must look at the other cards supporting it.

My second impression was that the left hand and the right hand sides were speaking of quite different parts of the question. This is usual for the "Sisters" spread: the left hand side is considered the younger sister, and the right the elder. What this means, in interpretation, is that the elder precedes the younger and influences her. In this case through the dominance of "The Witch Queen."

The younger sister in this case appears to be speaking of Arcadia in terms of her fairy tales, since both "The Changeling" and "The Bride" are deeply connected with the hearth stories of our land. And the elder sister is obviously speaking of the pitfalls and goals of Arcadian history. When "Pride" is seen at the top of the right hand side, this is traditionally thought to mean "Blindness" (although it may have other meanings in other positions in this and other spreads). When "Mortality" is seen in a middle position on either the left or the right side, the usual meaning attached to it is one of violence, particularly violent death. On the left side, this would most likely

228

refer to an individual fate, but on the right it refers to that of a community.

"Rebirth" at the bottom of the right side is a fortunate cast. In fact, this is one of the most fortunate of all the Luna, in no matter what position, though on the right hand side, it refers to a group, rather than an individual fate.

Also of note is how the cards balance each other on either side. "The Changeling" balances "Rebirth." "The Bride" balances "Mortality," "Time" balances "Pride." And overseeing all, the two fold meaning of "The Witch Queen."

This is therefore how I read this spread. The stories of Arcadia will take it through cycles of violence and death, leading to a renewal. All of this will be overseen by two competing forces, each one labeled, for good or ill, a "Witch." On one side, we have the "Witch" as she has become by defiling her position in search of power. On the other, the "Witch" who acts in aid of love. The fact that the two cards on the lowest level of both the left and the right side are "The Changeling" and "Rebirth" gives me the feeling that it is the transformations that happen within Arcadia that promise a new spring.

HOPE

But the main feeling is of violence. A great conflict, then. Worried that my disinclination to predict a story of tragedy for my own beloved land led me to read this spread with an overly optimistic eye, I felt I needed more information. Troubled, I drew one last card to lie over the spread, a final say on the part of the Luna.

This card was "Hope."

I think no more needs to be said. "Hope," in Arcadia's story, then, will be the final word of the Luna.

THE MARMOSET, THE HEN, & THE LIZARD

Another Arcadian Fairy Tale

A rabbit judged a contest between a marmoset, a hen, and a lizard, to give the prize to the greatest animal. Each one promised him a gift if he would choose them.

The marmoset promised: "You will be the most beautiful of all."

The hen promised: "You will be able to lay as many golden eggs as you please."

The lizard promised: "You will always own whatever patch of ground you stand upon."

The rabbit thought it over carefully, and awarded the prize to the lizard. He reasoned:

"If I am the most beautiful, this will attract unwanted attention I cannot control. If I lay golden eggs, this will attract robbers, and those who want to enslave me to make the gold their own. But if I own the ground I stand on, no matter where, I am free from that day on."

"A smart, funny, and thought-provoking read for readers of all ages, *Snotty Saves the Day* has me eagerly awaiting its sequel." —DAVID GUTOWSKI, *Largehearted Boy*

"The most audacious and unusual book I have read this year. Framed in a "we found this on our doorstep" ala *Spiderwick* sort of way, it is ostensibly forwarded to the publisher by a professor from the land of Arcadia. . . . If you are intrigued by how [fairy tales] are manipulated with such ease by pop culture mavens and movie makers . . . you will find the cheekiness of Davies' story to be wildly appealing." —COLLEEN MONDOR, *Bookslut* Summer Reading List

"Awesome. . . . There's plenty of humor in the book. . . . And the best is the truth—what Is, as the book calls it—Snotty discovers about himself. He doesn't just see the error of his old ways; he re-becomes an entirely different person. And that possibility, that ability—that we all might re-become what we were born to be—raises a wonder, a "sympathy with the idea of 'changing the world'" that beats louder than does a superficially bleeding heart." —KRISTIN THIEL, *Nervous Breakdown*

"[An] amusing debut . . . dressed up with footnotes, scholarly introductions and a bibliography, as well as lovely line drawings by Gary Zaboly, Snotty's story seeks to prove that fairy tales rank with quantum mechanics in their ability to establish parallel worlds." —*Publishers Weekly*

"Like Susanna Clark's magnificent *Jonathan Strange & Mr. Norrell* . . . and many works by Nicholson Baker, *Snotty Saves the Day* features fictional footnotes that add another layer to the novel. . . . Give it to a smart, precocious young person in your life, read it yourself, and see what kind of interesting conversation develops." —*Bookconscious*

Praise for *The Lizard Princess,* the third book in The History of Arcadia series

"Complex and gripping. . . . Newcomers to Arcadia will be captivated by the rich history, while those familiar with it will find that Sophia's legend grants them a new perspective on the earlier tales."
—*Publishers Weekly (starred review)*

"This fantasy quest lends a hand toward making our contemporary world a little better."—*Foreword Reviews*

"The impressive *The Lizard Princess* continues Tod Davies' imaginative History of Arcadia series with her trademark brilliant storytelling."
—*Largehearted Boy*

"[*The Lizard Princess*] encourages big-picture thinking. . . . The combination of a straightforward quest complicated by hindsight, with magic, science, and meditations on the building of myths and the role of stories, makes for a book not like much else out there. . . . Gorgeously written and complex." —*New York Journal of Books*

"A fantasy novel that includes a conflict between a world that admits of the supernatural and skeptics who deny anything beyond the material, it is a tale for our time. "—*Sects and Violence in the Ancient World*

"Look inside this world and find wonder."—KATE BERNHEIMER, editor of *My Mother She Killed Me, My Father He Ate Me* and *Fairy Tale Review*

"Innovative form and spellbinding content. . . . Stories, as Tod Davies's History of Arcadia novels ultimately suggest, serve as civilization's backbone, and it is therefore in stories too that we can discover the potential for fundamental change and a better society." —*Marvels & Tales*

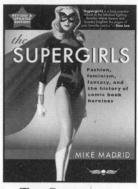

MORE BOOKS FROM EXTERMINATING ANGEL PRESS

"Change the story, change the world"

THE SUPERGIRLS
Feminism, Fantasy, and the History of Comic Book Heroines
(Revised and Updated)
Mike Madrid
$16.95
ISBN: 9781935259336

DIVAS, DAMES & DAREDEVILS
Lost Heroines of Golden Age Comics
Mike Madrid
$16.95
ISBN: 9781935259237

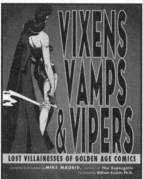

VIXENS, VAMPS & VIPERS
Lost Villainesses of Golden Age Comics
Mike Madrid
$16.95
ISBN: 9781935259275

JAM TODAY
A Diary of Cooking With What You've Got
(Revised and Updated)
Tod Davies
$15.95
ISBN: 9781935259367

JAM TODAY TOO
The Revolution Will Not Be Catered
Tod Davies
$15.95
ISBN: 9781935259251

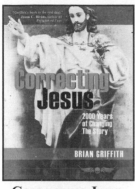

CORRECTING JESUS
*2000 Years of
Changing the Story*
Brian Griffith
$16.95
ISBN: 9781935259022

**GALAXY OF
IMMORTAL WOMEN**
*The Yin Side of
Chinese Civilization*
Brian Griffith
$16.95
ISBN: 9781935259145

PARK SONGS
A Poem/Play
David Budbill
Photos by R.C. Irwin
$14.95
ISBN: 9781935259169

3 DEAD PRINCES
An Anarchist Fairy Tale
Danbert Nobacon
Illustrations by
Alex Cox
$13.00
ISBN: 9781935259060

*Request E.A.P.
books in print and
electronic editions
from your favorite
bookstore or library*

GREENBEARD
Richard James Bentley
$14.95
ISBN: 9781935259213

Tod Davies is the author of *Snotty Saves the Day*, *Lily the Silent*, and *The Lizard Princess*, the first three books in The History of Arcadia series, as well as the cooking memoirs *Jam Today: A Diary of Cooking With What You've Got* and *Jam Today Too: The Revolution Will Not Be Catered*. Unsurprisingly, her attitude toward literature is the same as her attitude toward cooking—it's all about working with what you have to find new ways of looking and new ways of becoming ever more human. Originally from San Francisco, she now lives with her husband, the filmmaker Alex Cox, and their two dogs, Gray and Pearl, in the alpine valley of Colestin, Oregon.